# JANE CLAIRE BRADLEY

# DEAR NEIGHBOUR

SPHERE

SPHERE

First published in Great Britain in 2023 by Sphere
This paperback edition published by Sphere in 2024

1 3 5 7 9 10 8 6 4 2

Copyright © Jane Claire Bradley 2023

Extract on p.19 from 'It's Not Right but It's Okay' lyrics by Rodney Jerkins, Jason Phillips, Lashawn Ameen Daniels and Fred Jerkins III. Copyright © Emi April Music Inc, Emi Blackwood Music Inc., Universal Music Corp., Sony/atv Melody, Music of Windswept, Mic'l Music, Fred Jerkins Publishing, Siphosong.

Extract on p.19 from 'So Emotional' lyrics by Tom Kelly and William E Steinberg. Copyright © Sony/atv Tunes Llc.

Extract on p.127 from 'Didn't We Almost Have It All' lyrics by Michael Masser and Will Jennings. Copyright © Universal Music Publishing Group.

The moral right of the author has been asserted.

*All characters and events in this publication, other than those clearly in the public domain, are fictitious and any resemblance to real persons, living or dead, is purely coincidental.*

All rights reserved.
No part of this publication may be reproduced, stored in a retrieval system, or transmitted, in any form or by any means, without the prior permission in writing of the publisher, nor be otherwise circulated in any form of binding or cover other than that in which it is published and without a similar condition including this condition being imposed on the subsequent purchaser.

A CIP catalogue record for this book is available from the British Library.

ISBN 978-1-4087-2592-4

Typeset in Caslon by M Rules
Printed and bound in Great Britain by Clays Ltd, Elcograf S.p.A.

Papers used by Sphere are from well-managed forests
and other responsible sources.

Sphere
An imprint of
Little, Brown Book Group
Carmelite House
50 Victoria Embankment
London EC4Y 0DZ

An Hachette UK Company
www.hachette.co.uk

www.littlebrown.co.uk

*For Carl*

Dear reader,

Thanks for being here. Being published by Little, Brown is a literal dream come true for me, but it would mean nothing without readers like you. So I want to share with you some of the story behind the story that went into this book.

I was born in Liverpool in the eighties, spending my earliest years in squats and shared flats in areas like Toxteth: places with a history of protests, riots and community campaigns against issues like racism, police brutality and poverty. I entered that world six weeks into my mam's final year at uni, and from birth onwards I was surrounded by the students, artists and activists who shared our first few homes. We lived in perpetual poverty-line chaos, but the shambolic, rebellious vibe sowed some formative seeds about the inextricable links between politics, creativity and community.

Several years later, my mam, our kid and I moved from Liverpool to Salford, our years of squatting, sofa-surfing and insecure short-term rentals finally over once we got our first council house. The estate was a notoriously violent shithole (and a valid caution against over-romanticising council housing), but the house gave us a level of safety and security we'd never had before.

Once I left to study in Leeds, I ended up in Woodhouse, renting the attic in a dangerously unmaintained Victorian terrace let by a sleazy rental agency renowned for ripping off students. The electrics were so antiquated that changing a bulb or fuse was a dance with death, the bath almost fell through the kitchen ceiling, mould blotted our bedroom walls and the roof leaked whenever it rained. But despite all that, I recollect that time with fondness. It's a cliche, but the people mattered more. My time on that street involved a lot of traipsing in and out of my neighbours' houses: creating dubious concoctions in each other's kitchens, splattering each other with fake blood or paint for the constant theme parties, dragging out decks or drumkits into overgrown front yards, or just spending countless evenings sitting on our front steps, chatting endless shit over infinite cups of tea until it got dark and then light again.

That intimacy and connection was truly magical, made all the more special by the reputation our street had. I didn't know it when I moved in, but in earlier decades, it had been infamous within the local arts and music scenes. Renowned for its eclectic, ever-shifting population of weird and wonderful residents, it was a safe haven for misfits, musicians, activists, artists, punks, pagans and queers. I didn't know about psychogeography then, but the idea that a location's history can echo through the years is one I often think of when I recall my time there. Chapel Allerton – where Dear Neighbour is set in Leeds – has its own vibrant history of protest and community action, and I like thinking of the novel's characters being influenced by, and honouring, that legacy.

Years later, I moved back to Manchester: writing, performing, setting up a non-profit and collaborating with community groups and charities to deliver workshops on writing, creativity and storytelling. I became a mental health practitioner, working first in a women's centre and getting my heart smashed to bits every day. For all the years that had passed inbetween, the women there – almost exclusively single mams like mine had been – were grappling with the same old harms being done by threadbare support systems, undiagnosed trauma, insecure housing and austerity. And yet over and over again – in that job and other community work I've done – I've witnessed the way the darkest of griefs can be made lighter when they're shared, whether it's over biscuits and brews, while making a mess with glitter and paint, or fighting for something that matters.

Writing this book during a pandemic and the accompanying mental health crisis reinforced to me more than ever how important community is. The characters in this book have all survived a lot, and yet their connections to each other are a source of comfort, challenge, strength and hope. We all need those things from each other. And I hope reading their story brings some of them to you.

All my love,
Jane x

# CHAPTER ONE

The news keeps threatening an Easter heatwave, but so far there's no sign of it. Monday has been relentless grey drizzle, and Alice curses herself for not bringing Mollie's pram. She stops halfway up the hill to reshuffle her handbag and tote bag full of lesson plans, then hefts Mollie into a more comfortable position on her hip. The toddler's knackered from nursery, her arms snuggled around Alice's neck, giving an occasional drowsy mumble in her ear.

Things at school have been hectic. The kids have been getting increasingly hyper as Easter approaches, the classrooms are chaos, and there's never enough time for everything that needs doing, but noise and mess have never fazed Alice. She'd rather spend her breaks mopping up paint or prepping worksheets than in the staffroom, listening to the other TAs complain about school politics or comparing notes about their diets, boyfriends and book clubs. Alice tried bonding with the others when she started, but found herself spacing out so often that almost two years down the line she's come to terms with keeping their interactions surface level and her real concentration on the kids.

Alice and Mollie weave past the lads breakdancing on rain-spotted sheets of cardboard outside the off-licence, a speaker blasting hip hop next to an upturned baseball cap with a collection of coppers and one grubby note, clashing with the techno from the Caribbean takeaway next door. In every cafe window, students type at laptops with ferocious caffeine-fuelled intensity, looking far younger and more fashionable than Alice remembers ever being when she came to Leeds for uni ten years ago. Pushing away a pang that accompanies that image of her teenage self, Alice focuses on that night's to-do list. *Sort the tea. Bath for Mol. Council tax bill. Get a wash on.* Mollie's becoming more of a dead weight with every step, but they're almost back, turning onto Leodis Street just as the first spits of a harder downpour start.

Oppressive grey clouds leach the colour from the narrow red-brick terraces, casting the curved row of council houses in a murky gloom. Alice suppresses a snort, picturing her mum giving a theatrical shudder at the sight of the street accompanied with the words 'grim up North'. Once Alice made it clear she wasn't moving back to Liverpool after graduation, her parents had traded their own terrace near Anfield for an apartment in Nice. Her mum never tires of evangelising about expat life, her messages full of sunshine and passionate descriptions of nearby vineyards, markets and beaches. But while Alice can usually brush off her mum's jokes about Leodis Street looking like something from a Mike Leigh film, today Alice grudgingly sees her point. The weeds snaking up through the cracked paving slabs, the damp-blotted brickwork and the potholes on the street can't be masked by all the hard work Alice has put into making this little corner of Leeds a home. Alice glares at the dark patch above her bedroom window, weighing up its size. Is it bigger since last time she looked? She's so distracted that she doesn't immediately see the man sitting on the low crumbling wall that joins their house with its neighbour.

He's slumped over, face hidden in his hands, so it takes Alice a moment to recognise Bill from next door, looking strange without his usual flat cap and coat. *What's wrong with him?* Alice's mind flashes to the first-aid course school sent her on, but blanks on retrieving anything useful. She nudges Mollie from her doze and sets her down, then bends to touch Bill's shoulder.

'Bill? You okay, love?'

From behind his hands, Bill mumbles something Alice can't make out. There's a letter folded in his lap, a brown envelope and a white sheet of paper. Bill rubs his face hard, then lowers his hands, revealing a weathered face set with mistrustful blue eyes.

In the three years Alice has lived on Leodis Street, Bill's barely talked to her. She only knows his name from the grunt he gave her when she first introduced herself. Since then, his only other communication has been the bangs on the wall whenever she and Mollie get too loud. *Moody old codger.* Alice knows she's not a bad neighbour, but she needs music to get going in the mornings. She can't help the occasional noise of her ongoing self-taught DIY, or Mollie's sporadic nightmare shrieks. There *had* been that couple of wearing weeks when Sam idiotically gave Mollie a harmonica, but following a headache-fogged fortnight, Alice banned the instrument to Mol's weekends with her dad. But Bill's narkiness long pre-dated that incident, so while it might not have helped matters, Alice knows it's not the cause.

Alice's wariness about Bill isn't helped by the fact he hardly ever seems to go out. *If only he went down the pub or whatever, we wouldn't have to tiptoe around or risk pissing him off.* Alice imagines her and Mollie cranking up the stereo and bopping round the living room, then scrambling to turn it down when they see Bill making his way up the path. But she never sees him go anywhere, though she assumes he must do his errands while she's at school. He seems independent enough for his age, and he never wants help. In the cold snap last February, Alice had worried about him slipping – the street's uneven pavements were annoying enough without the extra danger of black ice. But when she'd knocked to ask if he wanted any shopping, Bill scowled and told her not to fuss.

'I'm fine,' he snapped, the door already closing. 'I don't need anyone bothering me.'

'Thanks but no thanks would've been an acceptable answer too, you know,' Alice snarked back to the almost-shut door, but the only reply was the clunk of the Bill's lock.

Even though Bill's a miserable arse most of the time, it's still unnerving seeing him crumpled over like this.

'What is it, Bill? Has something happened?'

He's still staring into space, but the second time she asks his pale eyes come into focus and he shakes his head, meeting her gaze.

'You'll find out soon enough.'

*What the hell is* that *supposed to mean?*

'Do you need me to do anything, Bill? Call someone? A doctor?'

'Don't fuss me,' he grouches, creaking himself up from the wall and heading back towards his front door.

'What will I find out?' Alice calls after him as he goes, but before Bill can answer Alice hears footsteps behind her.

She turns. It's AJ from three doors down, hurtling towards them in his scrubs from the hospital. He's another one whose name Alice knows but not much more: they'd said hello about a year back, Alice passing AJ as he unloaded boxes from a banged-up gold Vauxhall with a Sheffield United pennant in the window, but their paths have hardly crossed since. Bill never goes out, but AJ's never in. She imagines he's got plenty of places to go when he's not working. Alice has never seen him with anyone else, but AJ's designer stubble and dimples make her suspect he's not short of admirers, so she assumes he has endless options for company he's taking up on the nights his car stays gone from the street.

AJ skids to a stop just before he crashes into them.

'You get one as well?' he demands, waving a brown envelope the same as Bill's. The sight of it puts Alice even more on edge. Clocking Mollie's look of panic at his sudden arrival, AJ pastes on a bright smile.

''Ey up, trouble,' he says to the toddler, exaggerating the Sheffield lilt in his accent and holding his hand out for a high five. 'You being good?'

Mollie smacks his palm with a nod, then wanders away up the path.

Alice turns to AJ. 'What is it? What's going on?'

AJ's expression moves from stressed to uncertain, then understanding. He nods to the tote bag stuffed with papers over her shoulder. 'You just getting back from school, yeah?'

Alice nods. 'Not been in yet. What's going on?'

AJ grimaces, but his voice is gentle, and that makes Alice even more worried than before. ''S not my place to say,' he tells her, tilting his head towards her door. 'But you'll see.'

Alice glances over to where Bill's still standing, watching them half-hidden by his partially shut door. For a moment, their eyes meet, and Alice thinks she can see something shifting in him, like he wants to say something more. He looks towards Mollie on the next doorstep, singing a low song to herself and colouring in the path with pastel-pink chalk. Bill's face softens, just for a second. Then his door slams shut.

Alice turns back to AJ, who's got a worried puckering between his eyebrows and the envelope half-crumpled in his hand. It must be something bad to have given him this knock. Alice usually only ever sees AJ whizzing past in his car, munching toast and doing his hair in the rear-view mirror, a blast of house music or Whitney Houston disappearing with a screech of tyres. His face and hands are always animated, drumming on the wheel or gesticulating in energetic conversation with whoever he's got on speakerphone. Alice can't imagine him having that calm grit that nurses need. He doesn't even look old enough to be a nurse. That's what she'd always thought, but facing him now Alice realises AJ must be mid-twenties or thereabouts, older than she'd first thought.

'Come on,' she says. 'Tell me.'

But AJ just shakes his head. 'Get yourself in,' he replies, turning to go. 'Don't stress yet.' He leans round her to shout bye to Mol, then slouches back towards his house with none of his usual bounce. Left alone on the street, the cool air and the still-spitting rain suddenly make Alice shiver.

Mollie bounds through their unlocked front door like a puppy. She's collected the post from the doormat and decided it's all boring before Alice has even set her bags down.

'Oi. Get back here and give me those.'

But Mollie's already in the kitchen, stretching onto her tiptoes to copy Alice's usual process of dumping each day's post onto the countertop. Following her, Alice retrieves the bundle and sifts through it, separating flyers, takeaway menus and the monthly listings magazine from the bills and bank statements. It's there, in among the others: a brown envelope matching the ones Bill and AJ had been holding.

Alice's stomach goes hollow and an icy, ominous sensation rockets through her. There's no way that envelope contains good news. She spins through possibilities, but can't think what it could be. Surely the council haven't put the rent up again? She glances at the messy pile of paperwork on her makeshift kitchen table desk and crosses her fingers it's nothing that's going to cost her. She makes ends meet but it's a tightrope act. When everything's in balance she even manages to stash a bit away each month in Mol's savings account. But it wouldn't take much to wobble them. *Later*, Alice decides. She makes a mental note of the things she needs to do before Mollie's bedtime, sighs and gets to work.

Once Mollie's in bed, Alice heads back downstairs. The letter is a sinister presence in the room, but she can't bear to open it yet, so she grabs her phone from the side instead.

There's a flurry of new messages in her old Leeds University girls' group chat. The messages are mostly cocktail-glass and thumbs-up emojis, so Alice has to scroll up to understand what's going on. The original text is at the top, sent an hour ago.

Anyone about tonight? Two-for-one happy hour at The Alchemist while the lads are at the football?

Alice turns her phone off. She can't be arsed with the inevitable strawberry daiquiri selfies later. She tries hard not to begrudge them their fun, but it's tough being the only mum. She has to bite her tongue on the occasional times she still gets to hang out with them, and take care not to talk too much about breastfeeding, or sleep schedules, or her constant heart-dazzling pride and amazement every time Mollie does or says something she's never done before. The messages have only made her feel worse, so she retrieves a half-bottle of white wine from the fridge and pours herself a glass, sits down at the little yellow table and takes a deep breath.

Alice grits her teeth as she opens the letter. The first two words are a punch in the gut.

**EVICTION NOTICE.**

*Bollocks.*

In a sudden sick wave of panic, Alice lets the letter fall from her hand. She downs her glass, the chill of the wine sharp against her teeth and slowing the tornado of thoughts storming through her head. She counts to ten, then twenty, and back down again.

Dear Ms Clarke,

This letter is to inform you of the impending purchase of Leodis Street land and properties from Leeds Housing Federation by Gatsby Luxury Apartments Ltd.

You are hereby notified to vacate the premises described in the address above within twenty-eight days of the date of the delivery of this notice to you, at which time your tenancy will be terminated.

Demolition of the property is scheduled for this date, therefore, if you fail to vacate the premises within this period, you will be considered to be trespassing on private property. Legal proceedings may be taken against you, with our security operatives taking immediate action to remove you from the premises if required.

If you wish to discuss this matter further,

you are invited to do so at the forthcoming
meeting with a representative from Gatsby
Luxury Apartments (details enclosed).

We apologise for any inconvenience this may
cause you, and thank you for your understanding and swift cooperation.

Paul Buchanan

Gatsby Luxury Apartments Ltd

*A month? That's all they give you to get sorted and get out before
they bulldoze your house? After three years?* And even as the
thought pinballs through Alice's brain, the nausea returns,
because she knows other residents on the streets have been
here longer. From his stubbornness and the old-fashioned
nets in the windows, Alice reckons Bill's been here decades.

*They can't.* The two words loop in her head, between
phrases like 'security deposit' and 'three months' rent
required upfront'. She can't do it. Not in a month, not without
more time to plan, to do the sums, to look for somewhere else
in between all the swanky places aimed at 'young profession-
als' with coke habits and actual career prospects, or the sorts
of students who won't do their own washing up. She can't
afford anywhere like that.

She could go back to the council, but Alice is already
envisioning the shit places they showed her last time: the flat
in Beeston with black alien tendrils of mould creeping from
the bathroom ceiling, or the place in Armley with smoke and
water damage from the fire that had destroyed next door.
Alice had still been reeling from the conversation with Sam
when they'd both finally been forced to recognise that it
wasn't going to work. She went to the viewings in a daze, big
vintage sunglasses hiding her swollen, tear-tired eyes, a Leeds

Housing Federation officer with neon nails and ladybird earrings cooing over six-month-old Mollie's chubby arms and long-lashed eyes. Alice knew how much hinged on her next move, the fog lifting just a fraction as she assessed the issues with each property. Even with its wheezy boiler and treacherously steep staircase, it was obvious that Leodis Street was their best choice.

*I mean, it wasn't exactly paradise, but come on. Look at it now.* Terrified but determined, Alice had dismantled Mollie's cot and borrowed Sam's car for an Ikea trip where she'd maxed out her credit card. Once they were in and sorted, Alice had relied on strategic rinsing of the B&Q sales and canny scouring of the posh charity shops in Ilkley to slowly turn the house into a home. *If you call it bohemian, you can get away with anything.* And it works: everything clashes but it all goes together, and it's *theirs*.

Alice goes back to the envelope and examines it again, fishes out a flimsy slip of paper with the meeting details. Next Monday, at some offices in Meanwood, chaired by Paul Buchanan. *Slimeball dickhead*, she decides, head collapsing into her hands. *But maybe I can appeal, or something. If they're holding a meeting, maybe it's not final yet.* The capital letters of the eviction notice have a grim finality to them, but Alice makes her breathing as slow and calm as she can, and decides she's got to hold out hope. *I'll go to the meeting, and I'll fight it. Even if I'm the only one on the street who shows. They're not taking this away from me. Not without listening to my case first.*

She doesn't want to have to change jobs. She doesn't want to move Mollie to a different nursery. She doesn't want to have to explain to Mollie that their home is worth more to someone smashed to bits than with them in it.

*They can't, they can't, they can't.*

The last of the wine gets poured into Alice's glass and by the time that's empty, she's empty and exhausted too. But there's something else – a tiny ember of defiance. She's not being evicted without a fight.

# CHAPTER TWO

B ill makes boiled eggs and buttered toast for breakfast. The estate and its surrounding area have changed a lot in the time he's been here, but the local bakery is still going strong. Each time he goes, the prices seem to have crept up and he no longer recognises the names of half the things on the chalkboard menu above the counter. Still, it's part of his ritual: once a week in a slow loop that stops at the market, the library, and sometimes the doctor's or the post office, to pay his bills and withdraw his pension. The bakery is on the way back, saved until last so the loaf keeps that soft flour warmth and smell. He does other excursions when he has to, but for the most part his life has shrunk to a one-mile radius, especially since the bus he used to get to the Yorkshire County Cricket ground changed its route. He doesn't know where it goes from now.

It's early, only just gone six, but the sun is already streaking the sky pink and gold. That and the birdsong that comes with the sunrise are a comfort to Bill; his body clock seems set for early mornings, once it's past a certain time he's awake with no chance of further sleep. It's harder in winter, when he's always been up for hours by the time the sun comes sneaking up and the few buzzy street lights still working finally flicker all the way out. When his day has been in progress for what feels like for ever by the time it even starts for anyone else. When the cold gets in his bones so that his arthritis becomes tight, knife-hot knots in his knuckles and hips, and it's hard not to get trapped going round in circles remembering when things were better. The noise from next door doesn't help: Bill knows it's not Alice's fault that their houses share a wall, but when he's knackered and in pain every sound grates on his nerves. Some days, it sounds like pandemonium next door: the little one caterwauling, the hairdryer blasting, cartoon theme tunes mixing in with the high motorised whine of the washing machine. The chaotic image it conjures up for Bill makes him bristle even more when he recalls Alice's intermittent attempts to bond with and help him. *Needs to get her own house in order before she starts mithering me. I've told her I'm fine, haven't I? Wish she'd bloody well just take me at my word and leave me well enough alone.*

Breakfast made, Bill eases himself into the armchair by the window, thankful for the temporary peace. The leather on the chair's arms is soft and splitting, and Bill smooths his fingers over the familiar texture like a good-luck talisman before reaching for his pint mug of tea. He still thinks of it as Dad's armchair, which is daft because Dad's been dead and buried half a century at least. But Bill can't unstick that way of thinking: the entire house is layers of people and memories, all pasted over each other. There are little echoes of Mam, Dad and his brothers all over the house. The bookshelves in the alcove by the fireplace: his dad built those for Mam, and for years they'd housed her sewing and recipe books. When Mam died, Dad boxed them away, using the shelves for his collection of battered murder mysteries and sci-fi paperbacks. A few of Bill's favourites remain there even now, kept from when he and Sally took the house over after Dad's death. There's a dint in the bannister from the impact of Bill's six-year-old head, the casualty of a zealous battle with Alfie on the landing that ended in Bill roly-polying down every thudding step of the steep staircase. He'd bounced back upright with a dazed expression, swearing vengeance and only realising he was bleeding when he sprayed red everywhere. He'd nearly bitten through his lip, and Mam's shrieks at the blood had been a long-standing joke on the street for years after. She'd hurled Alfie and Eddie out into the street to play while she bundled Bill to hospital, but his brothers put their exile to good use. By the time Bill and Mam got back, Alfie and Eddie had been begging at all their neighbours' doors, doing a dramatic retelling of his injury and promising future errands in return for a few donated pennies. They spent their scraped-together windfall on tin soldiers and sweets, presented to Bill with utmost solemnity on his return.

Sally's still everywhere, of course. She was always far better at the domestic side of things than Bill, and he can't bring himself to undo her hard work. Besides, it suits him to have reminders of her. His bedroom now is the same one he was born in, but it was his and Sally's so long he can't remember it being Mam and Dad's. Darker, he thinks, and not as comfortable. All through her cancer, Sally had fretted about what he'd do when she wasn't there to take care of him. He'd taken care of her as best he could, but taking care of himself is harder. Keeping to his routine helps: after rinsing his breakfast plate, he settles down with yesterday's paper and its halfway-done crossword. That letter is still on the mantelpiece. How long is it since it came? *Three days*, Bill thinks, scowling. He never used to have to check himself that way.

Since Sally died, Bill only opens the official-looking envelopes. Their friends sent so many cards and letters after her death that the weight of replying to them all started to crush him. He'd never been good at knowing what to say. Now he just deals with what he has to. But this one is too much for him even to think about.

Bill's tolerance for interacting with people is pretty low at the best of times, but he's almost grateful when the knock at the door comes. His thoughts were starting to get all twisted up again. When he opens the door, a man holds out his hand.

'Bill,' he says. 'Levon. I know you by sight, of course, but I don't think we've ever been properly introduced. I live just down there, on the corner. And I work at the library, so I sometimes see you in there.'

The man is softly spoken and well mannered, with an accent Bill can't place. *What does he want? I recognise him, I think, so he must be telling the truth. Not from round here, though, is he?* Bill gives a suspicious acknowledging grunt, scrutinising Levon more closely as they shake hands. Even though he must be in his fifties, the lapels of the other man's denim jacket are covered in badges. Without his glasses, the words on them are too small for Bill to read, but he recognises some of the political symbols. *Oh aye*, he thinks. *One of them, is he? Seems a bit long in the tooth to be rattling the collection tin or whatever this is going to be.*

Levon clears his throat. 'Bill, please forgive the intrusion, but I just wanted to check in and see how you were doing, after the letter. It must've been such a shock, what with how long you've been here.'

*Couldn't have been about owt else, could it? And what's it got to do with him how long I've been here?*

'Decades,' he huffs, purposely keeping it vague. 'Too long to keep count.'

Levon's eyes widen and he gives a hissing sympathetic sigh. 'And here I was thinking I was doing well with my nine years.'

Another grunt from Bill.

'So how are you doing?' Levon presses, rocking back on heels. 'What did your kids say?'

'No kids,' Bill says. 'Just me.'

Levon stumbles through an effusive apology. 'I thought I remembered seeing you have visitors, not long after I moved in. I just assumed ...'

*How many years did he say? Nine.* Around that first anniversary of Sally dying, then, when everything had just about started becoming the tiniest bit less black than before. But the days had still been a grey numb sludge, and when Danny turned up on his doorstep after his phone calls and letters had gone unanswered, Bill hadn't been in the mood for cake and sympathy. He'd let Danny in, but not for long, and the lad hadn't been back since.

Bill realises he's got caught up in his reminiscing and drags his focus back to Levon.

'Foster kids,' he explains. 'We had a few, over the years. Don't stay in touch. Almost all of 'em turned out to my Sal's funeral, though. Couple of 'em tried to keep the contact going after.' He rubs his nose, blinking fast like he might sneeze. 'I'm not too good at that, though.'

'So it's just you. And me. And all of us. We're all in it together, aren't we? That's why I'm here, really. I wanted to ask whether you'll come to the meeting on Monday?'

'Wasn't planning on it,' Bill grumbles. *Where did he say he were from? Can't be anywhere round here with all this talk of togetherness. I can't be doing with that. Fancy words that don't do owt real. And that's all that meeting will be, won't it? So what's the point?*

Levon tilts his head, an owlish look on his face like he can read Bill's mind. 'I wish you'd reconsider. If we join forces, all the neighbours, it'll be something. A show of solidarity, you know.'

That word – *solidarity* – that's another giveaway. For someone with ideals. Bill remembers Sally, all lit up with that sort of talk during the 1970 strike at the clothes factory; she and her work friends bundled up against the snow with their flasks and brollies and handmade signs. It had taken a month but they'd got their three shillings an hour pay rise. *Always a fighter*, Bill thinks, fondness flushing through him, and the recollection is enough to stop him from telling Levon to sling his hook.

'Don't see as it'll achieve owt, but I'll think about it,' Bill says, after a few more minutes of soft insistence from Levon, but it's more to get rid of him than anything else. After another handshake, Levon finally lets him go, and Bill rests against the closed front door for a moment before moving back towards his armchair. He was being honest when he said he thought the meeting was a waste of time, but that's not the only reason he's so reluctant. He's been rattled by Levon's visit, and he's not ready to face anything else that'll make the looming threat of that letter any more real than it already is.

# CHAPTER THREE

Nineteen minutes until the meeting starts. Should be enough to make it, as long as the lights aren't against him. Still damp from the shower, AJ scrambles into jeans and a T-shirt, then his car, revving the engine and cranking Whitney up to full volume as he speeds away up the street. *Every time*, he thinks, grimacing at his growling stomach and the grittiness of his eyes. Every time he's on the night shift, the next day's always upside down. Tea and cereal before bed after fourteen hours in A&E, putting on a film to wind down from the night's dramas then falling asleep within minutes, waking up to the credits and a crick in his neck. He'd snoozed his phone alarm six times before he remembered the meeting, then panicked.

*Bang.* AJ's tyres crash over the deep pothole at the end of the street, rattling his suspension, his spine and his teeth. Hoping he's gotten lucky again, and that the tyres have survived another day of him forgetting to swerve, AJ edges the car through drizzle and school-run traffic, tilting the mirror down at the lights to faff with his twists and wipe a smear of toothpaste off his cheek. *It's not right but it's okay*, Whitney croons. The car groans as he guns the gas, and AJ winces when he sees the fuel gauge needle nearly on empty. He doesn't want to have to transfer to another hospital. The one where he works is only ten minutes' drive away: a short enough journey that he could walk if he was more organised and less exhausted all the time. But he likes having the option, even if he doesn't ever take it, a surge of gratitude at the end of every shift for the close distance between work and home. He loves his job, but the idea of a long commute on top makes him want to go back to bed and hide. Looking at possible places to live back when he was interviewing for the job he has now, the proximity of Leodis Street to the hospital was what won him over. He'd looked through the photos of the house, with its wonky ceilings and ancient radiators, and imagined himself collapsing into bed under the sloping sky-light after his shifts. He was still at the housing office when the hospital phoned to offer him the job. He's loved Leeds since coming here for Carnival every August as a kid, but that was the day he started to build a picture of what living here could be like. He'd bombed it down the motorway back to Sheffield afterwards, blasting *I get so emotional* and fizzing with pride to tell his mam he'd got the job and hopefully a house all in one afternoon.

One minute before the meeting's due to start, AJ screeches up to his destination, banishing his fantasies of food and more sleep. Inside, the place is a maze of intimidating chrome as AJ scans the lobby for some clue as to where he needs to go. There's a receptionist in a headset who looks like a villain from a graphic novel. Everything about her is sharp angles: her hair, her make-up, her clothes. AJ knows how to turn on the charm when he needs it, and his time in nursing means he's used to dealing with all sorts, but this woman's icy blankness is unnerving.

When he asks for directions, she gives an irritated sigh. 'You're late, you know.'

AJ checks his phone. 'Bang on time, actually.'

'Everyone's already in the boardroom,' she says, as though that settles it.

*Everyone?* AJ gives his most amiable grin. 'So can you tell me how to get there, then? Please?'

Her eyes roll. 'Take the lift over there. Fifth floor. Second door on the left.'

'Cheers, love.' He dashes off before she can reply.

*Everybody's already here? That must mean some of the others came. I hope that woman with the little kid is here. She seems like she could cope with anything.*

But when he hurtles through the boardroom double doors, it's not just Alice he sees, sitting on metal chairs around a swanky long table. It's all of them. *That old grandad in the flat cap, he lives next to the woman with the kid. She called him Bill, didn't she? And that other older guy, must be a few decades younger than Bill. He's been on the street as long as I've been there. Iranian, or something. Didn't he post a leaflet through my door, a petition for the local library?*

AJ realises everyone's staring.

'Ah, I see we have a straggler,' a smooth voice announces. 'Mr Campbell, I assume? Nice of you to join us at last.' A man in a designer pinstripe suit with gelled-back blonde hair offers AJ a hand, wrist rattling with a chunky silver watch. 'Paul Buchanan,' he says. 'Come on in, take a seat.'

*Slick*, AJ thinks, but he's not impressed. He recognises the tone; he's had it used on him enough times before. Cut-throat arrogance wrapped in charisma and politeness like a magic trick. He can imagine Paul in a hospital waiting room, bitching about waiting times but in that veiled, well-mannered way that means there's no answering back.

AJ grits his teeth, gives the man an apologetic mock-salute and slopes towards a seat. The conference room is more gleaming metal and glass, and AJ gets the sense of being in a villain's lair again. It feels like the sort of place where evil deals are brokered. The only empty chair is next to the pale punky teenager who lives next door. He's let on to her before, but she always seems in her own world: stomping up the street with her headphones on, mirror shades hiding her eyes. He didn't see her when he came in because she's sitting hunched over, knees hugged up to her chest. *Bit weird she's here on her own. Shouldn't she be at school?* He slides into the space next to her and gives her a nod, but like always there's no acknowledgement: her eyeliner-ringed eyes just stare straight ahead.

'Now we're all here,' Paul says, with a sarcastic bow to AJ, 'we can get started.'

He clicks a remote control with a flourish. The lights dim, and a projector beams an image onto the wall behind him. It's their street, AJ can tell that much, but only from the position of the curve of the road and the church spire in the background. Because instead of their row of Victorian terraces with crooked stone steps leading to skinny doors, there's one mammoth apartment block. Like the offices they're in, it's a fusion of dark grey and reflections; walls made entirely from windows, balconies with potted palm trees, everything sleek and clean. Nothing crumbling. No litter. No potholes. No rust. No rain.

'As you can see,' Paul says, as he clicks through more pictures, 'our plans for Leodis Street are ambitious. Innovative. We see transformative potential. The Leodis Street Village will be a *real community*. An asset to the area. High-end contemporary living spaces *and* investment where it's needed most.'

His buttery evangelist voice pauses like he's expecting applause. Alice mutters something under her breath.

'Pardon?'

She blushes, but meets Paul's gaze without fear. 'I just said I don't know how you're going to make it a *real community* when only millionaires will be able to afford to live there.'

Paul smooths down the front of his suit, checks a piece of paper which must list their names. 'We appreciate your feedback, Alice. And I acknowledge this is an inconvenience. I understand you're upset. But if this is anyone's fault, it's the council's. They've failed to do anything with your street for decades. They've let it deteriorate to a point where it'll cost more than they've got to do all the jobs it needs. If you're going to lay the blame for this with anyone, that's been their failing. Luckily, we're always looking for opportunities to help improve the neighbourhoods that need it most. And your neighbourhood *really* needs it.'

'So that's it? You gave them that flashy speech and they believed it? What a joke,' Alice murmurs, and Bill, still staring at the table like he has been the entire time, gives a grunt. Paul ignores them.

'We've made Leeds Housing Federation a very generous offer, and they've accepted. The paperwork's in progress, but we expect the contract to be finalised any day.'

'It's *wrong*,' Alice says, and though AJ catches the little shake in her voice, it's clear and loud enough that this time Paul can't pretend not to hear. He motions for Alice to continue, smirking. *Go on, Alice*, AJ thinks. *Rip him a new one.*

'You can't do this. You've got no right. These are our *homes*

22

you're talking about. It's not ethical, to do this. There should be consultations, advance warnings. You've not given us any say. And you're not giving us any time.'

'Legally, we are only required to give tenants twenty-eight days' notice.'

'I'm not talking about legally. I'm talking about morally.' Alice folds her arms and leans back in her chair. 'Have you heard of morality, Mr Buchanan?'

'Damn,' AJ puts in softly, and thinks he hears a snorting noise as the teenager next to him hides a laugh in her sleeve.

'I'm happy to hear your comments,' Paul tells them. 'That's what we're here for, after all. But I'm afraid that beyond that, there's not much I can do. This is a done deal.'

The man whose name AJ doesn't know raises his hand. 'And you don't think you have any ethical responsibility to support and rehome the existing tenants?'

'Mr . . . ' Paul consults his list and hesitates over the surname. 'Amiri. Levon Amiri.'

'Mr Amiri, we have gone above and beyond our responsibilities by hosting this meeting. This was a gesture of goodwill, to allow you to share your thoughts. Your tenancy agreements are with the council, not us. Those agreements are being terminated. That's all there is to it.'

Levon cocks his head, listening hard to this response, and jots down a scribble in a notebook before he answers. 'I came here as an asylum seeker. Did you know that, Mr Buchanan? I was ten. I've lived in many places, and I've been very lucky. People have mostly been kind. But I can tell you, separating people from their homes has consequences. It's cruel. Forgive me for saying so, but you don't seem like a man with much of a conscience. But if you do have one, somewhere, please hear this as a direct appeal to it. Reconsider. Please.'

AJ gives a *hell-yeah* finger-snap while Alice nods, dewy-eyed. 'You should be ashamed of yourself,' she tells Paul. 'There's no way this is right. There's got to be a way this can be stopped.'

'Yeah, man,' AJ puts in. 'We can appeal to the council or something. They can't just sell off our houses without telling us.'

'They can,' Paul says. 'And they have. Because they're not really your houses, are they? They belong to the council. Or they did. As soon as the contracts are signed, they'll be ours. And I'm afraid we have a vision for Leodis Street that means they'll have to come down.'

'"Vision" being code for bullshit,' the punk kid chimes in. 'Just say you want us out so you can get rich suckers in and make another few million quid, why don't you?' Her deadpan tone's at odds with her laser glare, and the combined effect just makes Paul's patronising smirk wider still.

'And your name is?'

Her scowls deepens. 'Jessie Cassidy.'

Paul checks his sheet of paper. 'I assume the Donna Cassidy I have down here is a relation?'

Jessie juts her chin. 'That's my mum.'

'Ah. Well, I'll tell you, Jessie.' Smug wolfish smile. 'However you want to describe it, this has gone through all the correct legal channels. Your tenancy agreements are being terminated in three weeks' time. So I suggest you all start packing.' He glances at his Rolex. 'And now, if you'll excuse me, I have another meeting. Thank you for coming.'

Then he's gone. The receptionist ushers them out of the building, no hint of warmth in her demeanour as they emerge, shell-shocked, onto the street. The rain has stopped and the sun is harsh after the cool dark of inside. They squint at each other, unsure what to do next. Somewhere between the meeting room and here, Jessie's already disappeared.

'We've got to do something,' Alice says, finally. 'We need a plan.'

Levon nods. 'Absolutely. There's power in numbers. The more we can join forces, the better chance we've got.'

'I've got to go and get Mollie from her dad's. But can we meet up soon, start getting some ideas together?'

'I'm up for that.' AJ pulls up his phone calendar, scrolling through his shifts. There's something in his diary he'll have to move, but he's done it before and he can do it again. *Least it's a real reason this time*, he thinks with a dark smirk to himself. *Being made homeless is a better excuse than just being too tired from work, right?*

He makes his decision and looks up at the others. 'I'm on nights at the minute, but I can do tomorrow, as long as we're done in time for me to get to work after?'

'Come to mine,' Alice says. 'You know which one it is, right? I'll get Mol to bed early, then you can come any time after seven.'

'This is a good idea,' Levon says. 'I'll check some things out in the library tomorrow too. Try to find other incidences of things like this happening. What the tenants did then.'

'Brilliant. Bring anything you think might help.'

'What about you, Bill?' The three of them look to the older man, hopefully. The combined impact of their staring clearly makes him uncomfortable and his gaze lowers to the ground.

'Don't see the point,' he grumbles, after a moment. 'He said it's a done deal. Nothing we can do.'

'Just come, Bill. Please? The contracts aren't final. It's got to be worth a try.'

'My bus is due,' he huffs, turning away from Alice's

beseeching expression and pointing towards the bus stop with his walking stick.

'I've got the car,' AJ tells him, scrabbling in his jeans to retrieve his keys. 'If you want a lift home.'

'I'll get the bus.' Bill's tone doesn't invite further discussion and AJ wonders, for a second, whether he's ever compromised in his life.

They all watch Bill slowly make his way in the opposite direction, then look back at each other.

'He'll come around,' Alice says, but her voice wavers like she's not sure.

AJ pats her shoulder. *She better be right. Because we need all the help we can get.*

# CHAPTER FOUR

I t's nearly nine the next morning when AJ finally gets off the ward. It was supposed to be six, but then his colleague Deb phoned to say her entire family were projectile vomiting with suspected food poisoning, and there was no way she could make her shift. Everyone's faces tightened when they heard, the knock-on impact of being one person down too much to take when they were already stretched to their limits. AJ stayed on after his shift until he knew someone else was coming in as cover. Dawn's long been and gone by the time he makes it out of the hospital and across the puddle-blotted Tarmac to his car. It lashed it down overnight, rain hissing against the windows in those dim-light dream-like hours between night and morning, then vanishing into the milky morning April sun.

In the driver's seat, he lets his forehead rest against the wheel for a minute. It's been a tough night. Around three, a little girl on his observation round was rushed down to ICU. She'd been on the ward for days, coming in with abdominal pain and awaiting appendix surgery. When her pain levels spiked in the early hours, AJ's suspicions that her appendix had perforated were soon confirmed, and everyone scrambled to get her down to the emergency theatre in time. She was still there when the ward nurse made AJ go home. He loves it on paediatrics, most of the time. During his degree, he spent most of his training hours at Northern General in Sheffield, revolving through the different departments and absorbing as much knowledge as he could. Pain management. Oncology. The acute medical unit. They'd all taught him a lot, but it was AJ's final placement at the children's hospital that made his mind up about who he wanted to be once he graduated. Those weeks had been the hardest, but the best, and he'd finally felt his confidence building, felt himself becoming good at what he did. AJ never gets bored of seeing how tenacious the kids he treats are, even when they're scared, in pain, far away from home. He loves the daily reminders that recovery is possible, that it's possible to go through the worst kinds of hurt and come out the other side. But when the heartbreaks come, they're hard to take. Between AJ's training and his time in paediatrics since, he's seen a lot. Deaths, slow and sudden, the aftermaths of injuries, accidents, abuse. It's made him tougher over time, but his mam's always saying she doesn't know how he copes, or how he can stay cool in a crisis now when he was such a soft, caring kid. AJ's learnt to compartmentalise, but he still feels the knocks. Fumbling for his phone for music to keep him awake on the drive home, AJ realises a message has come through while he's been in his trance: Still on for later? Can't wait to finally hang out x

Giving a soft groan of frustration, AJ lets his head thud back down onto the wheel. He was supposed to do this yesterday, wasn't he? *Such a shit look to cancel on the day.*

*Again. He's gonna think I'm a right knob. But I've got to be at that meeting tonight.*

Gritting his teeth, he sends a reply: So sorry, something's come up. Rain check?

AJ turns the key in the ignition. *No point waiting for an answer, because he's definitely gonna think I'm taking the piss. Wouldn't blame him if he just ghosted.* AJ's lost count of how many times this date's already been rescheduled because of work, and after multiple attempts it was a reluctant compromise to organise it for an evening when AJ had a night shift afterwards.

Not exactly gonna be a wild one if you're on the lemonade, Luca sent, when AJ originally suggested it. But better than nothing ;)

AJ got it: the vision of them slamming back shots on a heaving strobe-lit dance floor was more exciting than soft drinks or coffee and polite chit-chat, but it turns out he's not going to get either. The date had initially been set up by one of AJ's mates, exasperated by AJ's perpetual inability to do anything other than work and convinced that Luca – a half-Italian social worker and weekend triathlete who shared AJ's obsession with Whitney Houston – would be the answer. AJ wasn't so sure. *But I'll never know now, because I've blown it before we even met.*

AJ drives home on autopilot, swearing when he forgets the pothole yet again as he turns onto Leodis Street, his tyres slipping on the wet, worn-out patches of road where the original cobbles show through from underneath. Luca's reply comes through just as he pulls up. No offence but I'll leave it. You're too elusive for me + I don't like wasting time x

*Called it*, AJ thinks, resigned but also relieved that now he can give up continually moving the date around his calendar. *Another one bites the dust.*

Inside, AJ drops his keys on the counter and sleepwalks straight to the shower. He won't be able to sleep until he's washed off last night's grime, stress and sadness. The hot water and bright menthol smell of the eucalyptus shower gel suds ease the aches in his muscles and slowly make him feel more human. Once he's out, towelled off and in his trackies and a clean T-shirt, he's with it enough to identify that some breakfast and a big sleep might not fix everything, but they'll go a long way to sorting him out.

When a poke through the fridge and kitchen cupboards leaves him empty-handed, AJ heads back out. *Get some oxygen and some Vitamin D*, he thinks, *and ingredients for a proper meal.* That'll see him right. No more passing out after his shifts and getting bollocked for being too thin when his mam sees him next. *Mawga*, she'd cluck if she could see him now, the patois rolling off her tongue in disapproval at his waistband slipping down. *Skinny.* Keeping her imaginary admonitions in mind, AJ loads up his basket with bread, eggs, cheese and beans, making his purchase from a headscarfed teenager and heading back out into the weak sunlight. Turning the corner back onto the street, AJ gets a wave from Levon, who's crossing towards the main road in the direction of the library in his John Lennon glasses, satchel hanging from one shoulder. With his upside-down schedule, AJ's not seen much of Levon before now, but his hazy impression of him was the sort of out-of-touch do-gooder and dreamer who'd be in his element in an endless dinner-party argument about where Corbyn went wrong. Someone who comments on every *Guardian* article about politics and dresses like a mature student at art college as a protest against the middle class. AJ hadn't expected him to be so practical: he'd felt reassured hearing Levon's calm, clear voice in the meeting, and liked his unflappable attitude despite how shit and hopeless things seem.

With everything that's happened overnight, AJ's not had much chance to process yesterday's meeting. But replaying it now, he comes to a sudden halt at his gate. *That girl, what was her name again? Jessie. She went before we made the plan. She doesn't know that we're getting together to try to fight. Someone needs to tell her, and her mum.*

He squints at his phone for the time. He swapped out his contacts for glasses after his shower but his eyes are still itchy and tired. *She'll be in school now, won't she? Maybe I could write a note to put through the door?* But as he dithers at the end of the path, AJ realises he can hear the shudder of drums and guitars coming from the house next door to his. Someone's in.

It takes ages for anyone to answer. *Am I being ignored or can they just not hear me over the music?* AJ's stomach growls and he's about to give up when the noise abruptly shuts off. He knocks again and sees a shadow coming towards the door through the frosted-glass panel. There's the clunk and scrape of bolts and locks being undone, then Jessie's face, pixie-like and suspicious, peers through a gap in the door. She's wearing a black dress with so many buckles and straps that it reminds AJ of a straitjacket, with stripy tights and giant monster feet slippers. Since last night, she's dyed her hair neon green, and a banana-yellow fringe falls into her heavily made-up eyes. AJ can tell it's a DIY job from the splodges on Jessie's scalp and ears.

'Yeah?'

'AJ,' he says, in case she doesn't recognise him. 'I was at the meeting yesterday. I live next door.'

'I know.' Jessie leans on the door frame. 'I've been here a year,' she says. 'I know who lives where.'

'Right. So. You were at the meeting yesterday. And then at the end you disappeared. And I wanted to let you know that we're going to try and fight it. The evictions.'

'Who is?'

'Us. The neighbours. All of us.' He thinks of Bill, grumbling and plodding off on his own. 'Or anyone who wants to, anyway.'

'What are you going to do?'

'Not sure yet. But something. We're going to get together tonight. At Alice's, you know ...?' He makes a gesture towards her house, with its psychedelic flower stickers on the bins and Mollie's chalk drawings decorating the path, and Jessie gives a grudging nod of recognition. 'She says we can do it at hers. Get our heads together, come up with some ideas.'

Jessie scoffs. 'You kidding me? Prim and proper's gonna plan a revolution? I'll pass.'

'What?'

'I'm just saying, I don't know if I wanna join a rebel alliance run by someone who dresses like a primary-school teacher.'

AJ screws his face up, remembering the scant details he'd got about Alice on the journey back the night before. 'I think she is one, actually.'

Jessie rolls her eyes and gives a sudden hiccuppy giggle. 'So predictable. Swear down, I'm psychic sometimes.'

'Well ...' AJ scrambles to get them back on subject. 'We're meeting later, and I thought you and your mum might—'

'Mum's not here.'

'Is she at work? You could let her know when she gets back, then you could come together, later? If you're up for it, I mean.'

Jessie chews a chipped black thumbnail. 'I don't think so.'

'She won't be up for it?'

'It's not that. She just ... doesn't really live here at the moment.'

She shuffles on the doorstep and AJ gets a glimpse over her shoulder at the room beyond. There are art supplies spread out all over the floor, and a mammoth wall hanging of lotuses and mandalas, picked out in such intricate detail that even from the front door, AJ can see the glint of beads, sequins and mirrored discs reflecting the light.

'What do you mean?' he asks. 'You're here on your own? Where is she?'

Jessie gives a snorting little grin and squints at AJ like she doesn't trust his intentions. 'Mate, you ask a lot of questions.'

He holds his hands up in apology. 'Sounds like you're telling me to mind my own business.'

'It's okay,' she tells him, but she still sounds annoyed. 'Everyone always asks. At college, they're always at it. Asking me things.' She puts on a daft spooky voice. 'Must be because I'm such an enigma.'

AJ returns the grin, but his voice is soft when he replies. 'You also look pretty young to be living on your own, you know? That might have something to do with it, too.'

Jessie rolls her eyes. 'Whatever. I'm eighteen. I'm fine here on my own. It's better that way, really.'

'So what about your mum?'

Jessie sighs, shuffling the monster slippers. 'At her boyfriend's. She's pretty much moved in. Doesn't come back much.'

'And you didn't go with her?'

She shakes her head. 'There's no room for me in his flat. He's got a kid, and a dog. One of those massive husky ones that looks like a wolf. Add my mum into that and he's more than got his hands full. And me and Mum get on better with a bit of distance, anyway.'

'So what about everything that's going on? You know, the evictions? The demolition?'

AJ thinks Jessie looks young for her age anyway, but the fear and then defiance that flash across her face in answer to his question make her seem even more childlike.

She does a half-scowl, half-shrug. 'Don't know.'

'But your mum would want to know, right? Even if she's living on the other side of town, surely she'll still care about what's happening? To this house, and to you?'

'I messaged her when that letter came.'

'And?'

'She's not replied.'

AJ winces. If he misses a call from his mam he gets at least three texts and usually a voice note or two demanding to know if he's alright.

'What about you?' he asks. 'You could still come.'

Jessie glances around, anywhere but at AJ, her gaze settling on Alice's front door before hardening. 'Nah. Don't think so.'

'Why? You were brilliant last night, telling that Paul Buchanan what you thought of him. We could do with more of that.' Suddenly AJ really wants Jessie to come, to show her that it's okay to care about things.

Jessie gives a lopsided smile, but still shakes her head. 'Can't.' She gestures behind her, at the sketchbook on the carpet surrounded by a messy halo of pens and paints and crumpled-up balls of paper. 'I've got a deadline for college. I need to get this coursework done. The teachers all give me enough grief as it is.'

'I bet,' AJ says, in a conspiratorial tone. 'Because, based

on the time, I'm guessing you should probably be there by now, right?'

'God, you do ask a lot of questions, don't you?' Jessie folds her arms. 'I get the work done. I'm the best at art in my class. And English as well, I'm good at that. But I don't really go to classes. I just get on with it from here.'

'How come?'

Jessie fiddles with one of her dress buckles, waggling its metal tongue back and forth. 'I can't cope with it. All the noise and strangers and people telling me what to do. It does my head in. My brain gets overloaded. I get stressed and then I get moody, and then they get at me about my attitude and I end up in fights or telling the teachers to fuck off, and everything just gets way more dramatic than it needs to be. I think that's part of what stresses Mum out about me. I don't know, I can't really explain it. But I get the grades. I wish they'd just leave me to it.'

'But they don't?'

'They write nasty letters, threatening all sorts. Saying they might not let me do my exams if my attendance doesn't improve. When I missed the UCAS deadline, they got really pissed off about that. I don't know. I'm always doing something wrong. I usually just bin the letters they send. I nearly did that with that one the other day. But it was a different envelope to the ones from college, so I thought I'd better open it.' She huffs a sigh. 'Wish I hadn't now, though.'

'Me too,' AJ says, shivering as a cloud drifts over the sun. He's hungry and tired and wishes he could do something to make it better, and it makes him sadder still that he can't. But he makes one last attempt. 'We'll be at Alice's from seven tonight. If you change your mind.'

'I won't.' The door closes and then AJ's alone on the doorstep, stifling a yawn. He half-expects the music to start blaring again but everything stays quiet. He heads indoors towards bed.

# CHAPTER FIVE

Teatime over, Alice half-regrets hosting tonight's meeting. *Probably be more worth my while to be looking at rentals, right?* Or sending up the bat signal to the chat groups she's in – her old student mates and the other teachers from work, see if any of them have heard of anything that might suit her and Mollie. But something stops her. She doesn't want to tell anyone what's happening. Not yet. Alice gazes round at the cosy home she's made, her fury returning when she remembers Paul Buchanan's smug reptile smile. They're fighting. That's what matters.

So she plumps cushions and tidies toys, raids Mollie's treat cupboard and arranges cookies on a plate. Dashes upstairs at ten to seven, sorts her face and gets changed. She's in her comfiest leopard trackies and matching hoodie, but her clothes are clean and free from stains, which is as good as it gets with a toddler in the house. Alice blitzes round the room, wincing at the occasional cough coming from Mollie, burritoed in a blanket in Alice's bed. She's been subdued and snuffly all evening, and Alice is worried. She can't afford time off if Mollie comes down with something. Before the thought sends Alice spiralling, there's a knock at the front door.

'Levon. Thanks for coming.' She ushers him inside. He's in his library clothes; smart dark jeans and a sky-blue button-up shirt under his usual denim jacket, holding a potted plant and a clingfilmed plate.

'Thanks for hosting.' He passes her the plate and the plant. 'I brought these.' The plate contains creamy-coloured slices the consistency of fudge, studded with jewel-like chunks of pistachio, while the plant sits in a dark ceramic bowl, its leaves spiking up in glossy yellow-green tongues.

'That's so thoughtful. But you didn't have to do that.'

He smiles. 'Ah, but one mustn't go to someone's home without bringing something. It's tradition. So that's a snake plant, for luck, persistence and happiness, and some halva. There's no symbolism to that, but it's delicious. And I thought it might keep us well fuelled.'

'Levon, that's lovely. Honestly. Come on, let's go through.'

She leads him into the kitchen and puts the kettle on, then peers through the jungle of plants on the windowsill over the sink.

'I was debating whether to knock on for Bill, to remind him about tonight.' Alice bats aside the yellow star-shaped flowers on a spindly tomato plant, stands on her tiptoes and cranes her neck in an attempt to see from her kitchen into Bill's. Lights glow from behind closed curtains. 'I don't want to hassle him. But surely the more heads, the better?'

Levon makes a small humming sound accompanied by a politely sceptical head-tilt. 'If he wanted to be here, he would be. He might need time to come around.'

'Not like we've got an excess of that, though, is it?'

'Suppose not,' Levon says, and they share a grimace as Alice passes him a mug of peppermint tea.

'You've been here the longest, haven't you? Apart from Bill.'

Levon nods. 'If we're talking time served on the street, he's certainly got a few years on me, but I've been here nearly a decade.'

Alice takes a sip of her own scalding builder's brew. 'You said in the meeting you came here as an asylum seeker. Do you mind me asking where you're from originally?'

'Not at all. I was born in an Iranian city called Khorramshahr, right on the border with Iraq.'

'So you left to escape the conflict between Iraq and Iran?'

Watching Levon turn his cup to inhale the peppermint steam, Alice is embarrassed by how little she knows about that part of the world. She read some of the history in the deep-dive features that seemed to be being published everywhere the last time the two nations clashed, but her memory of the details is murky.

Levon nods, voice slow and gentle. 'Khorramshahr was *not* the place to be at that time: territory disputes, skirmishes over the port. There was a great deal of bombing, even before the battle.'

'The battle?'

'We were out before then, *Alhamdulillah*. Thanks be to God,' he translates, seeing Alice's face crease into a question at the Arabic. 'One of my mother's oft-repeated phrases. Anyway, the clashes between the Iranian and Iraqi governments were escalating every day. My parents knew it was only a matter of time before it truly turned to war. We managed to get on one of the last trains to Tehran. And not before time. The next day was the first of the air strikes. Thousands killed, the station destroyed, the city essentially erased off the map. We got out just in time.'

'I'm so sorry,' Alice breathes. 'That's awful.'

Levon takes a delicate sip of his tea, then shakes his head. 'I was lucky. My parents had friends over here. It took some coordinating, but they were generous enough to take me in.'

Alice is suddenly aware of how intimate it is, learning about Levon like this. His words summon up smoke and chaos and bloodshed, so vivid that she leans back against the counter until its sharp edge digs into her back, the sensation helping clear the violent fog fuzzing her head. He seems to realise it too, because he places his mug on the table and crosses his legs, shaking himself out of the memories and giving a rueful smile.

'I'll never forget the generosity of the couple I stayed with. Taking care of an Iranian eleven-year-old transitioning to school in Cheshire, in the eighties ... that must have been a challenge. But it kept me safer than I would have been otherwise. I'm grateful for that.'

*Safer, he said. Not safe.* Alice pictures Levon, young and far from home. She doesn't want to imagine ever having that much distance between her and Mol. There must be more to Levon's story; he's probably had a few knocks over the years, and Alice's respect for him rises further as she realises they've made him wiser and more solid, instead of turning him hard or bitter or numb.

'And you,' Levon asks, 'you're settled here, too? Just because you've only been here a couple of years doesn't mean it's not a blow.' He gestures with his mug round the room, with its framed art prints and posters, Mollie's neon paint-splodge masterpieces on crinkled pastel paper, magnetted to the fridge. The cluster of tiny ceramic hedgehogs guarding the herbs in the spice rack, the collection of chipped charity-shop teapots on top of the cupboards, some of them repurposed into plant pots, with long, trailing tendrils of leaves. The glass mannequin head filled with soft-pulsing fairy lights, wearing a bobbed tinsel wig and heart-shaped sunglasses.

'It's definitely a blow,' Alice says, leaning back against the counter again. 'I moved here after splitting with Mollie's dad. I've never been on my own before. I got with Sam while we were at uni and we moved in together in second year, in a shared house in Hyde Park. Then into our own place a few years later. All those grown-up things, we did together. Having Mollie. Being a family.' Alice hesitates, taking another glug of tea to cover her moment of weighing up how much she wants to share, then puts on a tone so cheery it almost comes out sounding sarcastic. 'Let's just say it took me a while to work out how to do it by myself.'

Alice has had some practice of putting what happened into a story that could be shared, eventually, with her parents and their friends. But the succinct summary still sticks in her throat. It's incomplete, and it makes things seem so tidy and simple, when the real experience of it was terrifying and sometimes brain-meltingly impossible to move forward from, even though she did, in the end. It feels like a lie, to tell such a matter-of-fact version of it when it actually nearly ripped her apart and even now, years later, there's so much of it that's never been said. Alice suspects that Levon, with his calm descriptions of how the city he was born in was razed to the ground, might know something about this, if she could find the words to explain. But she can't: it's still too hard to remember how hollow and black she felt in that sick hormonal thunderstorm the weeks and months after Mollie came, the post-birth pain and exhaustion eclipsed by a numb fear, a creeping sense of impossibility, knowing in her bones she couldn't do even the most basic of tasks, that there was no

41

hope and might never be again. How even after she got the medication, when those minuscule increments of hope started to gradually creep back, Sam still felt irreversibly different to her, their relationship never the same as before. *Bit of a downer, doing all that as well as bombs, blood and war in a first chat, eh?* She drags herself out of her reverie and addresses Levon again, dismissing the thought of confiding further.

'I mean, I've got Mol, and that's amazing. But this place is important to me. It was such a hard thing, deciding to stay in Leeds after things with Sam fell apart. But I know it was right. And, honestly, I don't know if I've got it in me to start all over again somewhere else.'

'I'm sure you would if you had to,' Levon says, raising his mug again in acknowledgement of everything they share. 'But let's hope you don't have to.'

'Cheers to that.' Alice gives a wistful grin and raises her mug to meet his just as the door goes again.

It's not even ten past seven, but AJ's full of apologies as he bounds inside. Alice makes him a coffee, clinking the spoon against the side of the cup as she stirs and watching the liquid swirl. The chat with Levon's swirled her thoughts up, too, and she's trying not to let her eagerness to get started put her in a nark about AJ being late. She wants to know what he's been doing that could be more important than this, but when they decamp to the living room he beams at her appreciatively as she hands him the mug.

'Legend, cheers. This'll sort me out. I've got the feeling it's gonna be one of those nights where I need all the caffeine and sugar I can get to power me through.' He rubs his face, and Alice wonders whether what she'd taken to be a deliberate shadowy dusting of stubble is just the hangover of him not always having time or energy to shave.

42

Levon waits for Alice to sit down first in the big blanket-covered armchair by the open window. He takes the sofa, open-faced but serious with his cup balanced on his knee. AJ grabs a handful of cookies and a thick slice of Levon's halva, then toes off his trainers and curls up at the other end of the settee.

'Right, it looks like this is us,' Alice says, once they're settled. 'What are we going to do?'

# CHAPTER SIX

It takes a while, but eventually they come up with some ideas.

'I spoke with a colleague of mine at the library,' Levon tells them. 'She's a bit of an expert when it comes to housing associations, co-ops, that kind of thing. Much as it pains me to say it, she says we're probably wasting our time lodging an appeal with the council. There's no denying Leeds Housing haven't put the funding that's been needed into the street, and this is an opportunity for them to get it off their hands and make some significant money at the same time. It's going to take more than us putting our complaints in for them to turn that down.'

'So the official route is going to get us nowhere,' AJ says, thinking out loud. 'That sounds like we need to get creative. Cause so much stress and drama for the council that it's not worth their while going ahead.

'You mean go to the press?' Alice asks. 'Would that work?'

'Gotta be worth a go,' says AJ. 'Think about it. If we can get it in the papers and on the news sites, it's not going to look good for them, right? Surely they'll think twice about this entire thing if it'd mean their name getting dragged through the media.'

'So what do we do? Make a list of local places that might cover it and contact them?'

'Not just local,' Levon puts in. 'National, too. This could be something that could get attention. People are already so vulnerable under austerity, their situations so precarious. And something like this just highlights the reality of that.'

'Yeah,' AJ asserts. 'You can be going along like everything's fine, then bam. Evicted. Get out. There's no way that's okay.'

'It's not okay,' Alice agrees. 'And if people know it's happening to us, maybe we can get public opinion on side. Maybe we can make enough noise that the council will think twice.'

'Nothing to lose, right?'

'This is good,' Levon says. 'A call for help to the community could work. We're not the only street that's been hit hard by austerity measures and budget cuts. For all we know, they could be doing this in other streets. The more we get the word out, the better – for us, and for anyone else who might be in the same position.'

'So what should we do next? Write emails to papers?'

'I'm not bad at writing,' AJ says, sheepish like he's been taught it's not good manners to sing his own praises. 'I mean, I'll need help. I'm dyslexic, so spelling's not my thing. The other nurses always give me grief for it; they say they can't make sense of my notes. But I'm good with words.' He blushes, downs what's left in his mug and leans over to put it on the floor.

'Brilliant,' Alice says. 'You must be, doing what you do.'

There's a mumbled deflection of the compliment from AJ, but he smiles into his cup.

'If you want to write something, I can go over it,' Levon offers. 'And I can find the contact details for the newspapers. TV, too, and radio.'

'Wish Jessie had come,' AJ says. 'She'd know other ways, I bet.'

'What do you mean?'

'Well, she's young, isn't she?' He explains about how he'd tried to convince her to come and how he'd hoped she'd change her mind and turn up. 'Bet she'd have something to say if she could hear us talking about newspapers and radio. Not that they're not good ideas,' he adds, in a rushed tumble of words, not wanting to offend Alice or Levon. 'But she probably knows other, faster ways of getting things out there. Ways we don't.'

'Sounds like you're calling us old,' Alice puts in, with a sly grin.

'Get lost,' he laughs. 'You can't be much older than me. And age is wisdom, isn't it?' he adds, with an acknowledging nod towards Levon, the oldest in the room. 'But I hardly have time to eat and sleep, let alone know what the kids are into these days. I've not got a clue how you make something go viral.' He laughs, a funny warm snorting sound. 'Other than actual viruses, I mean.'

'We'll figure it out,' Alice reassures him. 'Once we've got it clear what we want to say, we can put it online. That way we've got it in a format we can share.'

'And I've been thinking,' Levon puts in. 'It'd be good to have some proper legal advice, too. Get someone who knows their stuff to look over our contracts with the council, see if there's any chance we can challenge it that way.'

'Yeah! You never know, they might just be chancing it, seeing if they can scare us into doing what they want.' AJ gets a ghost of his usual bounce back as he says this, gesturing with half a biscuit in his hand. 'They put it all in those big words and hope we'll be too intimidated to do anything else.' His excitement catches, spending sparks of hope through Alice and putting a hesitant smile on Levon's face. Maybe this won't be the nightmare battle they thought it'd be. Maybe they can unravel this threat into nothing if they can just find the right thread to pull at.

'I've been doing some research into pro-bono lawyers,' Alice says, words tumbling out in a rush, pleased that she and Levon have had the same thought. 'You know, people who offer their services for free if it's for a good cause. There's a couple nearby. One's in Chapel Allerton, so that'd be best – they're so close they'll know the area. Might even know of our street. But there's another in Roundhay, and one in Holbeck. I can phone them and see if someone can make some time to talk to me about all this. Be good to know where we stand, right?'

'And if they're local,' Levon adds, 'they might have dealt with the council before. So they might know some things that we don't.' He hums, staring in deep thought at the ceiling, its fuzzy, cloud-shaped lampshade and dangling glass-bead raindrops. 'Come to think of it, we might have a list, at the library, of firms offering pro-bono services. People come in and ask us for all sorts; it's useful being able to signpost them to what they're looking for. I'll dig that out too, if I can. That way if you can't get an appointment with the ones you've found we've got some back-up options.'

Alice takes another piece of halva and bites it in two, sweetness crumbling onto her tongue. 'I'm really scared about this, you know. Or I was. But it's good to be in it together.'

The other two nod, then continue chatting more about

their collective to-do list in determined murmurs, so they don't hear the noise on the stairs. But Alice, with her finely tuned mum-hearing, hushes, tilts her head and listens. Another creak comes, this time from the hallway.

'Mol?' she calls, getting up and moving towards the sound. 'Is everything okay?'

Mollie appears in the doorway, pale but with bright patches high on both cheeks. Her hair's rumpled, she's lost a sock and one leg of her pyjama bottoms is scrunched up, making her look even more haphazard and pathetic. She's carrying her favourite teddy, a grotty stuffed llama that once belonged to Alice, and her cough is a nasty hollow scrape that makes all three of them wince.

Alice scoops Mollie into her arms and collapses back down into the armchair with her. 'What's going on, baby? Don't you feel well?'

Mollie blinks at Levon and AJ, baffled, before focusing back on her mum. Her face scrunches in a slow-motion wail, which turns into another spluttering cough, making her bury her head in Alice's hoodie with a series of sad little snuffles.

Alice rubs soothing circles on the toddler's back, murmuring reassurances to her.

Over Mollie's head, she makes an apologetic grimace to AJ and Levon, but they both seem more bothered about Mollie than any intrusion to the meeting.

'She didn't seem this bad earlier. Just a cough, and I hoped it'd sort itself out ... ' Alice trails off, then gives her head a small shake, gritting her teeth and steeling herself. 'Can you give me a few minutes to try and get her settled? Then I can see about getting her a doctor's appointment tomorrow.' *In between work, and phoning lawyers, and knocking back the coffee because, between everything else and now this, it's shaping up to be*

48

*another anxious, staring-at-the-ceiling-at-three-a.m. sort of night, and if I keep turning up at school looking like a sleep-deprived zombie I'll be in the shit there too and that's the last thing we need.*

Alice doesn't say any of it out loud but the other two must sense some of what's going through her head, because Levon starts gathering the mugs, saying he'll put the kettle on again. AJ leans forward.

'Want me to check her over?' he offers, in a whisper, making sure Mol doesn't hear and freak out even more. 'Make sure it's nothing serious?'

'Really?' Alice's voice is hollow with relief. 'AJ, that'd be amazing, thank you so much.'

'You got it,' he says, and slides off the settee onto the floor, scooching round so Mollie can see him.

''Ey up,' he says, gentle, and Mol stops sniffling for a minute to stare at him with suspicion.

'Can I have a little look at you, please, trouble? Would that be okay?'

*She's never going to let him*, Alice thinks. *Any minute now she's going to start shrieking at maximum decibels and Bill will hate us even more than he does already. AJ's probably going to get twatted in the face with a transformer, then I'll have that on my conscience as well as everything else.*

But Mollie's stare-down with AJ ends in a series of confused blinks and then a hesitant nod. She wriggles free from Alice's arms and goes over to him, plopping herself in a cross-legged seat that mimics his position. She coughs again, worse than before, but she doesn't seem as bothered this time.

*Wow*, Alice mouths at Levon, as he edges back into the room with more brews.

AJ goes through a brisk examination, asking permission each time he touches Mol, whether it's to take her pulse or temperature or listen to her chest. By the end, Mollie's made a game of it, shaking her head at first and then changing her mind.

'Thank you,' he says, solemnly, when they're done. 'You did grand.' They fist-bump with utmost seriousness, then Mol crawls back into Alice's lap.

'She'll be reet,' he tells Alice, retaking his seat on the sofa. 'If you've got Calpol in, dose her up on that tonight. I don't think it's an infection, but if she's still like this into next week maybe give the doc a bell and see about antibiotics. But it should clear up before then. And just make sure she drinks as much as possible. When they get feverish, it's easy for them to get dehydrated, then that causes all sorts of other trouble.'

'You absolute star. That just saved me hours of stress waiting at the doc's. Or the hospital.' *Because, knowing me, I'd have bundled her to A&E in the middle of the night, then regretted it but had to stay, and who knows what a nightmare that would have been.* 'Thanks, AJ. Really.'

'Nae bother,' he says. 'Glad to be able to help. Especially when it's nowt to worry about.' He moves back onto the sofa, his face distant for a moment. 'If I can have a few more like that tonight, I'll be laughing.'

'I'll see if I can get her back to bed,' Alice tells them both, hefting the toddler onto her shoulder, but Mollie has other ideas, squealing to be put down, giving a series of sandpapery coughs into her pyjama sleeve, then curling up like a kitten on the middle sofa cushion between AJ and Levon, eyes closed.

'You're honoured,' Alice tells them, mildly suspicious that Mol's faking sleep to stay up, but decides to leave her to it. 'She's not used to having people round.'

For a moment, Alice thinks about how few of her friends have been here, how few people she'd even want to invite round. On her sporadic attempts to force herself to be social, those things happen in other places. Trips to Hyde Park Picture House, or adventures to the leisure centre by the uni campus for the roller derby championships. The annual psychobilly all-dayer at the Brudenell. But single parenting and teaching just take up *so much* of her energy, and she usually wants to spend what's left over on adventures for her and Mollie: she's had it in her head ever since Mollie was born that they need to visit the Butterfly House at Tropical World, and she's still not made that happen yet. So having people round to theirs hasn't really been on her radar since they moved to the street. But the sudden recognition of its absence sets off flares of sadness in her chest. That was such a highlight of her student days: that casual, communal intimacy, everyone up late, pretentious wine-soaked chat and laughter until sunrise sneaked in and they stumbled to bed in the hope of being up again for lectures a couple of hours later. Or getting in from nights out and dancing round the kitchen with Sam, concocting elaborate 3 a.m. feasts for anyone who was still awake. The flicker of candles and the gas flame from the hob, Sam headbanging and stirring the pot while Alice channelled her inner rock-goddess in the two-foot space between the cooker and the sink, bare feet sticking to the grimy tiles, a sauce-crusted spatula for her microphone. The memory seems ancient and cinematic, like it's not even hers. Alice wonders whether AJ and Levon have ever noticed her lack of visitors, and fumbles for a joke to mask her uncertainty.

'Anyway,' she says. 'You two seem to have been a hit.'

'Bairn's got good taste,' AJ cracks, then checks his watch. 'But I'd better get going in a minute. Are we good with our plan?'

'Think so,' Alice says, as Levon nods, too. 'Thanks for coming tonight.'

*I've got to tell Sam what's happening. I've got to tell someone. And I don't want to. I* really *don't want to. And if we can find a way to stop all this from going ahead, maybe I won't have to.*

They must see some of her emotions on her face, because Levon tilts his head. 'Everything all right? Under the circumstances, I mean?'

'It's nothing. Just being daft, really. But ever since opening that letter, I've had such a grotty feeling. That I'd done something wrong to end up in this position. You know, like I should have known or anticipated it. Done a better job at saving up or moving to a better neighbourhood or something. Somewhere this wouldn't have happened. But tonight, while we've been chatting, I've realised what a load of –' Alice pauses, glances at Mollie to make sure she's not listening before silently mouthing the word *bollocks* '– that is. Because I would never think that either of you two had any kind of responsibility to somehow psychically foresee this and stop it from happening. Like we said before, it's just circumstances, isn't it? Could happen to anyone. And I don't know, it's really helped me get my head right. I can't afford to get all bogged down in shame and self-pity and what I could've done different. What matters now is how we fight it. And I feel so much better about doing that with the three of us joining forces.'

They cheers their mugs together, the mood still serious but lighter than before, and some of the weight that's been dragging Alice down all week evaporates, just a bit.

# CHAPTER SEVEN

When Bill hears Mollie's wail through the wall, he sighs and puts down his book. *Bloody eyes are going anyway*, he thinks. He's been rereading one of his dad's old mystery novels, but for the last hour it's been getting harder and harder to focus. He's tired, and distracted. He knows he's read the story several times over the years. He pulled it off the shelf expecting the familiarity of it to be a comfort. But as he turns the pages, he realises he doesn't remember the plot at all and that's unsettled him just as much as the sinister descriptions of double-crossing, tense meetings in strange places, mysterious lurking villains with secret, malicious agendas.

*Poor mite*, Bill thinks, as the sound of Mollie's crying gets louder then settles again. He and Sally never had it, really: their foster children came to them older than Mollie, already fierce and stubbornly self-reliant, determined not to need anything despite how young and small Bill remembers them being. But always, *always*, there would be a moment, when they finally let their guard down enough to let Sally and him see their hurts. Neither of them could ever predict how long it would take. He remembers Danny, eleven and warier than a feral cat, bawling an hour after arriving when he'd ventured outside to play with the others and been stung by a bee, the allergic reaction swelling his elbow to the size of a plum. Charlie, who'd refused to say a word for weeks, staying tough and silent through trips to the dentist, the doctor and starting school, but sobbing into Bill's jacket when they found a dying baby sparrow that had fallen from its nest. Little Lou-Lou, who had nightmares but refused to admit it, sneaking coffee at bedtime to stay awake with a torch and a library book, who finally told Bill everything when he thought she'd gone missing, searched the entire neighbourhood in a frenzy of worry, then found her asleep on the floor of Sally's wardrobe, curled up in a nest of coats. So he feels for Mollie, he does, even if he can't imagine what it must be like for Alice looking after her all by herself. He's heard Alice shushing the toddler before, her babble of animated chatter hushed when they come up their path. He knows it's well intentioned, but it rankles. *They must think I'm a right cantankerous bugger. And they wouldn't be wrong, would they?*

Sally knew how to set him right on his blue mood days. They'd happened a lot less back then. And even when they did, she knew how to handle it. *Alright, mardy bum*, she'd say. *This won't do, will it?* She'd give him an affectionate smack on the arse, then get down to business, whipping up his favourite baked custards or sending the kids down the park so they could have some quiet, her knitting needles clicking beside him. At times, she'd take advantage of the empty house, bossing him into the bedroom and kneading her knuckles into the gristly knots in his back to siphon off some of the pain. Sometimes after that they'd double-check the lock on the door and find other uses for the time to themselves. For all he frets about his memories disappearing, Bill remembers the sweetness of those times well, the softness of Sally's skin on his and her dark curls spilling over the pillows afterwards, the sun on the walls and the ancient windows rattling in the wind and the two of them content with the home and family they'd built, even if they'd got there a different way to what they expected when they got wed.

Bill finds the remote control, turns the TV on and clicks through the channels. The first scene that comes on is a violent horror film: a man with a mask and a knife chasing a screaming woman through a shadowy house. It's too much like the mystery novel he was reading: the ominousness of it puts him on edge, and then when the killer sinks the knife into the woman's shoulder, the grisly sound effects and the bloom of blood on her clothes make him change the channel. There's a game show next, hosted by a man in a lurid lime suit who talks way too loud about the couples who'll be competing, and even when Bill fumbles for the volume so he can make out the words, he still can't understand the rules. The next channel is the news, which he knows will just depress him more. He turns it off. Night's coming, and even if Bill had the energy to get himself together enough to go for a walk or a pint, he doesn't think it'd help. It's just him, on his own, facing down another long night.

*Nowt I've not done before,* he tells himself, in his gruffest tone. *Get yourself together, man.* But it's no good. Between the lapses in memory and the times he seems to be nothing but memories, there's something else that's bothering Bill. It's been sneaking up on him, but it's got to the point where he can't ignore it any longer. Bill's starting to suspect that, if she could see him now, Sally would be ashamed.

No, not ashamed. Concerned. He's let himself get lonely,

even after all the promises he made her that he wouldn't. That he'd keep going, afterwards. He doesn't like to think about those times: the vivid moments that spit forwards out of nowhere in the long nights and early mornings by himself. Holding tight to Sally's hand and promising her anything, *anything*, if there was even the most microscopic chance it'd make her feel the tiniest bit better. He can't even remember if he meant them at the time, if he even knew what he was saying. He can recall hearing himself speak and wondering how the hell something as normal as putting words into sentences was still somehow possible, when everything felt so consumed by the pain, the fear, the grief. He promised Sally he'd keep going, and he has, but his heart hasn't been in it. He's let her down.

Next door, everything's gone quiet. No sound from Mollie or Alice. Bill can imagine Sally and Alice getting along. The timeline's all wrong, he knows that much, but in Bill's mind Sally is every age. When they met and when she died. She's all of them at once. And he knows she'd have loved Alice's stubbornness, that combination of compassion and grit that he loved so much in his wife. And that young lad, the nurse, she'd have liked him as well. Ahead of the curve, was his Sally, in the way she thought about things. She'd have enjoyed knowing someone like AJ was in nursing, she'd have said it was proof that the world was changing, that things were getting better, that they were moving towards a better future. That even if the journey was long, and painful, and knackering, it was still worth it, in the end, because it was moving them all towards better things.

Levon, too, he never knew Sally. Bill can't remember the details of their conversation clearly. *How long did he say he'd been around? Was it just before or just after she went? Doesn't matter*, he thinks, shaking off the thought, the image of Sally skeleton-thin in that hospital bed. She'd have liked him if she'd got the chance, that calm insistence on doing the right thing. Bill's seen Levon at the library, though they've never spoken there. Levon's always talking to someone. Always helping. Bill gets the sense that Levon believes in change the way that Sally did, that perhaps that belief is what keeps him going.

But the thing is, Bill doesn't know if he can keep believing in hope and change in the same way as Sally. The disloyalty of that thought makes him feel sick. *You daft bugger, don't be such a traitor. What would she say?* She'd fold herself over his armchair, a gentle palm at the back of his neck, a playful tug on his earlobe, a barely there kiss against his hair. Try as he might, he can't summon her touch any more. But he knows, in his bones, that if Sally was still here, they'd both be in Alice's house next door right now. Sally would've made scones and taken round the massive red teapot with the rainbow polka dots. She'd have ideas, and reassurances, and faith.

*She's not here though, is she? And the thing's bloody hopeless. Stop living in the past, you stupid old man. Face the facts. They're taking it away, everything you've had and built. They're doing it because they can, and there's nowt you can do to stop them.*

Bill's sick of it: the arguing with himself and the not having answers, the feeling that he's letting her down and not knowing what to do about it. And even though he knows it'd kill his Sally all over again to see it, Bill's not sure he's got it in him to keep fighting.

# CHAPTER EIGHT

I am writing to you from Leodis Street, a
street in the Chapel Allerton area of Leeds.
The Victorian terraced council homes where my
neighbours and I live have been here for over
a hundred years, having stood through two world
wars and relentless gentrification, which has
in the last decade changed the surrounding area
virtually beyond recognition. These houses and
the land they are built on are owned by Leeds
Housing Federation, who are in the process of
selling to developers, evicting all of us with
only the bare minimum statutory notice. At the
time of writing this letter, we have less than
three weeks remaining.

My neighbours include a single mother, an
Afro-Caribbean nurse, a young person still
in education, an elderly pensioner who is
already isolated and vulnerable, and myself,
an Armenian-Iranian immigrant who has lived

in the UK since the age of eleven, and worked
here for more than three decades. Collectively,
we have been here for many years, with time
on the street ranging from decades to just
eleven months.

Levon pushes his glasses into his hair. 'I'm still not sure
about this bit,' he says, looking up from the paper to where AJ
stands on his doorstep, making the most of their commutes
crossing to go over the letter again. They've been piecing the
draft together by text message over the last couple of days, with
AJ sending screenshots from the notes app he'd been dumping his thoughts into, then Levon collating the fragments into
coherence. 'I'm concerned we're putting in too much about
ourselves. This issue transcends the five of the us, surely?'

'I know it's cringe,' AJ says, leaning against the door frame.
'But we gotta do it. Gotta go human interest. It's the only way
anyone will go for it.'

'I just worry we're diluting the key message.'

'And it sounds like the letter from *The Breakfast Club*. I
know. But we've got to pull some heartstrings here, right? The
facts alone aren't enough.'

Levon tugs his glasses back into position, his eyes shrewd
behind the lenses as he examines the draft again. 'You don't
think there's benefit to being clear and matter-of-fact?'

'We need that too. But we also need to show we're real
people. Not just numbers. Not just statistics. Real.'

'You're right,' Levon says, finally. 'The more human, the
better.' But he's still troubled by the letter's subtle implication
that they can only hope for understanding and compassion if
they meet the right criteria. For now, he lets the younger man
convince him.

Once the letter's been rewritten several more times, Levon's confident it's there. At his desk in the library the next day, he checks over the final paragraph one last time, praying it'll be enough to get someone's attention, that it'll connect with someone enough to set off a chain of events that'll save them.

We believe our eviction to be unjust and negligent. We believe that all people deserve safe, secure and affordable housing, no matter their age, occupation, race or sexuality. We call on our community — including the media outlets that exist to share news and stories — to support us in stopping this from happening. While we acknowledge that regeneration is often seen as a form of community investment, and a process which can raise house prices and benefit the community, we are deeply concerned about the wider impact of this sort of gentrification occurring without challenge. Neighbourhood change should be driven by the changing needs of its community, not pursuit of profit, a practice which typically hits already marginalised and vulnerable people hardest. Already in our area, funding cuts have forced the local women's centre to close and the library to reduce its opening hours. While crime and anti-social behaviour are issues faced by our community, we believe this to only amplify the need for sustained community investment at a structural level, rather than selling off much-needed council housing to the highest bidder.

Will you help us? My contact details are included below, along with those of some of my neighbours on the street. All would be happy to speak with you in more depth at your convenience on this matter of utmost urgency.

*Convenience* and *urgency? Is that too much of a contradiction?* On his phone, Levon scrolls back through the chat thread of their deliberations and decides to leave it in. Over the past couple of days, he's already combed websites and directories for the editors' contact details of every national newspaper, and a smattering of smaller locals, too. His master list has radio stations and TV stations and even the informal news sites by and for the students. *They'll probably be giving their all to their studies, this time of year, but can't hurt to try, can it?* He's heard horror stories about the conditions in some of the student houses in Woodhouse and Hyde Park, dilapidated terraces more run-down than their own, and can't help but wonder whether some of those streets could be earmarked for demolition too. *Who knows where will be next?* He pictures the city changing shape, luxury apartments rising up from rubble and ashes, everything he'd loved about it eroded. The thought makes him shudder.

How to send the finished version had been the subject of some debate between Levon, Alice and AJ. Real-life letters may seem old-fashioned and slow, but Levon knows their physicality is an advantage. After all, someone has to physically go through the post, open the letters, read them and decide on their onward journey. Whereas an email could get snagged in a spam filter and never even get seen. All that hard work, time and emotion, zipped through the ether, across entire counties into someone's inbox, then disappearing before reaching its destination. They'd settled on doing both, Alice posting the letters on the way to school that morning while Levon had volunteered to do the emails and print out copies of the petition he's already talked a few of the library's most loyal service users into signing.

When Jessie comes in, Levon recognises her at once. But she doesn't see him. She skulks through the library's glass double doors looking distracted, giving darting glances in every direction as though she's not sure she's in the right place. Her shifty expression makes Levon put down his mug, questioning what Jessie's doing here. She's wearing paint-spattered black jeans with rips at the knees and a faded T-shirt with an illustration of manga-style animals playing heavy metal in an enchanted woodland grove, the sleeves hacked off to leave only frayed threads. Levon assumes it must be a band he's never heard of, maybe the one whose music is audible even through the huge neon yellow headphones Jessie's wearing, her head bopping to the beat as she scans something on her phone screen.

'Morning,' Levon says. 'You need any help?'

She either doesn't hear him or deliberately blanks him, because Jessie stomps halfway past him before she doubles back, pulling her headphones off to rest round her neck, a muffled cacophony still playing.

'Wait, don't you live on my street? You were at that meeting with that billionaire property bellend?'

Levon offers his hand. 'Levon. It's nice to meet you properly. I don't think I've seen you here before.'

'First time,' she tells him, screwing her face up in uncertainty. 'But I've got this project for college, and it's doing my head in trying to research it online. And then I remembered this place. Thought it was worth a go.'

'Good initiative.' Jessie's eyes glint at the praise, half-pleased and half-suspicious. 'Our collection is pretty good, all things considered.'

Jessie's already looking past him, scanning the shelves. 'Yeah,' she says, with a smile. 'I get that.' She fumbles with her phone again, and waves Levon off when he offers to help her find what she needs. 'Nah, I'm good. Thanks, though.'

Levon returns to his emails, refreshing the page. There are a couple of bouncebacks, from people who've left their jobs or whose inboxes are full. *Not a recognised address for this mail server.* A couple of auto responses from people on holiday. Nothing else. *Yet*, he reminds himself. No replies *yet*. After making sure no one needs him for anything at the information desk, he starts making calls. It's slow going: to start with, he mostly gets voicemails and polite robot voices asking for extension numbers he doesn't know. The next person on his list is the local Leeds correspondent for the BBC. It rings for a long time, and Levon's about to give up when a no-nonsense Scouse accent that reminds him of Alice comes on the line.

'Hello?' The woman's voice is cheery but distracted, and there's a lot of background noise: a static crackle of blustery weather and people talking close by.

He introduces himself. 'I'm calling about a story. About me and my neighbours being unfairly evicted.'

'Uh-huh.' She sounds like she's trying to do a million things at once. 'Look, I'm on location at the moment, I can't really hear. Can you put it in an email?'

'I did. I have.'

'Great. Cheers. Bye.'

He moves on to the next one. Gets as far as explaining the situation to some of them, but most don't even give him the chance. 'We don't really cover things like that,' one tells him, between muffled eating sounds. 'Why don't you try Citizens Advice?'

'Gatsby?' asks another, in a hacking smoker's cough, when Levon's repeated his summary of why he's calling. 'They're corrupt as anything, pal.'

'So is that something you could report on?' Levon asks, adrenaline flickering at the possibility.

'Sorry, mate. No chance. They've got me on courts reporting. Who gets sent down for what, and how long, that kind of thing. That and celebrity gossip is about all our team get to do these days. Stuff we can do from our desks, you know. Field reporting takes too much resource.'

'You could cover this from your desk, couldn't you? I've emailed you all the information, and if you need more, I'm happy to help however I can.'

'Don't think so. Sorry.' And he's hung up before Levon can even reply.

Levon's good with people, always has been. He learnt that from his mother: she could charm anyone, and was always so proud of Levon being able to hold his own around the adults, to chat to his parents' friends even from a young age. He can remember the dinner parties, with all the grown-ups in their smart dark clothes, the wine being poured and the intense murmured conversations about politics, art and culture. Levon can picture his mother playing her violin afterwards, swaying in the centre of the room with the instrument tucked under her chin, her long hair swept to one side out of her way. Everyone watching, spellbound, as the music swirled around them, a magical combination of sad, ethereal and defiant. Levon on his cushion by the bookcase, the taste of baklava and honey still in his mouth, pulling the tassels on the cushion corner apart then knotting them back together.

He knows being soft-spoken and articulate goes a long way. It was one of the things his mother had clung to, when they were making the arrangements to send him abroad. That his education and his manners would stand him in good stead, hopefully ease his transition to another place and culture, so many miles from home. He knows he can put people at ease, even if it sometimes takes more effort than he'd like. He's quietly proud to be so unfazed by the prospect of working his way through these calls. Still, he can only take so much at a time, so after leaving another couple of voicemails, he decides to have a break.

He sorts and re-shelves the returns pile, then gets a local group making decorations for an Easter egg hunt set up with their craft supplies, glitter and glue. The library's small, free-to-hire reading room functions as the home of many of the community organisations, the scrappy non-profits and charities and the more informal groups, from the queer teens' book club to the mothers against violence meetings. As he's making his way back to his desk, Levon sees that Jessie's dragged one of the beanbags from the children's corner to make a makeshift nest for herself in an alcove in the history section, surrounded by her laptop, sketchbook, pens and phone. Levon hovers, watching as Jessie gnaws a thumbnail, glaring at her computer screen.

When she glances up and sees him, she scrambles upright. 'Er, hey. That offer of help. Can I take you up on it now, please?'

'That's what I'm here for. What do you need?'

'A book. About what happened in Leeds, during and after World War Two.'

'A specific one, or will any book do?'

She consults her notes with a frazzled expression.

'Something that says what the main impacts were. As clearly as possible.'

Levon raises his eyebrows.

'History's my worst subject,' Jessie adds, with a shrug. 'And I can't get my head round this essay. Like, at all.'

'Smart move to call in reinforcements, then. Let's see what we can do.' He motions for her to follow, and shows her to the right shelf. 'See, we've got all sorts here. Reference books, local history, personal accounts and memoir. Not all of these are focused on Leeds specifically, but we've got an archive of local newspapers, going back several decades. They could be a good resource. And most books on post-war Britain will explore the regional impact. You could have a look at some contents pages and just consult the sections you need?'

Jessie runs a finger along the spines, nodding but still looking confused.

'What about starting with this one?' Levon asks, pulling a book from the shelf and putting it in her hands, the words YORKSHIRE AT WAR on the cover. 'This covers the Blitz and the fallout from it, as well as how Leeds contributed to the war effort by building bombers and munitions manufacturing.'

Jessie flicks through the first few pages, scanning the contents and nodding to herself.

'Okay. Cool. I think I can work with this.' She meets Levon's eyes, then glances away, looking sheepish. 'This essay's been mashing my head, but this should help get my teacher off my case. Or, I don't know, maybe she'll hate what I write, but at least I won't get a zero for not submitting.'

'Why would she hate it?'

'Probably because I get zeroes so much. But also because I want to write about the social and cultural angle, and I think college want more of *this happened, then this*. Like the specific sequence of events rather than everything else that was going on.'

'And that's the side you're interested in?'

She gives an exasperated growl, slams the book shut and jokily bashes it into her forehead.

'I don't know. I don't even know why I'm doing this stupid subject. I thought it'd be cool to find out *why* stuff happened rather than just what. But I've changed my mind. I don't care what happened, or why. It's all irrelevant now, anyway. Why do we even need to remember it?'

'You know what they say. Those who can't remember the past are condemned to repeat it.'

'What does that mean?'

'Well, I suppose the war was so awful that people hope that by studying it, they can learn enough from it to make sure it doesn't happen again.'

'But wars are still going on all the time.'

Levon gives a sombre nod. 'I suppose we need empathy as well as knowledge. That's where things stumble.'

'Riiiight.' Jessie drags the word out, examining the book he's given her again. Levon can't tell if she's listening or not.

'So history's not your favourite subject, I take it?'

'I'm good at art. And I liked art history, at GCSE. I thought it'd be more like that. The emotions, you know? The cultural shifts that make different things possible at different moments. But it's not. It's just disconnected lists of events that I can't get my brain around.'

'And doesn't your college have a library where you could research this?'

Jessie's eyes flicker to the floor, then back to Levon's face, a stubborn set to her jaw. 'I don't go in if I can help it.'

'You don't attend classes? What do your teachers say about that?'

'They don't like it, obviously,' she snaps in a tired voice. 'But I've got my reasons.'

'I'm sure you have,' Levon reassures her, his tone thoughtful. 'And your teachers are there to support you in learning in the way that's right for you. If they're not doing that, that's them letting *you* down, not the other way round.'

Jessie screws her face up, baffled by this response. 'Are you for real?'

'I mean it. People learn in all sorts of different ways. Shouldn't stop you getting your education.'

Jessie's eyes go glimmery with tears, but she blinks the sheen away and scowls again as she confides in Levon further. 'It's like they've written me off. And then I get in a mood about it, and start thinking there's no point even trying. I go round like that in circles, and then before I know it the deadline's been or it's the night before and I'm nowhere near where I need to be. It does my head in.'

Her defeated tone summons up memories of Levon's own schooldays. He'd spoken English since childhood, along with his native Farsi and his mother's Armenian. So he hadn't been prepared for the relentless mocking from the other schoolchildren about his accent and mannerisms. He hadn't told anyone. Hadn't want to make a fuss. He knew he was lucky to be far away from all the violence and death happening at home. He understood his parents wanting to keep him safe. He just hadn't understood why they couldn't come too. He missed them so much it was like having his oxygen cut off.

At night, the whole house asleep, Levon would creep from his single bed over to the window, easing it open and curling his knees up to tuck them into a sitting position on the wooden sill. Looking out at the garden, fluttery with night-birds and bats, was as connected to his parents as he could get. Same moon, same sky. But the air there was damp and so cold that inhaling it sent spikes through his lungs, and he'd have to admit defeat and slink shivering back to his sleeping bag. He was always tired, what with the worries and the nightmares, and his exhaustion didn't help him at school. But he's grateful for everything he learnt during those years – in lessons and out. Suddenly, it seems important to give Jessie another perspective, to make her see that however hard things are now, the unknown expanse of the future might change her outlook later.

Levon rocks on his heels, deliberating over his words. 'You know, Jessie, this is just a moment. Whatever happens, remember that. You've got your entire life still to live. Take it from me: I had some truly hard times at school. But the knowledge and skills I learnt during that time have served me well ever since. I made it through, and you will too. Your teachers are supposed to be supporting you, and maybe they're letting you down, but it's your responsibility too. You've got so much still to come, and a good education is like your foundation. It'll be there for you to lean on later. And when that time comes, you'll be glad of it, I'm sure.'

'Eurgh. Whatever. Fine. Does it have to involve so much learning about gross old white men competing with each other for power and money, though? It's so predictable. And annoying.'

Levon gives her an acknowledging nod, along with a wry smile. 'I won't argue with you there. But it shows you've got the critical thinking skills, that you can recognise those patterns. That's a good start. That's what college should be helping you to do. Develop your understanding of the world and how it works.'

Jessie dismisses the compliment with a scrunch of her nose. 'Sure. I'd better go and see if I can get my head round it, then.' She gives him a goofy mock-salute. 'Thanks for the book, dude.'

'Come back whenever you need. I'll be here.'

Jessie returns to her essay-writing nest, chewing a nail and thinking about what Levon said. It's been a while since anyone stuck up for her like that. *How can he care so much when he doesn't even know me?* She turns the pages of the book he found for her, realising he's chosen wisely: all the key details she needs are in there, presented in a format she can actually understand. *Right,* she thinks. *Let's smash this stupid thing.* She pulls her headphones back into position and cranks the volume up.

She stays for two hours, finally giving up when her rumbling stomach gets too loud to ignore. Jessie shoves her stuff back into her bag and ducks out of the library without saying goodbye to Levon, but she returns the book to its proper shelf before she does. Outside, the sun's just burning through drizzle, a weak slice of rainbow visible above the chimneys beyond the high street parade. Jessie keeps her music on loud, taking pleasure in the way it clashes with the sights around her. Pigeons grubbing in a gutter for someone's discarded chips transformed into an epic battle by a dramatic guitar solo score. Three girls on the roundabout in the playground, sharing a bottle of pop and heckling the players of a nearby football game, set to driving drums and witchy orchestral synths, the girls' hair whipped back and forth by the breeze. Protected by her bubble of sound, Jessie stamps towards home, mentally exploring the contents of the kitchen cupboards to decide what makeshift meal she can improvise for tea. The train of thought makes her realise how long it is since she or her mum have done any shopping, and she gets her phone out to send a message.

When ru next coming home?

It's not her mum's usual style, but the answer comes back in seconds. Not sure luv. U ok? How's college?

Poop emoji, Jessie sends. Exploding-head emoji. Books, computer, skull.

Eye-roll emoji, Donna sends back. Then two words: Drama queen.

A few moments. The flashing dots show Mum's still typing. U can do it clever clogs.

Jessie grits her teeth. Mum always talks about how clever Jessie is. Donna barely scraped through her own GCSEs before leaving school at sixteen, so it's a point of pride for her that Jessie's always loved books, and writing, and art. That for every parents' meeting she's been dragged into, there's always been an acknowledgement from the teachers about how bright her daughter is. But it irritates Jessie, her mum's rose-tinted view of her educational abilities. Because Mum doesn't see the letters from college. Doesn't understand how anxious Jessie gets about going in, her brain cells frazzled just from the prospect of the bus journey and the echoey din in the canteen. She's not there to see it. And it's been like this for years now, but Jessie still doesn't know how to handle it other than to pretend it's not happening and just get on with things.

She still remembers the first time her mum hadn't come home. Jessie woke up in the middle of the night, thirteen and feverish, and traipsed into Mum's bedroom. This was several houses ago, long before Leodis Street. She'd had cramps that day and her mates at school had teased her that her period

71

was finally coming, that she'd wake up in the night to a slasher film bloodbath. When she woke up the sheets were their usual unstained lightning-bolt pattern, but she still felt sweaty and shivery. The flat had an eerie quiet; even the next-door neighbour who accompanied their daily movements with a round-the-clock soundtrack of techno and video games had apparently succumbed to sleep. Jessie padded in her socks to the room next door. Mum's empty bed was baffling. Jessie stared for a long time at the floral duvet as though the image might shift, dream-like, into Mum's sleeping body, eye mask on and arms wrapped tight around her pillow. Then she lurched to the kitchen, dug in the drawer under the microwave, took two painkillers and returned to Mum's room, collapsing between the sheets.

She woke to a grotty, milk-coloured sky and a noisy lash of rain. Mum still wasn't home. *She'll be fine*, Jessie told herself. *Must've stayed out with a friend.* She forced herself through the motions. Coffee. Toast. It scraped as she swallowed but she felt better afterwards. Jessie gave herself the day off school and determinedly didn't turn on the TV because she didn't want to see the news. She'd seen enough headlines about women's bodies being discovered by dog walkers, and she was already barely keeping her panic at bay. Instead she flumped herself on the sofa, dozing through her favourite horror film until she surfaced to Mum's cool hand on her head.

'What's wrong, Jessie-boo?'

Jessie fought her vision into focus. 'Where were you?'

'At Dawn's, you know that.'

*'All night?'*

'We had a bit too much wine. I must've fallen asleep. You weren't worried, were you?'

'Yeah,' Jessie had croaked. 'I was.'

'Well, I wasn't far. Just round the corner, really. And I'm here now. Shall I make you some soup? Did you phone school already?'

Donna only seemed to worry about Jessie's absences when the school's snotty letters started mentioning fines. And the older Jessie got, the more Donna did her own thing. Since Jessie started college, they've become even more like roommates than mother and daughter.

Jessie looks back at the message. U can do it clever clogs. And then she thinks about Levon finding her the books she needed, and the word count on her essay, much higher now than it was on the way to the library. She sends back a thumbs-up and an emoji in sunglasses. *It's cool*, she means. Then another thought comes and she types one more text: What r we gonna do about the house?

The dots appear again, then vanish. Start again, then stop. Jessie keeps the app open the rest of the way home, but Mum still doesn't write back.

# CHAPTER NINE

The next time they assemble at Alice's house, there's a distinctly more subdued mood than before. With only two weeks left, they're all feeling the ticking time-bomb pressure of their deadline. Alice has been having trouble sleeping; even on the nights when Mol sleeps through and she gets her double bed to herself, she's found herself staring at the ceiling, wondering whether the others on the street are awake and worrying too.

When the knock at the door comes, Mollie gives a squealing cackle. It's AJ who arrives first this time, in a smart dark shirt, holding a bunch of sunflowers.

'What are these for?'

'You. And Mollie, of course.' He gives a dramatic bow and presents them to the toddler, who curtseys in response and takes them. 'You feeling better, love?'

Mollie nods, shy again for a second, and potters past Alice to take the flowers to the kitchen.

'Is she?' he asks, watching her go.

'Much.' Alice huffs a relieved sigh. 'Still not back to her

usual form, but getting there. Come through, I'll put the kettle on.'

Mollie has managed to shred the paper the flowers were wrapped in, but hasn't yet fought her way through the twine around the stems. She's sitting cross-legged on the kitchen floor giving it everything she's got, the effort purpling her face.

'Come here, Mol, let me help.' Alice confiscates the flowers and puts them into a tall jug, then hands them back to the toddler.

'She's definitely on the mend,' AJ comments, leaning back against the kitchen counter once Mollie's disappeared to find a place for the flowers to go. 'But what about you? No offence, but you look tired.'

'Bloody hell, AJ. Coming from a nurse, that's got to be bad.' Alice makes her voice light, but she can't help feeling a bit wounded by his comment. *And here was me thinking I had everyone fooled.*

'Nah, I just meant . . . you know. Are you holding up okay?'

'I don't know,' she admits, blowing ripples across the surface of her tea. 'Anxious, I suppose. Scared.'

'Me too.'

'Are you going somewhere after this?' Alice asks, nodding at his clothes. 'I hardly ever see you not in uniform.'

AJ gives a bashful smile. 'Going for a drink with a mate in town. Make the most of having a night off for once.'

'Sounds fun.'

'It won't be owt wild.' He puts his tea down. 'I'm not in the mood, to be honest, but my best mate's over from Sheffield for work and I haven't seen him in ages. Didn't want to let him down again.' AJ cringes, thinking about how distant he's been since he started at the hospital – his friends scattered across the country, living their lives, going on holidays and finding partners while he can't even find the time to make new friends, let alone date. He's tempted to cancel, but given how far he and Jordan go back and how rarely they get a chance to hang out, AJ reckons he owes it to them both to drag himself into town for a drink.

'God, I can't remember the last time I had a proper night out,' Alice tells him. She must have had one since Mollie was born. But the only thing that comes to mind is her and Sam in his parents' kitchen at their annual Christmas party: Alice eight months pregnant and massive, Sam mulled-wine-merry in a crooked paper crown. The two of them laughing as Sam caught Alice sneaking yet another helping of chocolate yule log and cream, before prising the bowl from her hand and leading her out onto the snow-damp back steps. Lit by the stars and the blinking Christmas decorations, their sugar-sticky kisses had been as intoxicating to Alice as any festive booze. *That doesn't count as a night out. Not when you only got as far as the garden.*

AJ cocks his head. 'So you're not out dancing on tables when Mol goes to her dad's?'

'No way. They're my recovery weekends. A lie-in and catching up on marking. Living the rock'n'roll dream. Besides, I don't know who I'd go with even if I did have the energy.'

'I know what you mean. Between doing my training and moving for this job, I've let a lot of old friendships fall by the wayside. Not intentional, like, but you know. Just happens, doesn't it?'

Alice grimaces in recognition. When she got with Sam, she'd let a lot of friendships slip. The dopamine whirlwind of their developing romance had intoxicated her so much that everyday details like replying to friends' texts or remembering birthdays had frequently passed her by. Since having

Mollie and separating from Sam, she's spinning so many plates that just keeping the essentials in place takes all her time and energy. Alice used to have so many friends, and she knows it's her own fault they've almost all fallen away. It's a sad thought, and one she shrinks from, shifting her focus back to AJ.

'So where are you off to tonight, then?'

'Just Queen's Court,' he says, and Alice pictures the bar, the rainbow flags in the window and strung like bunting across the cobbled courtyard. The recollection transporting her back to Pride afterparties every August, her and Sam's old housemate Jamie mixing Pornstar Martinis in a silver cocktail shaker, twirling and dancing behind the bar. Alice gets the impulse to thank AJ for trusting her with this detail, then checks herself. He's an adult, he saves lives on a daily basis, he doesn't need her patronising him. But even so, she feels the few years' age difference between them. Alice thinks about how young she felt before she had Mol, how unready she'd felt at twenty-four, sitting on the edge of the bath while the pregnancy test developed on the sink. Emerging from the bathroom in a daze, knowing everything was going to change. Chatting with Sam that night, the two of them soft and giggly with excitement and shock, Alice's gaze travelled round the Hyde Park house she shared with Sam, Jamie and their two other housemates. *This is it*, she'd thought. *Less than nine months until you have to leave all this behind.* Even now, she sometimes still feels impossibly young. And at any age, it takes guts to show someone who you are. The reflection warms her as much as the tea, but all Alice says to AJ is that she's sure he'll have a brilliant time.

'You deserve it,' she tells him, and takes back his empty mug to refill as Levon knocks on the door.

He's empty-handed this time, and effusively apologetic about it despite Alice reassuring him it's fine.

Alice clocks the dark circles under his eyes and decides she's not the only one being kept awake by their respective eviction notices, the letters loud and ominous wherever they've been left.

Once they're all settled in the lounge, they compare notes.

'All dead ends,' Levon reports, sad and solemn. 'Most people don't want to know at all. I barely managed to get through explaining our situation to most of them. Others were more sympathetic, but what they say is always the same. Not enough of a story.'

'People being made homeless with only a month's notice isn't enough of a story?' The bluntness of Alice's disbelieving words make all three of them wince.

'The reporters said it's not exciting enough. Not unique enough, not shocking enough. People are desensitised to this kind of thing. As long as it's not happening to them.'

'But don't people have any empathy? If I read about this happening, I'd want to help.'

'I know,' Levon says. 'But most people haven't got it in them to care. Surviving takes so much of their energy, there's none left for empathy. Or the empathy they do have is para-lysing. The world's got so much grief in it, hasn't it? I think most people are scared that if they let themselves properly face it, they'd be too heartbroken to ever do anything again.'

There's a prickling sensation behind Alice's eyes, and she gets the icy pre-sneeze itch in her nose that always comes before she cries.

'It's true,' AJ puts in. 'Everyone I spoke to said the same – that they'd need more of an angle. It did me in a bit, to be honest. I don't know what we're going to do.'

'Well, I've got that meeting with the lawyer tomorrow,' Alice tells them, blinking fast to keep her tears back. 'Sounds like we'd better hope she's got some advice.' Her voice comes out harder than she intends, followed by an immediate worm of worry. *Don't be such a hard-nosed bitch. They've done their best, it's not their fault.* To Alice's relief, the others don't show any sign of noticing. She's got herself in trouble for this before. *Passionate to the point of argumentative*, her school report said once. *Needs to work on her temper.* When her emotions surge, they're a tidal wave that might carry her away, just like Levon described. The stroppiness under pressure is a mirror of her mum's patterns, one that gives Alice something to focus on and help push the tidal wave back.

Levon gives a sad smile. 'We have to stay hopeful. We lose that, we've lost everything.'

Alice's phone gives a low rumble from where it's fallen off the side of the armchair and down between the cushions. 'Hang on a minute, sorry. Thought I'd put it on silent.'

She scrambles to retrieve it, secretly grateful for the interruption, the chance to turn away from AJ and Levon's faces and gather her thoughts for a moment.

She expects it to be the staff chat from school or something else that's supposedly urgent but essentially meaningless. But when she opens the messenger app, she sees the message is from Sam.

Sorry Lish, can't have Mol 2moz. Family emergency, Mum in hosp. Make it up 2U soon xxx

Alice's internal organs turn to scrunched origami swans. They fold in on themselves, making everything sick and hard and tight. Sam's mother Michelle had been so good to her while they were together. The epitome of glamour nana: down-to-earth in manner but always done up to the nines, a cheerfully bossy matriarch unfazed by any crisis. The idea of Michelle being ill or injured is too unrealistic for Alice to comprehend.

Levon and AJ watch her with concern.

'Why,' she snaps, looking up, 'is it always such a bloody drama when you come round mine?'

'Dramatic times.' Levon shrugs, a wry kindness threading through the words. 'Everything alright?'

'I don't know.' Alice stares down at the glowing screen. She's scared for Michelle, and for Sam, but she's also pissed off. The anger starts as pins and needles in her toes and rises like a warm blush through her limbs and chest. *Why has this got to happen now? As if I've not got enough to cope with.* As soon as she's had the thought, guilt follows.

'Sam just sent me this message …' Alice recaps its contents. 'And I know it's dead selfish of me to even be thinking about myself, but I've got that meeting straight after school tomorrow. I was already going to be cutting it fine to get out on time and over to the lawyer's office, even with Sam collecting Mollie. I've no clue what I'm going to do now.'

She could send up an SOS on the old uni chat group, but she can't imagine any of them volunteering for toddler-wrangling duties. Besides, they're all in office jobs. Even if someone was up for it, they wouldn't be around until hours after Mollie gets out of nursery.

'I can take her,' Levon offers.

'No,' Alice tells him, so fast she wonders where the reflex came from. Sam's voice echoes in her head: *Babe, no offence, but you do know you're a nightmare to help?* Behind his glasses, Levon's eyes widen at Alice's sharp tone, a placid expression returning to his face a moment later. The change is so smooth Alice is tempted to dismiss it as a trick of the light, but she doesn't want Levon to be offended, and stumbles to explain her abrupt refusal.

'Levon,' she says. 'I can't ask you to do that.'

'You didn't ask,' he points out, voice cooler now. 'I offered.'

'Even so.'

'I understand if you wouldn't feel comfortable,' Levon adds. 'But the option's there, if you need.'

'But won't you be at the library?'

Levon nods. 'I will, but if you can get her to me then I can keep an eye on her there. We've got a children's corner with loads of activities. Toys, books, colouring crayons. And the storytelling group is tomorrow afternoon, so she'd be in good company.'

'Seriously?' Alice weighs up the options, then realises this is the only proper one she's got. 'That could work.'

'Well, it won't be entirely selfless, will it?' Levon gives a kind laugh, and it melts away the momentary tension of Alice's initial reaction. 'We want you to be able to go to that meeting. So if this helps that happen, that's what we'll do.'

'I'm still really grateful.'

'Well, that makes two of us.'

'Three,' AJ says. 'Now fingers crossed you come back with good news, eh, chuck?'

'No pressure or anything,' Alice laughs, and the other two join in. But there's still that squirming worry in her stomach as she looks down at her phone.

They say goodbye not long after, Alice wishing AJ a good night and Levon loitering for a few minutes to chatter to Mollie with the hope it'll help her not fret when Alice leaves her with him the following day.

Alice locks the door behind them, slumping against it for a moment. She wonders again whether she should have knocked for Bill. She's not seen him for a few days, and while he's never gone out much, not seeing him at all is jarring. *Is he avoiding us?*

Once Mol's in bed, Alice rereads the email from the lawyer with the details of her appointment. Then she plans out the route she'll take to get there now she'll be going from the library instead of school, and rummages through her wardrobe in search of something smart and serious that'll do double duty for work and afterwards. With her bed half-buried under discarded clothes, Alice consults the weather forecast, sees it's going to be warm again and decides she'd be better off being comfortable. She digs out a nineties-style denim pinafore, and after some deliberation balls up a jumper and a pair of tights to shove in her handbag, forearming her in the event of the forecast turning out to be unreliable.

And then, one by one, she goes through every single step she can think of to ensure a good night's sleep. Half an hour of low-volume YouTube yoga followed by a bubble bath, then slathering herself in cocoa butter in the hope the soothing massaging motions will diffuse the adrenaline still rocketing round her system. She listens out for any sound of unrest or coughing from Mollie, but everything's quiet. *It's okay*, she tells herself. *She's fine. You're both fine. Tomorrow will be fine. It will all work out. Just stay calm. Get to bed. Face tomorrow when it comes.*

It's gone midnight by the time Alice crawls into bed.

It's getting light by the time she gives up on sleep and decides just to get up.

In the subdued grey-pink light of the sunrise, she fills the kettle at the kitchen sink, watching a cat slink down the back alley and spacing out for a second, not really taking in the plants, or the windchimes, or all the other bits and pieces of her and Mollie's life. Kettle on, Alice scoops three spoons of coffee into a mug, examining her bleary reflection in the shiny chrome surface. *Okay*, she thinks. *Today's the day. Better give it everything you've got.*

# CHAPTER TEN

E ven with everything that's going on, the library is a comfort to Levon. More than that: it gives him hope. He'd
felt that way even before he worked in libraries. The hushed
library of the private school he'd been sent to in England
had been a sanctuary; a place where he could disappear into
other people's stories and temporarily escape from his own.
He devoured every book he could, his imagination bubbling
with possibilities, with medieval fantasies and heady sci-fi,
Shakespeare and Sherlock Holmes. Memoirs and myths and
locked-room mysteries. Levon read as though possessed,
searching for answers to a question he couldn't yet articulate.
Levon felt more real when reading than he did anywhere else.
In his host family's home, there had been bookcases lining
the stairs: towering shelves full of serious texts. Levon, with
his ritual of trailing his fingers over their foil-lettered spines
as he went up and down the steps, wondered if any of them
could help him understand the intricacies of how he'd ended
up so many thousands of miles from home.

Levon's visited some incredible libraries over the years.

As a student in Manchester, he spent as much time as he could soaking up the Gothic grandeur of the John Rylands, and thrilled at being a member of The Portico, an institution almost two centuries old with its glass domed ceiling, dark wood shelves and soft lamplight. For his fiftieth birthday, he treated himself to a weekend at Gladstone's, a residential library with its own chapel, annexe and gardens. But this library, where he works now, is the first library that's truly felt like *his*. After graduating, Levon spent his time on youth work, literacy projects and activism, but it took him a while to find somewhere that felt like home. *When your roots get ripped up at such an early age, you don't really know what you're looking for*, he thinks. It's hard to find somewhere that feels right when the memories of what home should be are so far and so long ago. This library is the closest to it that he's found, and since the last round of funding cuts, that's been the case even more, because it's more often now that he's there on his own. Even when his colleagues are there, it's on the days when there's more to do, and they end up being satellites engrossed in their own tasks and to-do lists. But most days, it's him and the books, him and the service users, and there's pleasure and pride to be found in that even if sometimes it's lonelier than he'd like.

Setting out to walk to work, Levon edges round the scummy stagnant puddle that's ever-present around the apparently permanently blocked drain at the end of his path. The puddle is eternally expanding and contracting, depending how much rain has fallen, but Levon doesn't think he's ever seen it vanish entirely in the nine years he's lived here. Past the puddle, he strides over starbursts of toothy dandelion leaves coming up through the cracked pavement, crossing at the corner near Alice's and passing the bent rusted railings by the park before he turns towards the main road. The chill in the shade makes him pull his denim jacket tighter around himself, and he's glad to turn onto the high street, the sun warming his back as he passes cafes, a yoga studio and the medical centre. At the library, he turns the key to raise the metal shutters over the doors and window, a vivid spray-paint mural grinding noisily out of view. Levon should report the vandalism to the council, but he hasn't. The mural's a memorial tribute: a smiling face, dates and a tag. He knows it'd only be another grief for the artist to have their work scrubbed away or painted over, so he admires the portrait until it disappears out of sight, deciding to leave it be for now. Then he unlocks the doors and makes his way inside, turning on the lights and the ancient computer behind the desk. The pile of flyers with the information about their petition is still topped up; only a couple have been taken, if any. Levon makes himself a cup of milky coffee, then he sets to work.

The day disappears in a blur. In between fielding enquiries, issuing membership cards, shelving returns and helping who-ever needs it, Levon works his way through a pile of damaged books, mending the salvageable ones and submitting a budget request to order replacements for those that are beyond repair. So it momentarily confounds him when Mollie comes hurtling through the doors and up to his desk, Alice trailing after her. He soon rallies, returning the toddler's greeting and smiling at Alice's grimace behind Mol's back.

'Are you sure you don't mind doing this? She's been proper hyper on the way over, you know. I've got a sneaking suspi-cion you're going to have your work cut out for you.'

'I'm sure we'll survive,' he says, watching as Mollie spies the fairy-costumed volunteer who's here for today's story time, the toddler scampering towards the kids' corner with a soft gleeful hoot.

Levon turns back to Alice. 'How are you feeling about today?'

Alice frowns. 'I don't feel prepared enough. What if I don't ask the right questions?'

'You'll be fine,' Levon reassures her. 'Whatever you can find out will be helpful.'

'Eurgh,' Alice groans. 'I don't know. Lawyers scare me. I suppose I should be glad Sam and I never got hitched. No messy divorce, you know? But that leaves me with films and TV as my only lawyer reference points, so I don't really know what I'm walking into here.'

'Fear of the unknown. Classic. "We'd enter a tiger's lair before a dark cave."'

'What?'

'Joseph Campbell said that. I'm paraphrasing, but it still stands.'

Alice thanks him at least another six times for minding Mollie before checking the time and saying she'd better go. She stops in the corner to give Mol a goodbye kiss that she barely even notices, then disappears out the door.

Once story time is over, Levon sets Mollie up with a pile of books she's compiled from the nearby shelves. He recognises the cover of the Basquiat-illustrated edition of *Life Doesn't Frighten Me* by Maya Angelou, praising Mollie for her excellent taste. His to-do list is waiting, but he gives himself a moment to sit back down behind his desk and watch her for a minute. Out of habit, Levon refreshes his emails, just in case any journalists have replied, but there's nothing. He's tired. Levon's been keeping his fears at bay as best he can, but they creep up at night. He's had nightmares since childhood:

waking up in panic in his host family's house, simultaneously clammy and freezing, staying awake in an attempt to evade the images of his parents being bombed into bits. Between those nights and the ones where sleep wouldn't come at all, he's got plenty of experience of long nights, and he has his ways of coping: books, mostly, and never silence; the radio kept on low at all times, a soft background lull he can focus on instead of his thoughts. For the most part, it works. But today he's content to let time creep past him for a few minutes, listening to Mollie's whispered burbling to her books, occasionally glancing up like she's checking he's still nearby. *I hope this isn't the last time you get to come here, little one*, he thinks. *That'd be such a shame, wouldn't it?*

His reflections are interrupted by the blast of noise that wafts in when the door goes. It's Jessie again, this time with her hair in spikes, wearing a vest that seems to be mostly made from straps, and massive mirrored sunglasses that Levon thinks make her look like a character from a post-apocalyptic film.

'Back so soon?'

'Yeah ... hey.'

'It's nice to see you again, Jessie. Another essay, is it?'

'What, how did you ... ?' She trails off and removes her sunglasses to focus on him properly. 'You remembered my name.'

'Of course. And you remembered mine, I'm sure?'

'Err ...'

'Levon,' he reminds her, with a smile. 'So, what's the assignment today, then?'

'More history coursework. And the internet's down at mine so ... this place has wi-fi, right?'

'It does. Come on in, get settled. There should be a little sign on each table with all the log-in details.'

'Nice one. Cool. Thanks.'

Levon watches as she makes her way to a table in a corner not far from Mollie. She gets her things from her bag and assembles them round her in a constellation of organised chaos. She doesn't check the wi-fi details taped to the table, confirming Levon's suspicions: Jessie's returned to the library for more than just their internet.

*So young to be spending so much time on her own. Makes sense she'd want some company. Not that she'd ever admit it, I'm sure.* He recognises her spikiness as a self-protection strategy, wonders what it'll take other than time for her to learn to let people in. *Still*, he thinks. *She's here. That's something.*

Levon knows the library's not perfect. There's a continual and inexplicable soapy fish smell in their tiny staff kitchen, the roof leaks whenever there's a thunderstorm and Doris who does Wednesdays swears on her labrador's life that the reference section is haunted. But Levon's also seen how the library softens people's hard edges.

The next time Levon passes Jessie to check on Mollie, the teenager looks up from her screen and slides her big head-phones down to loop her neck.

'You need anything?' he asks, just as Mollie gives a banshee laugh and frisbees a book towards their heads.

They duck. *Funnybones* goes skidding across the table.

'No offence, dude, but you seem like you've got your hands full.'

'You might be right about that. Excuse me a minute.'

He goes over to see to Mollie, who gabbles happily to him in her own language while Levon answers back in a calm, patient voice as though he understands perfectly. While they're occupied, Jessie grabs one of Levon's petition flyers, reading it over then keying the link into her phone.

When Levon comes back to Jessie's table, it's with Mollie trailing after him, fists full of paper and pens.

'Wanted to sit with you,' he explains, with an apologetic shrug.

Mollie nods, gives Jessie a shy grin, then immediately retrieves the copy of *Funnybones*, props it up so she can hide behind it and engrosses herself in her colouring.

'Makes sense,' Jessie deadpans. 'I am the best.'

Then she holds up the flyer. 'Mate, most people are not going to type in this long link. I'm going to do you another version you can put on here. That'll make it more shareable, yeah?'

'That'd be wonderful, Jessie, thank you. But don't let me take your attention away from your essay. Have you got everything you need?'

She hums. 'I wouldn't go that far. But that last one you helped me with got a much better grade than I usually get. And now the teacher thinks I'm like ... getting my act together or whatever. So I want to do a good job.' Jessie fiddles with a spike of hair, folding it over and around a finger. 'Whatever. It's stupid. But I really thought I didn't even have a chance of passing history. And now I think I might. Have a chance, I mean.'

'That's fantastic, well done. So what's the topic this time? Are you still on the World War Two module?'

'Yep.' She spins the laptop screen to show him her Word document, where she's typed out the title but not much else. 'Displacement in Leeds during the war. You know anything about that, mystical library genie who lives on my street?'

'A little. And I can find you some material from the archives that can probably help more than me. Can you watch my friend here a minute? Then I can go and find them.'

'What do you say, mystical library genie's child friend? You good with that plan?'

Mollie moves the book she's been hidden behind and gives a solemn nod.

Jessie repeats the nod to Levon. 'We're cool.'

'Good. Won't be long.'

As he moves off to search the shelves, he hears Mollie describing her drawing of the family of skeletons from the *Funnybones* book.

'Oh, cool,' he hears Jessie telling the toddler. 'You're a baby goth. Brilliant.'

Mollie's awed laughter tells him that she's taken this as a compliment. Levon wanders out of earshot, meandering towards the corner of the library that houses old newspapers, pamphlets, zines, maps and the various miscellanea that make up the local history section but can't be filed neatly on a standard bookshelf. Levon only knows a little about Leeds during wartime, but he's picked up bits and pieces during his time in the city. He knows about the museum being bombed, its collection detonated into the surrounding streets: no fatalities but the losses included dinosaur bones, an Egyptian mummy and a taxidermied tiger. He knows about the abandoned church nearby that housed one of the area's biggest bomb shelters, and about Waddingtons making Monopoly games with secret additions of maps and money to send to POW camps. Scouring the collection, he assembles a selection of resources covering wartime changes in labour force, post-war immigration of refugees and the evacuation of Leeds children at the start of the war. On the shelf, there's a memoir by one of them: the back cover describes the author as one of almost twenty thousand sent by train to the countryside to escape the risk of bombs. The correlation with his own experience gives Levon a bittersweet pang of recognition, and he makes a mental note to read the book once Jessie's done with it.

When he returns, Jessie and Mollie are conferring in whispers, heads close together, each adding their own details to a piece of paper between them.

As he gets closer, Levon recognises the scribbly drawing as their street. One of the stick figures carrying a towering pile of rectangles he imagines are supposed to be books is undoubtedly him. A stick version of Mollie has a red crayon smile. A manga cartoon illustration added by Jessie has her blue spiky hair. Levon can't help his grin.

'Here we go,' he says, depositing his picks in front of Jessie. 'And I can help keep this one occupied, if you need to concentrate.'

'Nah, she's good there. You're inspiring me, right, Mol?'

Mol gives another serious nod and starts another artwork as Jessie opens the first book on the pile.

# CHAPTER ELEVEN

B y the time Alice leaves Mollie at the library and gets back to the bus stop, she's behind schedule, and she sends a prayer to whatever gods might be listening that the bus comes when it should. Opposite, a Rasta with fat locs down to his knees is playing the saxophone, a case open at his feet, the red velvet lining glinting with chucked coins. The busker sees Alice watching and winks, puffing his cheeks out to hit the high note, and she imagines the music making its way down the street, into the shops and the flats above. A candyfloss-haired old lady sitting in the bus shelter hums along to the melody from behind a Mills & Boon paperback that Alice recognises from the sticker on its spine as being from the library. *It's brilliant round here*, Alice thinks, surging with gratitude for all these everyday details she's usually too distracted to appreciate, loving even the litter and the bird shit, the pawn shop on the corner with its loud banners about payday loans. *Please let this lawyer meeting work out. Let the bus come on time and the lawyer come to our rescue so none of us has to move.*

As though she's summoned it, the bus wheezes its way round the corner just as Alice's skin starts crawling with panic about being late. She sits at the back, relishing for once not being dragged to Mol's favourite position at the front of the upper deck. She pulls up the map app again, checking how many minutes are left until her appointment. It counts down the stops for her and she focuses on that as the bus lurches forwards. When her phone vibrates in her hand, Alice glances down to see Sam's name on the screen. Another jolt of fear thuds through her. *Not more bad news. Please. Not today.* She's tempted to shove her phone back in her bag and leave the message unread. But she needs to know. Alice swipes to open it, biting the inside of her cheek.

Thinking of you today, Lish. Whatever it is, you got this.

Sam doesn't know what's going on. In the fragmented back and forth they had after his message about his mum, Alice decided not to tell him. He's got enough going on trekking back to Marple to see Michelle in hospital. But he'd still been apologetic about not being able to have Mol, and Alice eventually explained she had an important meeting but that she'd sorted childcare with someone from her street. *He doesn't need to know the details, but he's got a right to know who I'm leaving his kid with.* She deliberately didn't explain any more about the meeting, letting Sam assume that it's something for school. Still, the unexpected sweetness of his message makes her reel. She hadn't expected him even to remember, not with everything that's happening. She shoves down the twisty mix of feelings and focuses on the song still being hummed by the woman with the Mills & Boon book, the grind of the engine, the tinny rap rattle from someone's headphones, the ocean wash of her breathing as she recalls the mindfulness techniques she's shared with the kids at

94

school. She watches the little dot move on the map until it's time to get off.

Alice has been expecting the lawyer's offices to be scary and serious. Compared to her area, where austerity and gentrification are still bitterly battling it out, this street seems more upmarket: calmer and cleaner but a bit unsettling. When she gets there, there's only a door at street level, tucked between an estate agent and a flashy salon filled with shiny mirrors and fresh flowers. A discreet plaque by the doorbell confirms that Alice is in the right place, and a crackly but warm voice over the buzzer directs her through the heavy door and up the thick-carpeted stairs.

The lawyer is waiting for her with an outstretched hand.

'Afshan Tuli. Nice to meet you at last. Come on in.'

Her raspy voice makes Alice instantly calmer. Afshan wears a sharp asymmetrical dress that shows off a curvaceous figure, with chunky bangles at each wrist that jangle as she leads Alice into an office. It's small, two walls lined with shelves of books and framed certificates, and the other a large window with gauzy white curtains that soften the sunlight and give the room a serene glow. Opposite the window, a wooden desk covered in paperwork and an open laptop takes up most of the space between the bookshelves.

'So, Alice,' the lawyer says, once they're sitting either side of the desk, 'my assistant passed on the information you gave over the phone. Can you give me an update of anything that's happened since then that I might need to know about?'

Alice recaps the meeting at the Gatsby offices, the details about herself and the other tenants. She keeps her voice as steady as she can, but the absolute shock and upset of it all is still so raw that she hears her words speeding up and falling over each other as she scrambles to get everything explained. To her credit, Afshan listens with grave attention, making occasional notes on a leatherbound pad and never interrupting, even though Alice can't fathom if her garbled story is making sense.

'It can't be legal, can it?' Alice asks, in the moments of quiet after. 'To just evict us like that?'

'It certainly shouldn't be. Sadly, though, these things don't always work the way they should. But I can have a look. And if there's a way, I'll find it. Did you bring the documents my assistant asked for?'

Alice pulls the file from her bag, secretly thankful that, unlike much of her school marking, this folder has escaped Mollie's scribbles and chocolate-spread smears.

Afshan puts on a pair of large tortoiseshell glasses, reads through the letter from the property developer and then the original contract Alice signed with the housing agency three years ago, excavated last night from the vintage suitcase under her bed that holds all her important paperwork. She'd reread it herself, cross-legged on the bedroom rug in her pyjamas, but the smeary photocopy with its tiny text had been so full of incomprehensible clauses that it had headached her into giving up.

But as Alice watches Afshan's serious amber eyes flicking back and forth, she inhales, holds, exhales, holds out hope, willing the woman to find something that will help. *There's got to be something in there. Some word or loophole or archaic detail that everyone's overlooked. Something that will undo all this, make them have to retract those eviction notices and let us go back to how things were.*

Afshan lowers the contract, removes the glasses and rubs her eyes. And Alice knows even before the lawyer speaks that it's not going to go that way. She can see it in the sympathetic head-tilt and the way the woman seems to be weighing how best to break the news.

'I'm sorry,' she says, and Alice's stomach sinks. 'But there's nothing here to indicate that the council has broken the law. There's a clause in the original contract that reserves their right to end your tenancy at their discretion. So as long as they've given you the statutory notice period, in legal terms, they haven't done anything wrong.'

'Nothing wrong.' Alice echoes Afshan's words, her voice hollow and disbelieving.

Afshan puts her glasses back on and takes a sympathetic tone. 'Look,' she says. 'Ethically, this is horrendous. We both know that. What they're doing isn't right. But to challenge it, I have to work with the letter of the law, and I'm afraid I don't see how I can do that with this.'

'So there's nothing you can do?'

'I can signpost you and your neighbours to other resources that might be useful. There's a women's housing unit in Kirkstall that I know has spaces available. There are other charities that might be able to help your neighbours.'

'Right. Okay. No. I don't know. Can I get back to you on that?'

'Of course.' Afshan's face is kind but Alice can't stay in the room another moment.

'Thank you for looking, and meeting with me,' she says, standing upright and snatching the papers back from the lawyer's outstretched hand. 'I'm going then. I'm just. I'm going.'

She stumbles down the steps and into the street. There, Alice leans against the rough brick wall, taking deep breaths while competing emotions rocket around her brain.

*I need a minute*, she thinks. *To process*. In a daze, she sets off walking, finding a pub on autopilot and heading inside. She gets a distracted impression of antler chandeliers and framed film noir posters before she's at a blonde-wood bar and a grungy barman with model-beautiful cheekbones is asking what she wants.

Alice orders a gin and tonic, not even comprehending the bartender's flirting as she takes her drink and moves through the pub, looking for a quiet corner before finding a door that leads out onto a shady terrace with deckchairs and picnic tables. In one narrow section of the beer garden, the late afternoon sun cuts between the nearby buildings, and Alice sits down, angling herself to the warmth, ice cubes clinking in her glass. *Okay*, she tells herself. *Thirteen days left. What now?*

By the time she finishes her drink and leaves the terrace, the adrenaline in Alice's system has settled from a storm to a simmer. *Get yourself together. You've been through worse.* The endless Reddit threads from other desperate new mothers. The doctor's office. The words *postpartum depression.* The pharmacist passing her the flimsy paper bag with its box of medication. *You got through it, though. You can do this, too.* Alice's hands are strangely numb when she fumbles for her phone. There are so many thoughts crackling and zipping through her brain, like static and radio interference. She can't make them line up in a coherent way. All she can catch are fragments. *Moving boxes. Change doctors. Update CV. Redirect the post.* Her imagination flickers through different parts of the house, questioning the best way to pack and transport their contents. *The little sideboard with the elephants on, that could go in a car, if I can borrow or hire one. But the wardrobe, that'll need dismantling, or a van.* She gets on the bus in a trance. There are no seats downstairs so she goes to the upper deck, a dizzy

98

tug of vertigo making her grip the handrail extra tight. *Stop it*, she tells herself. *You can't spiral. Get your shit together.* The zoomed-out reality is too much, so she forces herself to focus in. *Just do the next thing, Alice. Then the one after that.*

*Get Mollie.* But that brings to mind the library, Levon's thoughtful face and questions Alice can't face yet. When she can focus properly on her phone, there's a message from him, with a photo attached. Mollie beaming, brandishing a book. Her dungarees are covered in stickers, and so is her face. When Alice zooms in, she can see they have the library name and a cartoon owl reading a book. There are more stickers in Mollie's hair.

Hope it went well. Mollie is the library's newest, youngest and best ambassador. Are you coming to collect her or shall I bring her back when we close?

Fingers crossed you + library still in one piece! Be brill if you can bring her back with you, thanks so much x

Then she sees the timestamp: Levon sent his message over an hour ago and realises he'll assume she's been with the lawyer all this time. *Will that have got his hopes up? What would I have thought if it'd been him or AJ who'd gone? Longer meeting = more to discuss? More possibilities to fight, more negotiation, more hope?* She can't remember how long she was there, but it can't have been long. *Never mind. It was worth a go. There could have been something. We have to try everything.*

Alice zones out for the entire ride home, only coming back to earth when she's at the stop for Leodis Street. She doesn't even remember passing the library. *Good job Levon offered to bring Mol home*, she thinks, guilt clawing at her and fighting with the relief she feels at being able to have some time to herself before getting back into mum mode once Mollie returns.

The trudge up the hill breaks her heart even more and makes her far more aware than she'd like of the lack of sleep the night before. Rounding the crooked railings at the corner onto the street, Alice deliberately doesn't look down at the snarl of nettles or up to the broken-off street name sign. She's fantasising about kicking off her shoes, about sloshing Kahlúa over the last bit of caramel ice-cream in the freezer and eating the entire melty mess straight from the tub. All she wants is some cool quiet, and to be able to cry without worrying about Mollie getting upset. So she's distracted as she gets closer to home, and it's like Bill materialises from nowhere, dragging his bin across the broken pavement ready for collection tomorrow morning. Jarred by his sudden presence blocking her path, Alice stops short, slipping off the kerb and into the road to avoid crashing into him.

'Watch it,' he huffs, halting in his fight with the bin to glare at Alice. 'You'll do us both an injury if you're not careful.'

His caustic tone stings Alice like a slap.

'Give it a rest, Bill. Your relentless charm and sunny disposition are too much for me today.' The clenched-jaw sarcasm is the best Alice can do to avoid a swearing showdown with him in the middle of the street, but Bill just grunts, leaning heavily on his bin.

Standing so close, Alice can see how much effort it must've taken him to get it to the kerb. His face looks clammy with sweat and his breathing comes raspy and fast. *Please don't let the grumpy old bastard have a heart attack. That'd just be the cherry on top of today's shit sundae, wouldn't it?* Until now, Alice's continual offers to help Bill have mainly been out of manners, and not wanting him to struggle. Not from thinking he can't cope. It's a shock seeing him look so fragile, the swollen knots of his knuckles white around the handle of the bin.

'Bill? You need to sit down a minute?' She waves vaguely towards the crumbling wall where they found him before.

'Gi' over,' he grumbles. 'I sit down, be a miracle if I get up again.'

'Is it the heat?' Alice angles them into a pool of shade on the path.

'Me hip,' he explains, with a wince. 'And me back. Bloody everything, these days.'

'Almost like you should take someone up on it when they offer to help, isn't it?' Alice tells him off in a ratty tone. 'I've told you tons of times I'll do the bins if they're too much for you.'

'Bloody 'ell, you never give up, do you?'

They glower at each other, but Alice is thinking about how soon it won't matter who's doing the bins, about how pointless and stupid this bickering is. She shivers, the contrast between sun and shadow leaving her suddenly cold. Bill watches her rub the goosebumps on her bare arms.

'What's up wi' you, lass? Don't tell me you're nesh 'n' all?'

Alice mentally translates his calling her soft about the chill and rolls her eyes. 'Lovely as always chatting to you, Bill. See you later. Don't let the bin win, yeah?'

'Don't be so mardy,' he grouches as she moves round him towards her gate. 'I don't like the shade, either. Much better, it was, when we had the sun all afternoon.'

Alice stares in confusion, then spins in place, trying to work out what he means.

'Aye, I'm not daft. Me dad had his veg patch here, for a bit. Grew so many tomatoes there was enough for the entire street. Then they built that thing,' he huffs, gesturing to the squat block of flats on the next council estate and the shadow it casts. 'Now it's dark nearly all bloody day. Not that it matters, really. I'm not up to owt like that any more. Knees wouldn't have it, these days.'

The building he's pointed to is one Alice has never even thought about. It's part of the background, always there. She focuses on it now. *That's not new. Far from it. So how long is he talking here?*

'How long have you lived here, Bill?'

'What?' He's been staring at the ground where the vegetables used to grow, shaking himself at the sound of Alice's question and making to slope back inside. 'Oh. Years and years. You know how it is. Hard to keep track at my time of life.'

The door closes behind him before Alice can reply.

# CHAPTER TWELVE

B ill moves down the hall with care, teeth gritted against the pain sparked by each step. Once he's in the living room, he lowers himself into his armchair, but at the last second his grip gives way, making the movement closer to a collapse than a graceful sit down.

*Bloody hell. I'm falling to bits. Better have a rest a minute, pull myself together.*

It's caught him out, the reminiscing to Alice next door about his dad's green-fingered phase. He hasn't thought about that in years. But the memories, when he lets them come, are still there in vivid detail, like being transported back in time. He and his brothers being given weeding duties and ending up sword-fighting with their hand-held trowels, Eddie tying one of Dad's handkerchiefs round his head, pirate war-cries bouncing off the other terraces and making all the street's mums come to their doors to see who'd been injured. Dad with his pipe held between his teeth at sunset, goofy with pride to show them the first green tomato starting to blush red. Mam roping in Bill as the most patient of the three to peel homegrown carrots and potatoes for tea. And whatever was leftover put into spare pans and left on the wall at the bottom of the path for the neighbours to take on their way past.

That was Bill's job, too: going up and down the street to collect the pots after, collecting compliments and thanks with the returned pans and counting them off on his fingers to his parents once he got back. He can remember his mam's glow of pleasure about it: that all their boys were growing up big and strong, and that no one on the street was going hungry if they could help it. Bill was only a kid, of course, but he can remember that being important. That if anyone on the street was poorly, or out of work, or battling some other mysterious issue that made the mums whisper at the doorsteps or the dads go quiet, everyone would help out if they could. Bill's best friend from three doors down had been round for tea every night for a month, at one point. *Something going on at home,* he supposes now, but at the time all he remembers is the sly victory of having an ally in games with his brothers, and his mam's constant baking to send his friend home with warm gingerbread or biscuits wrapped in a clean tea towel.

Bill only means to sit down for a few moments, but at some point his recollections must slip into dreams. Because when he comes back to himself there's a crick in his neck from leaning sideways in his chair, and the room has dimmed around him.

*Get a grip, man.* The name of the friend is on the tip of his tongue as he wakes, evaporating into nothing as he pulls himself upright. Bill's eyes fall to the black-and-white wedding photo on the wall. It's one Sally's uncle took; they hadn't been able to afford a proper photographer but Dom always fancied himself clever with a camera, he'd done all the other family weddings and his pictures always came out beautiful. This one, though, has always been Bill's favourite. Snapped after the proper posed ones assembled on the church steps, Bill hadn't known that Uncle Dom was still there when he'd leaned down to tell Sally how gorgeous she looked in her hand-sewn white lace, and how he couldn't wait to get her home and celebrate their marriage properly. In the picture, Sally leans against the church wall, laughing with her head thrown back, Bill holding her up and grinning in his smart suit with the carnation buttonhole, eyes glinting with mischief and desire. The photo's not entirely in focus, one of Sally's hands a blur of motion, smacking Bill's chest for his cheek-iness. But to Bill it couldn't be more perfect, and reminds him of carting Sally over the threshold in his arms that night, her protesting he'd put his back out and Bill telling her: *Don't be so soft, woman. We're only going to do this once. Got to do it properly. Now lift your head up, love, that's it. Don't want you getting concussed on a door frame, do we?* Sally's laughter had got harder with every step up the stairs, and by the time they got to Bill's bedroom, she was shaking so much he was worried he might drop her. But he managed to place her gently on the bed, Sal's laughter dying away but the smile staying on her face as he pulled at his tie and shoes then crawled onto the blankets to join her.

He gazes at Sally's face in the picture. *Long time ago, that, eh, love? All them promises, and look at me now. You'd hate seeing me like this, wouldn't you?*

He met Sally for the first time at Silver Blades, the ice-skating rink in Kirkstall that had only opened a month before. He was there for a friend's eighteenth birthday party, a gang of about twenty lads who'd taken over several lanes at the ten-pin bowling alley on the ground floor before goading each other into heading up the stairs to the ice rink. Bill remembers being part of that wild and boisterous group, pushing through the entrance to the rink and being blasted by the shivery chill, the music and the silvery light of the mirrored disco ball revolving above the ice . Bill had wobbled around the rink's edge while the others raced back and forth, the carve of their skates leaving deep lines in their wake. But when he bumped into Sally and started talking, he wasn't sorry for his lack of dexterity. The jukebox clicked over to the Beatles, the speakers blaring *I Want To Hold Your Hand* as Sally held out hers and asked Bill if she could show him some moves.

The pain from earlier has melted down into a creaking ache that's sharp when Bill shifts his posture but not so bad if he keeps still. Even so, he's out of sorts. He doesn't like Alice seeing him struggle. Doesn't want her thinking of him as a stupid old sod who doesn't even realise he can't cope. *Even if that's what I am. No need to make such a fuss.* But even as he thinks it, he knows he's being unfair, and that Alice means well. *She's a good lass, really, trying to take care of me even when I'm such an ungrateful bugger. She'd have got on with my Sal like a house on fire. Probably good for me they never met. Don't think I could've coped with them both fussing me. Sal was more than enough. Steel core and heart of gold. No messing about, everyone taken care of, even when times were hard. Like my mam and dad, that. And that Alice seems like that too. Wants everyone to have everything they need, and woe betide anyone who gets in her way while she's making that happen. Got her head screwed on right, she has, even though I don't always give her credit for it. Especially being on her own. Can't have been easy for her.*

Bill heaves himself up out of his chair and towards the

kitchen. As he fills the kettle, he finds himself digging through his memories for when Alice first arrived on the street. It was only a few years ago, he knows that much, after the Ellises moved out, the last ones on the street whose names he knew. But he can't fully remember when, only that since then the house has slowly become noisier and more colourful, with the windchimes by the front door, the plant pots on the steps, the chalk drawings on the path. It had annoyed him at first. Didn't seem proper, the messy chaos of the front garden. *No way to keep a house.* But now he's reassessing his earlier judgement. *It's what that place needed*, he thinks, stirring sugar into his tea. *Probably what this place needs, too.* Since Sally died, he's rattled round it on his own, the quiet getting to him in a way it never had before. He'd always expected the house to stay the way it was when he was growing up; loud, chaotic, never enough money, never enough time to get everything done, but full of laughter and kindness, a deep love that doesn't need saying to be understood.

He sips from his mug while staring out over the sink. Doesn't want to sit back down in case he dozes off again and ends up there overnight. *Dread to think what my joints would be like if that happened.* But as he drinks his tea and looks out, it's not the dark yard behind the house he sees. He's back in time, remembering being in this very kitchen, arms round Sally from behind as she stirred a pan of something on the hob. Kissing her cheek, her neck, every bit of her he could reach, saying *turn that bloody cooker down a minute, turn round and let me get a look at you.* Their infatuation with each other lasted much longer than their week-long honeymoon in Sal's auntie's caravan in Prestatyn. Lasted their entire lives, really, and Bill's counted his lucky stars god knows how many times for that. But the first ten years or so, they were pure magic;

the other lads at work teasing him rotten for always being so soft about her, for forsaking the pub on Fridays because he wanted to get back to Sally, for spag bol and red wine with the record player on, then sometimes they'd go out. The Scala had been their favourite, the sounds of the live band echoing down the road from the former cinema that had been co-opted into a dance hall, Bill and Sally pulling each other's hands to get there faster when they turned the corner and the music reached them. He'd spin her round that dance floor until they were both dizzy, the warmth of Sally's body coming through her dress to his hands. Other Fridays they'd go to bed early, the sun setting and them too distracted by each other to appreciate its beauty, dizzy with love and the prospect of a lazy lie-in the next morning.

Tea finished, Bill makes his way down the hall, using his stick to nudge open the cupboard under the stairs and knock loose an ancient shoebox full of photographs. The box has gone soft and feathery at the corners, and he pushes it ahead of him to the bottom of the stairs, then takes a heavy seat on the bottom step, hissing at the complaints in his hips when he leans down to pick up the box and examine its contents. The top few are more from his wedding, one of him and his brothers in their suits that sets his thinking along darker lines. He and Sally had their hard times too. Alfie's death, in an accident at the Scarborough docks the week before his thirtieth birthday, that had turned Bill inside out. Woebegone and sick with it, he was. It was only Sally's solid hold on him that had got him through the funeral, then the numb months afterwards, when one nip of whisky led too soon to the next and before long the entire bottle was gone, but it was the only way he could sleep. Sal had let him grieve but intervened on the drinking; they decided together enough was enough and stood side by side with her rubbing circles on his back while he poured the last half-bottle down the sink.

And Sally had her moments over the years. Once, she'd come home from the factory with her hair wild from the wind, a storm snatching the door from her hand as she tried to close it, whipping it back open with a bang. Bill knew something had happened. Sally said she was fine, fighting the door closed and latched, kissing his cheek and hanging her coat and scarf in the hallway, but her face wasn't right. Tight, it had been, like she was keeping something in, and as he trailed her into the kitchen, her movements were off, too, jerky and mechanical as she fumbled for her favourite mug to make tea.

As Bill watched, the cup slipped from her fingers, exploding as it hit the floor and sending shards everywhere. And then Sally had crumpled, her back sliding down the kitchen cabinets until she was huddled in a ball, surrounded by smashed crockery.

'What is it, love? What's going on?' He was beside her in a flash, picking his way through the wreckage and kicking the biggest pieces away so they wouldn't cut themselves as he sat next to her on the floor.

Sally said nothing for several minutes, face covered, snuffling into her knees.

'Nothing,' she said, after a while, wiping her face with a hand and turning a weak smile to him. 'It's nothing.'

'Doesn't seem like it. Did summat go on at work?'

She nodded, and Bill steeled himself for the blaze of fury that always came when Sally told him the stories about some of the factory supervisors; the ones who were flippant about the injuries the women got from the machines, the ones who ruled with nastiness and the ones whose lewd comments and actions made the youngest girls fear being called to the manager's office. But this time, there's no sign of Sally's usual righteous defiance. Instead, she shifted her body to curl into Bill's side, leaning her head on his shoulder so he couldn't see her face.

'It's Emma,' she said then, her voice wobbling with the mention of her best friend from two streets down, the one who'd got her the factory job. 'Turns out it wasn't the flu she had when she was off last week. She's expecting.'

Understanding engulfed Bill, and he put his arm around Sally, holding her tight on the kitchen floor.

It had taken years to get to that point. They always assumed it'd happen for them, and as time went on and Sally started to mention it each month, Bill would do his best to reassure her, grinning and reaching for her and saying it was a good excuse to keep trying. But then time wore on and the news of each coming baby in their extended circle became a series of blows they both found it harder and harder to take. They had a lot of friends, but they were all settling down, occupied with their own families, and it wrenched Bill's heart to see Sally get sad whenever they passed a mother with a pram. So it seemed like the obvious thing to do, when Sally came home with the leaflets one day.

'You know you're more than enough for me, don't you, love? Even if it's just you and me for the rest of our days, I'll be happy with that.'

'You daft lug,' she said, and kissed him. 'I know. But I also know how much love you've got in you. How much we've both got. Seems silly not to share it, doesn't it? This is a way we can do that. I don't care about the how any more.'

And so they'd made an appointment with the foster agency, dressed in their Sunday best and went to the office in the town hall, where they filled forms in and were interviewed for what felt like hours. Finally, they'd been told to wait to be contacted and sent off into Leeds city centre, dazed and clutching each other's hands extra hard. It'd been raining, Bill remembers that, one of those sudden storms that blitzes in from nowhere and soaks you right down to the skin. After the stuffiness and nerves of being indoors, the cool relief of the rain and the fizzy excitement of what might be coming for them was a combination that made Bill grab Sally and spin her in a circle right there in Victoria Square. She shrieked and laughed and tried to hide her curls inside his coat. They found a little cafe just off the Headrow, hidden down an alleyway close to the art gallery, and they'd huddled inside it until the rain eased, Sally ordering them both slices of Victoria sponge and strawberry milkshakes with whipped cream. They clinked the pink shakes together and watched each other's faces as they drank, and Bill loved Sally even more in that moment than ever before.

*Silly sod*, he says to himself, shaking his head and shuffling through the photographs. But he can't help but recall how it was for weeks after, Sally wondering out loud how soon it might be before they heard. And then, finally, the phone call from the agency came. They'd been approved, the voice said. They had a child in need of a place to stay. Not for long, likely just a few weeks while their mother was poorly. Possibly more if the situation didn't improve. Might the two of them be able to help?

That was it: Sally whirling through the house like a woman on a mission, cleaning, tidying, roping in her friends from the street to transform the room that Bill had once shared with his brothers. Between them, they scrubbed the floor, Bill heaving the rug over the line in the yard behind the terraces and beating it with a tennis racket until the dust made him sneeze, Sally whizzing up curtains on the sewing machine. Friends donated hand-me-downs: clothes, books, toys. Bill braved the rickety ladder up to the attic and rescued some of his own childhood treasures, the tin soldiers and the wooden train set. Teddy, when he came, had been too insular and scared for weeks to even notice any of it. But Bill and Sally had loved the shy six-year-old from the moment they met him.

Bill rifles through the box, suddenly desperate to find a picture of Teddy, a dawning sense of unease at the hazy memory of his face. He stayed for three months, in the end. It took him a while to be ready to talk, but Bill remembers the day he came home from work and found him baking with Sally, sleeves rolled up and stood on a chair to reach the counter, hands clotted with dough and a gleeful smile on his flour-flecked face. The apple pie they made together all the sweeter for the stories Teddy told them as they ate.

It was a wrench when they had to say goodbye, bundling Teddy onto the train to stay with other relatives who lived somewhere down south. But as they walked back towards Chapel Allerton together, Bill and Sally's subdued quiet also had an edge of pride. For a while, they'd given Teddy the best home they could. And even in the sad circumstances, the small crumbs of joy they'd been able to bring him had given them both a fierce, heart-aching satisfaction. The agency was thrilled with the way they'd adapted to the changing situation with this first assignment, and from there things escalated fast. Sally and Bill became the first call whenever there was a child in need of a foster home, and their house soon became a revolving door of different ages, circumstances and lengths of stay. Makeshift constellations of siblings that might last for weeks or sometimes years, and though Bill and Sally saw their fair share of scuffles, tantrums and tears, the chaotic whirl of good times more than made up for those.

Bill fumbles through the pictures, not finding any of Teddy but unearthing a handful of snaps of some of the others: birthdays and Christmases, jubilee parties and picnics. His chest feels too tight for his shirt. He returns the pile of photos to the box. *You'd better not be having a heart attack*, he scolds himself. *That's the last bloody thing we need.*

Perhaps because of their experience being passed from place to place, most of the kids soon found their place in the ecosystem of the house, and the street. Before long, it felt like how Bill remembered it from his own childhood: the street's kids always in and out of each other's houses, loyalties and betrayals and rivalries evolving every day, so fast he couldn't keep up, though he loved hearing them tell their stories. That was his favourite, was that, making time at supper for each of the children to describe whatever was going on in their world, and Bill dishing out the best advice he could and telling them their tales were better than any of Sally's soap operas. It had brought him and Sally closer to the other adults on the street, the open attitude they had to feeding and making time for whoever turned up for tea. For a good number of years, it felt like an extended family again, the way he recalled it being when he was young. Everyone helping each other with the hard bits of life and never passing up a chance to celebrate the good. A proper community, it was.

Not like now. Those days are long gone. *Stop living in the past*. He drags himself upright again and returns the box to its cupboard. *I'm on my own now, and I'll have to manage that way*. On his way up the stairs, he touches the bannister, with its dent from his head, its varnish long since worn away by so many hands: his parents, his brothers, Sally and the kids. *Be a shame to say goodbye to this place, though.* The memories and the house are all knitted together, and he doesn't want to lose any of it. But if he has to go somewhere else, he hopes the memories don't slip away, too. Not when they're all he has left.

# CHAPTER THIRTEEN

With eleven days left until they get evicted, AJ's hurling himself into his work as much as he can, but that ticking-down clock can't be stopped. Nothing's worked: it's like no one cares, and he's been holding onto their little scraps of hope so hard that he hasn't even done anything to start facing the possibility that maybe they'll be forced to leave. That nothing they do will make any difference, and in a week's time he'll have to cram his possessions into his car and retreat back to Sheffield, to Mam's cooking and fussing and hours of commuting back and forth down the motorway. From there, he'll have to somehow untangle this mess he's found himself in: find somewhere else to live or transfer to another hospital. AJ's scrambled thoughts go round in circles. He's got the start of a bad headache coming, a gritty, dizzy shimmering at the corners of his vision, and the fluorescents in the hospital corridors are only making it worse. One of the patients from his ward has just been sent down to ICU. It's only eleven o'clock, meaning there's still another nine hours left to his shift, and when he ducks into the bathroom between rounds, his reflection gets a stern talking-to. *You can do it, yeah? Those kids are scared and in pain. This is your chance to do your part in making them better. For tonight, that's all that matters. You can't do anything about any of that other stuff now. So set your own shit aside, and get on with it.*

During his time in nursing, one of the wildest things that AJ's learnt is how much people stay themselves, even when they're ill. He's had people minutes from death apologising for taking up his time. He's had gun-shot gang kids still trying to be hard, even with their consciousness being slowly sapped by blood loss. He's had ex-cons and marines and bouncers sobbing in grief or pain or because of their phobia of needles. He's had mothers like hissing wildcats threatening to rip his bollocks off if he doesn't bring their kids back from the brink. But on the paediatric ward, the thing that always knocks him sideways is how much power he has. How much the kids trust him, even when they're scared. Most of the adults in hospital, even when they're sick or vulnerable or terrified, their social conditioning holds on hard. They keep their fear at bay as best they can; they mask their anxiety or agony or impatience with bad jokes, nervous laughter, polite chit-chat. The kids don't do any of that.

They tell him how it is. They tell him what hurts and he can read it in their faces, and they don't return his smiles and chat unless that's what they want. They don't perform in the same way as adults, and AJ loves them for that. However complicated and exhausting and heartbreaking nursing can be, there's a purity to his role in this department that helps dissolve the strange floaty feeling he had earlier and helps put him back in his body, his shoulders tense and his face itchy with stubble.

He washes his hands and leaves the bathroom, checks the

fob watch pinned to the front of his scrubs and makes his way back to the nurses' station. The last brew he made at the start of his shift has long since gone cold, but he sips the milky sweet concoction anyway, sorting through the pile of patient folders on his desk. His colleague Mags is on the phone in the office, and AJ finds himself zoning out for a moment, thinking about how different it is now to when he first qualified. He remembers Leone, the nurse he shadowed for his first two weeks, her calming Edinburgh accent, the butterfly tattoo on the inside of her wrist visible in flashes as she deftly redid her silver plait when it inevitably came undone halfway through each shift. Remembers her continually telling him *just trust yourself and you'll be barry.* Which meant good, apparently. And here he is now, with no one to shadow any more, even though his job is so much harder these days. The last round of funding cuts was a blow, and AJ finds it tricky to navigate the gaps they've left: things that used to get sorted straight away now take hours, and there used to be six nurses on the ward at any given moment, whereas now they're lucky if they've got three. But AJ's glad of the distraction, necking the rest of his drink and then making his way around the ward, doing observations and making notes of temperature, time and heart rate on each patient's file. Most of them are asleep by now, but a few of the older kids are still awake: an owlish twelve-year-old watching *Riverdale* on his iPad with the volume down low, the punky fifteen-year-old who reminds him of Jessie, laser-focused and scowling as she types on her phone. He moves from bed to bed, returning to the nurses' station just as Mags emerges from the office.

'AJ, can you sort bed seven? There's someone waiting downstairs that triage want to send up.'

'Course, boss. What've we got?'

His colleague squints at a post-it note covered in green biro scribbles, fumbles for the thick-framed red glasses on a chain round her neck, puts them on and tries again.

'Five-year-old boy, dehydration, high temperature, nasty cough, struggling to breathe when he first came in but apparently not so bad now.'

'So could be a chest infection?'

'Sounds like it. Someone's bringing them up now. You good to go and meet them?'

'Got it. You got a name?'

Mags peers again at her notes. 'God, my handwriting is getting worse. Benji, I think that says. Benji Buchanan.'

A wave of recognition goes through AJ, remembering Paul Buchanan introducing himself in that sleek anonymous office, the flamboyant signature scrawled on the bottom of their eviction notices. *Can't be. Just coincidence.*

But Mags must see him dither. 'Something up?'

'No, nothing ... I thought I recognised the surname, but it's probably no relation.'

'Sure? I can do it, if it's a conflict of interest?'

AJ rubs the back of his neck, then squares his shoulders. 'Nah. It's fine. I got it.' *It's not going to be anything to do with him. And even if it is, I can do it.*

A few minutes later, AJ is rolling his eyes at his own wishful thinking, because of course it *is* Paul Buchanan who enters the ward, his son carried in his arms. He looks smaller than AJ remembers, wearing a leather jacket over a plain T-shirt and jeans. Benji's almost hyperventilating with panic and Paul looks equally stressed.

*Here goes nothing,* AJ thinks, and introduces himself. Paul doesn't even look at him. He's fixated on Benji. From the look of the boy's swollen eyes and flushed face, AJ can see how much he's been crying, and immediately sets to putting him at ease.

'Reet, mate,' he says, 'let's get you sorted. We've got a bed for you just down the way here.' He starts leading the way down the corridor, turning back to make a show of admiring Benji's pyjamas. 'Wow, look how cracking those dinosaur jim-jams are. They're amazing, they are. Do you reckon they make them in my size?'

The boy's breathing slows from its previous shallow shudders as he concentrates on AJ's question, then gives a subdued shake of his head.

'No? Too bad, I'd love some of them.' AJ shows them to the bed he's prepared. 'Here we are. You plonk yourself down there and get under the covers, then we'll get you some medicine and see if we can get your temperature down a bit, make you more comfortable. Then hopefully you can have a bit of a sleep before the doc comes to see you in the morning.'

The gloomy hush of the mostly-asleep ward seems to have calmed Benji down a bit. *Bet it's more chill up here than in A&E*, AJ thinks, waiting as Paul helps his son into bed. Benji gives a big juddery sigh, a snotty tearful sound that nonetheless tells AJ the boy's no longer as panicked. In fact, Paul looks more shaken than his son; he's pale and there's a barely there tremor to his voice that AJ can tell he's doing his best to disguise.

'Come on, son, kick them slippers off, that's right.'

'You good?' AJ asks, once Benji's settled in bed, and he nods. 'First things first. Can you show me how much of a big breath in you can take?'

Benji inhales, puffing out his cheeks. 'Cracking. Now do me a favour and hold it, just for a few seconds. Nice. Now blow it all out, as slowly as you can, like you've got loads of candles on a birthday cake.' Benji exhales in a long wheezy breath. 'Brilliant. One more like that? Amazing. You smashed that bit, well done. But I've got another big favour to ask you now, Benji. We need to get some medicine into you as fast as we can, and the best way for us to do that is through something called an IV.'

'But my dad already gave me Calpol.'

'Well, that's a good start, but we need something a bit more heavy-duty than that. And we want to get you feeling better as fast as possible, so we're going to put this medicine straight into your bloodstream.'

'Into my veins? *Gruesome.*'

Behind him, AJ hears Paul mumble an explanation about gruesome being Benji's current favourite word.

'I suppose it probably does seem a bit gruesome. But I prefer to think of it as us putting tiny little medicine superheroes straight into your system, where they can whizz round your entire body and start doing battle with that pesky infection.'

'So they kill the bad bacteria?'

'Woah, woah, hang on a minute.' AJ feigns shock, grabbing for Benji's notes. 'No one told me you were a genius. We should really get that written down in your file. Make sure no one else makes the same mistake.'

The boy gives a bubbly little snort of laughter. Paul glances, baffled, between AJ and Benji, as if he can't believe how much his son's calmed down. From the corner of his eye, AJ sees the look, wonders if he's imagining the flicker of recognition that crosses Paul's face, then returns his focus back to Benji.

'Okay, so now I know I've got a genius on my hands,' AJ continues, grinning at the boy as he pretends to make a note in his patient file. 'The first thing we're going to do is put in this IV so that can start working, and then if you've got any questions, I'll be happy to answer them, okay?'

Benji wavers, his face creasing like he might cry again, but then he takes another cheek-puffing massive inhale, and nods.

'Amazing. I'll just go and get everything ready, won't be a minute.'

AJ moves away from Benji's bedside, thankful for the chance to escape proximity to Paul for a moment. *Breathe*, he tells himself. *It's nowt you've not done a million times before.* He snags Mags' attention and she goes through the protocol of checking the drugs and the patient's identity, then it's just them again.

'Reet, Benji. I'm going to put something called a cannula into your arm first, that's how we get the medicine into your bloodstream. This might hurt a little bit, so you might want to hold Dad's hand for a minute in case you want to give it a squeeze.'

'Come on then, son, you hold onto me.' Paul threads their fingers together. 'Don't break my fingers, though, will you?' AJ recognises the Rolex around his wrist, the sight of it transporting him back to that gleaming glass and chrome meeting room, all of them around the table, begging him to reconsider his plans for their street.

*No empathy for us, was there? And now he's the one in need.* The injustice of it scorches through AJ's system, another sudden thud of emotion that's not what he needs right now. He steadies himself, returns his attention to Benji. The boy is watching, gaze fear-bright but steady, as AJ readies the equipment, then squeezes his eyes shut as AJ swabs antiseptic over the skin and gets ready to insert the plastic tap into his arm.

'Alreet, Benji, here we go. I'll be as fast and gentle as I can, and all I need you to do in return is keep as still as possible. Deal?'

The boy nods and AJ sets to work. Benji keeps his face screwed up and his grip clamped tight on his father's hand, but doesn't move other than that. Moments later, AJ's got the cannula in place, smoothly attaching the flexible tubing and manoeuvring the drip into position so it can start transporting the antibiotics into his veins.

'There you go, sorted. You can open your eyes now, if you want.'

The boy peers at the set-up. 'Gruesome,' he repeats, dragging out the word so that it sounds almost approving now. 'I can feel the medicine going in.'

Paul gives a mumbled scoff of disbelief.

'It can be a bit weird,' AJ tells him. 'And it can feel cold.'

'Yeah. Cold, but on the inside.'

'Well, you were totally brave just now. I'm going to put that on your notes as well, yeah? Brave *and* genius. That's pretty good for someone who's not well.'

Benji gives another subdued smile, but then another bout of shuddery scraping coughs convulses through his entire body. His dad rubs his back, and AJ ducks away from the bed for a moment and comes back with a jug of water and a glass.

'Here you are, chuck. You were dehydrated from having such a high temperature, so we've got fluids going straight into your system as well as medicine. But in the meantime, this'll help.'

The boy gulps from the glass and the coughing eases. He returns the glass to the bedside table and curls up under the covers, moving the arm with the cannula with utmost concentration and care.

'Okay, I'm going to leave you to get settled, but I'll be back to check on you in a bit. And if you need anything, you can

122

press this call button and me or one of the other nurses will be over in a flash, got it?'

Benji gives his assent, his face still blotchy and feverish, holding tight to Paul's hand as he glances round at his surroundings, the bright mural of a tropical jungle along one wall, the other patients in their beds, then burrows his face into his pillow like he's absolutely done with the world.

*What a mood*, AJ thinks. *Poor kid.*

He lowers his voice so as not to disturb the boy, facing Paul properly for the first time.

'You can stay, if you want. We've got a room for parents I can show you to. Or we can take it from here and call you with an update in the morning?

'I . . . I don't know. Ben'll want his mum when he wakes up, but she's not my biggest fan. I'll phone her in a minute, then get out of here once I know she's on her way.'

AJ nods. *Is he even going to let on that we've met before? I know he recognised me earlier. Maybe he's so used to wrecking lives he can't keep the faces straight.*

Paul still seems distracted; he's eased his hand away from Benji, so he can check his phone and fidget with his watch, spinning it round on his wrist. 'You'll call me, though, won't you? If anything changes?'

'Course. The main things are getting him rehydrated and bringing the temperature down, and the IV will do both of those. So he's in good hands.'

'Really good hands,' Paul concurs. 'Thank you.' And AJ gets the sense of the mixed emotions doing battle in Paul's voice and face. Gratitude, but also something else. Defensiveness. Or relief. *Did he expect me to take it out on his kid? Or start a screaming match by his kid's bedside? He should be ashamed. Of himself, of the situation. His sick kid getting cared for by the nurse he's making homeless next week.* And it's that thought that prompts AJ to usher Paul away from the bed and out of the ward.

There's paperwork to be signed, and then when the forms are filled in, AJ clears his throat.

'Mr Buchanan, I know you recognise me. I live on Leodis Street.'

'Ah. Right, mate. Thought I'd seen you somewhere before. Cheers for everything you did with Ben back there.' Paul shuffles his feet and glances down the corridor, calculating his exit strategy.

'Mr Buchanan, can I tell you something? I nearly didn't come in for my shift tonight because of you, and everything your company's doing. And I'm sure any of my colleagues would've looked after your son just as well, but it's ironic, isn't it? The way it's worked out? Me coming in because I decided taking care of other people was more important than my own impending homelessness. And here I am, looking after the child of the person who's created that situation.'

'Listen – AJ, was it? Like I explained at our last meeting, there were many contributing factors that led the council to want to divest themselves of those properties—'

'There's another child on our street,' AJ cuts him off. 'Younger than your boy. She was poorly last week, with the same thing. She's got a single parent too, you met her at that meeting. Alice. And you know, don't you, after what you've been through tonight, what it's like seeing your kid in that state?'

Paul fidgets; hands in his jeans pockets, then out. He's pale again, like when he first got to the ward with his son. 'Wouldn't wish that stress on anyone,' he mutters, but AJ's not done.

'No one would,' he says. 'But your kid isn't getting kicked

out of his house in the next few days, is he? You've not got to worry about getting him better at the same time as job-hunting and house-hunting and doing the sums and packing everything into boxes and not knowing where you're going to be living the week after next, have you?'

'It's regrettable, the situation. Like I said last time, I know it's an inconvenience, but—'

'Not just an inconvenience. These are our homes you're planning on destroying. Our community. And those homes are everything to us. They mean everything. Connection. Independence. Family. History. Think of all those stories, all that meaning.' He crosses his arms and keeps his gaze hard. 'And you just want to bulldoze them into nothing.'

Paul closes his mouth with a click of teeth.

'You could stop it, you know. There's still time. You could put an end to it, cancel the demolition. It's not too late to show some compassion. That's something we all need. Even you, sometimes. You're not invincible, Mr Buchanan. Even with all your money. But you could make a real difference, if you called things off, found another way to do whatever you need to do for your investors or whoever. You could be brave. Like your kid was tonight. You could show some compassion and make a stand for what's right.' *Has this even got a chance in hell of working? I don't know. I don't care.* Inside, AJ feels fizzy, shaky, but his voice comes out strong and clear.

Paul looks around at the blobby paintings done by patients and the thank-you cards taped to the noticeboard behind the nurses' station.

'Thank you for everything you've done for Ben,' he says. 'Really. I hear what you're saying, and I wish I could help. But progress is progress. And it's late, and I'm tired, and I bet you are too. So good night.'

Paul turns and makes his way down the corridor, shaking his head and typing on his phone. AJ watches him leave, continuing to stare after him for a long time once he's gone.

# CHAPTER FOURTEEN

*Didn't we almost have it alllll,* Whitney belts out when AJ cranks the key in the ignition of his car. The interaction with Paul had rattled round his head for the rest of his shift. Even as his brain buzzed with all the numbers on his rounds – temperatures, birth dates, medication dosages – underneath it was Paul's closed-off face and that phrase, *progress is progress,* worming through AJ's mind.

He drives down still-asleep roads as the sunrise turns the sky a vivid swirl of pink and orange. He sees dawns so often he's almost numb to them now, but it always used to be a beloved feature of nights out, to emerge from an all-nighter to find that the sun was already creeping back into the sky. Nights of MDMA and magic, skin on skin and music still a pumping heartbeat long after the clubs had closed. It's been longer than AJ cares to admit since then.

AJ was sixteen the first time he and his best mate jumped the train from Sheffield to Leeds for the annual West Indian Carnival. As a kid, his parents took him almost every year. AJ was dazzled and infatuated with the flamboyance and vivid colours of the dancers' feather-flashing costumes, and the infectious tropical rhythms of the steel drums. Even more so when he and Jordan went on their own, claiming their place on the parade route among the sunshine bop of reggae beats and clutching each other's arms every time they saw another ridiculously amazing sight. Intricate, imposing costumes, dark skin gemmed with sequins and rhinestones, stilt-walkers and fire jugglers dancing in the road, the movements mirrored in the crowds alongside the parade. Thousands of people, celebrating Caribbean culture and heritage, months of planning and costume-making all leading up to one week-end of wild joy and noise. Later, AJ and Jordan followed the boom of the sound systems down to Potternewton Park, the celebrations turning more electric towards night. The two of them were so transported by the music that they'd almost missed the last bus back to the city centre to get their train home. Within a year, he'd come out to his parents, the tension between his sexuality and his culture slowly chipped away with every re-watch of *Paris Is Burning*, every YouTube deep dive into videos of more recent vogue balls, watching people with his skin colour contort themselves into impossible positions, moving in a way he could never mimic despite hours of practising in his bedroom mirror.

Taking his coming-out with her trademark zeal, AJ's mam took him to his first Manchester Pride, outfitting herself in head-to-toe rainbow and enlisting his dad into driving. They'd had identical cynical responses to the corporate floats, and at first AJ had wondered if the entire thing was a mistake, the synthetic feelgood boppiness not even touching him. Then they saw the delegations from the teachers' union, the local charities for HIV and AIDS and homeless queer youth, followed by the NHS cohort: close to a hundred doctors and nurses dancing past in their uniforms, holding hands and waving. AJ was so grateful for his parents' love that day, but the next bank holiday Monday he'd gone back to Leeds Carnival instead, and by nineteen he was at Black Pride in London, dizzy with community in Vauxhall Pleasure Gardens.

As he pulls up onto the street, for once remembering to weave the car through the worst of the potholes, AJ sees Alice sitting on her front step in ratty leggings, bare feet and an oversized hoodie, clutching a coffee mug to her chest and staring into space. His gold car rattling past must have disrupted her trance, because she looks up and waves as he brakes.

"Ey up,' he calls, hovering on his side of the road as Alice puts down her cup and picks her way down the path. 'What you doing up this early?'

'Couldn't sleep,' Alice mumbles, hiding a yawn in her hoodie sleeve. 'You want some breakfast before you head to bed?'

AJ grins, still exhausted but cheered by the prospect of food and company. 'You know what, chuck? That'd be absolutely magic.'

In her kitchen, Alice sets eggs sizzling in a frying pan then brews another pot of coffee for herself, stirring sugar into AJ's tea, directing him to the cutlery drawer so he can dig out a knife to butter toast for them both. Sitting at Alice's tiny yellow kitchen table, they set the world to rights: AJ recapping his encounter with Paul Buchanan in between wiping his toast around his plate to mop up the last egg yolk smears and Alice describing the previous day's experience with the lawyer.

'And I'm just so scared for Sam about his mum; that's the last thing I need on top of everything else. He's been messaging with updates most days, and he says it's not as serious as they thought at first but I don't know if he's giving me the full story. Not that I'm one to talk about that, because it's not like I've told him what's going on here. Anyway!' Alice's voice shifts abruptly from scared to apologetically matter-of-fact. 'That's enough of me waffling on, that's probably the last thing you want to listen to after the night you've had.'

'It's cool,' AJ reassures her, as Alice stacks their plates and crosses to the sink. 'You've listened to me going on about that Buchanan prick. All in it together, aren't we?'

'True,' Alice says over her shoulder as she turns on the tap, her tone more real now, less brittle and fake-bright. 'But you've really helped me get my head right this morning. Thank you.'

His stomach full of eggs, toast and tea, the night's fatigue is chasing AJ down, so he says his goodbyes and slopes home. He doesn't expect to cross paths with Jessie leaving for college, art portfolio under one arm as she wrestles with the door's ancient lock.

'Mate.' AJ mock-faints from shock, grabbing at the broken-off gatepost to steady himself. 'Don't think I've ever seen you at this time. You sure you don't dissolve when sunlight hits you?'

The door finally sorted, Jessie pulls up her hood and puts on a pair of massive face-hiding sunglasses. 'Even night-dwelling evil must sometimes consort with daywalkers, foul peasant,' she intones, putting on a melodramatic Transylvanian accent.

'Fair enough. Good luck then, Morticia.'

'Morticia's not even a vampire,' Jessie retorts with an exasperated head shake, looping her headphones around her neck before stomping down the street towards the bus stop.

Making his way indoors, AJ wonders if she's going in for a specific deadline or lesson, and hopes the teenager's feeling better about college now than that first time they spoke. Jessie's still wary, keeping her distance, but AJ likes to think she's benefitting from not being so isolated. Although there's almost a decade between their ages, they're the two youngest on the street, and he likes the protective sibling vibe it gives their dynamic. Laughing at Jessie's imagined eye roll if she heard his thoughts, he sends himself up to bed.

It's weird to imagine that only a few weeks ago he knew his neighbours' faces, just about, but nothing more. It's strangely comforting to realise how much they know about each other now. He's lost count of the times he's heard other queer people say the words *found family*, but he's never really understood what that could mean for him.

He falls into bed, thankful for his clean bright room, the framed black-and-white Whitney print over the empty fireplace alcove stacked with his favourite books and a half-melted lemon and sea salt candle he lights after hard hospital shifts. A deep sleep disappears most of AJ's day, but when he resurfaces he's not surprised to see a missed call from his mam, followed by a bossy voice note ordering him to call her when he can.

'So, come on then,' his mam says when he phones her from bed. 'Tell me your gossip. When you go quiet, that always means there's something going on. Out with it.'

'Mam,' AJ moans. 'You think my life is way more interesting than it is.'

'It better be,' she laughs. 'You're only young. Plenty of time yet for being boring and serious. So why haven't you been speaking to me?'

'I talk to you nearly every day.' AJ attempts to sound reassuring, but he knows it's a lie even as the words are out of his mouth, and so does his mam.

'Not properly,' she contradicts him. 'Not for weeks. What's got you distracted, love?' A coy teasing tone creeps into her voice. 'Or is it a person? Go on, tell me who he is.'

'No one!' Then he realises his scandalised pitch is likely just to excite her, that she'll read into it like she always does. 'Really, Mam,' he tells her, burrowing deeper into his duvet. 'It's not like that.'

He knows he should be grateful for his mam loving him so much she wants to know all the ins and outs. Literally, if her obsession with his love life, or lack of, is any indication. Frustrated as he can get with it at times, it means a lot to him to hear her enquire so casually about prospective boyfriends. Not everyone has that, he knows.

'Is it so bad that I want you to find a nice boyfriend to treat you right?'

'Nah, it's not bad. But I've got no space in my head for anything like that right now.'

'"Space in your head"? Get making space, love. I know your job's important, but you can't let it be everything. I want you to have more than that. Big love affairs that make you feel like your heart's going to burst.' She's in full flow now, and even when she sighs, AJ knows there's no point talking at all until she's done.

'I'm not going to be around for ever, you know,' she continues. 'I want to know you've got love in your life that you can lean on when things get tough.'

'I know, Mam.'

'So what about coming back for a visit? Or haven't you got time for that, either?'

'I will. Soon, I promise. Soon as I've got my shifts for the next couple of weeks, I'll let you know.'

'I'll hold you to that, you know.'

'I love you, Mam.'

'Love you.'

AJ doesn't say he might be back sooner than that. Doesn't ask about moving back in, if it comes to that. Doesn't want to imagine piling his things into his car and rattling back down the motorway towards the Sheffield suburb with their semi-detached house, his former bedroom now a home office but its squashy blue sofa bed more than enough for him whenever he goes back to visit. Instead, he says goodbye, then sends his mam a row of heart emojis and tells her again not to worry. Even with the ever-present anxiety of the demolition countdown, AJ's not on his own. For the first time ever, he's connected to his neighbours: Alice's resilience and wicked grin when she's relaxed enough to show it, Levon's endless wizardly insights, patience and encyclopaedic knowledge, Jessie's deadpan humour and ferocious independence, her bizarre taste in music creeping through the walls from the house next door. Finally forcing himself out of bed, AJ suddenly can't take the idea that they might all be torn apart, just when they'd started forging these connections. He thinks about what Levon told him, about seeing Jessie in the library, and it gives him the initial rumblings of an idea. *We can't give up*, he thinks. *We've got to do something. Anything.* On impulse, he digs his phone out from where it's become buried in his pillows, scrolls through his contacts and hits call.

'Lev, hey,' he says, once the other man answers. 'Yeah, it's me. How are you, man?'

He listens to Levon's reply and continues. 'Yeah, I'm not bad, ta, but I've been thinking. There's got to be something else we can do. You're always going on, aren't you, about libraries being the heart of communities? Like that old indie song, you know? Libraries give us power. So listen . . . is there a chance there could be summat that'd help us, somewhere in the archives? Some other street that managed to fight off this kind of thing? Or some clue to some old council bye-law that means we'll be able to tell them where to go?'

Levon gives a humming sort of sigh, considering. 'Well, AJ, the library's never let me down yet, but this might be the one time I have to concede defeat. I've searched high and low. If there's something like that here, I haven't been able to find it.'

His voice has such a sad heaviness to it that AJ panics that Levon thinks he's being blamed, and scrambles to make himself clearer.

'Nah, nah, nah. It's not just on you, is it? We can all help. But I don't want to waste everyone's time. So I suppose what I'm asking is . . . is it possible? Is it worth a shot?'

'We have to hope,' Levon says, in his solemn quotation voice. 'We can't live on that alone, but life's not worth living without it.'

'Deep. Who said that?'

'Harvey Milk.'

He swallows. 'Did you learn it in a library?'

'From the film,' Levon says, and AJ can hear his rueful smile. 'Hyde Park Picture House. You know what else he said?'

'What?'

'Hope is being able to see that there is light despite all the darkness. The library's still standing, even after years of cuts and threats. And we've got the archives. Local news, oral history transcripts, old maps. You never know. We might find something.'

AJ decides he has to hold onto hope. 'I can't just do nothing,' he tells Levon.

'No.'

'And you've got the keys to the library, right? Like, if we needed to stay after hours?'

'I've stayed late lots of times,' Levon reassures him. 'As long as we lock up after ourselves, we'll be fine.'

'So what about tomorrow night? I can contact Alice and Jessie, see if they're up for it.'

'I'll be there,' Levon says. 'Come whenever you can. We'll stay as long as it takes.'

'Okay, man. Thanks. Catch you later.'

He phones Alice and relays the plan.

'I don't know, AJ. It's a good idea, but childcare is a nightmare at the minute.'

'Bring Mollie with you. Didn't you say she loved it last time she spent the day there?'

'Hasn't stopped going on about it since.'

'There you go, then,' he tells Alice. 'She'll be sound.'

'I suppose I could. You need me to do anything? I can bring snacks?'

'Now we're talking. See you then, yeah?'

He messages Jessie next.

SOS, he types. Street meeting tomorrow at library. Can you come?

She's online and typing back in an instant: Is this when we start our villain arc and form an evil plan?

There's a beat, then another few words. If so I'm in.

It's a good plan, AJ sends back. Not evil.

Jessie's reply is all caps and bold. BORING.

Then several messages, one after the other:

jk I'm coming.

What are we doing tho?

Do I need weapons?

AJ snorts. No weapons, he types.

Never mind then, Jessie sends. I'm out. Peace sign, wave emoji.

Bring your brain, he sends.

Nah soz can't.

He sends back a question mark.

It's melted from too much coursework.

Bring your melted brain. And no weapons. Levon says we can stay as late as we need.

LIBRARY LOCK-IN?! Jessie writes back, fast. That is punk af.

I can't even tell if you're being sarcastic.

No dude, she says. I'm serious.

Sick, he sends, and then immediately regrets it, suspecting he's about to get a schooling from Jessie about his use of slang. He nearly ignores the next blip when it comes through, then has to read it twice to make sure he's understanding right.

Is the library haunted? Do I need ghost-hunting equipment?

Nah, he sends back. Trust Jessie to make this even more surreal than it already is. Then he decides to troll her back, just a bit. Levon says the ghosts are nice.

I'M GOING TO HOOK UP WITH A GHOST IN A MIDNIGHT LIBRARY LOCK-IN.

Then a sequence of hearts and ghosts, then another sentence: omg this is so romantic.

AJ shakes his head. Texting you makes me feel so old, he tells her.

Dude no one says text any more.

Okay so library tomorrow. U want a lift?

Okay boomer.

JESSIE I'M NOT EVEN THIRTY.

136

Okay boomer, she says again. Old man emoji, kissy face, peace sign.

AJ chucks his phone back into his covers. *Okay*, he thinks. *We're on*.

# CHAPTER FIFTEEN

B y the time they start assembling at the library, it's started
to rain. The sky is a grimy cloud-streaked blue-grey,
but the wind makes things feel more miserable and shivery
than they have any right to at this time of year. The library
is almost empty but for one of the community groups getting their things together to leave. The raucous laughter and
Caribbean accents coming from the flamboyantly dressed
group of women in the reading room have been Levon's
soundtrack for the last hour, but before he knows it they're
almost done and making their way out of the door. He says
his goodbyes and they start bustling out of the exit, just as AJ
turns up. He holds the door open for them, beaming at their
clucks of approval at his lovely manners.

Jessie follows him inside, hissing about the rain messing
up her dyed hair, then lapsing into a hummed tune that
Levon thinks he recognises as the theme from *Ghostbusters*.
He shows them in, takes tea orders, then returns to hovering near the door. It's not that he's nervous about what
they're doing: he knows he could probably get in trouble

with the council if anyone found out, but he also knows all too well how minuscule the chances of that are. No one's going to be checking on them on a rainy Saturday night. It's more that he doesn't want anyone passing by and seeing that the lights are still on, doesn't want anyone asking what they're doing, doesn't want to have to tell anyone that they can't come in.

He's lowered the shutter halfway down when he sees Mollie and Alice making their way up the street, and he turns the key to raise it again and let them inside.

Mollie hurls herself at each of them in turn, hugging their legs and then spinning on the spot to show off her shimmery unicorn onesie complete with rainbow mane and silver holographic horn on the hood. Alice follows behind her, in a sundress, rain-damp slouchy cardigan and stompy yellow Docs, hair in a messy bun that's haloed with frizz, carting a thick black canvas tote bag emblazoned with a cartoon Maya Angelou and swirling text saying AND STILL I RISE.

'I brought supplies,' she announces, and unpacks a make-shift picnic: crisps, dips, biscuits; baklava for Levon; pistachios for AJ; vegan flapjacks for Jessie; 95 per cent dark chocolate, her own ultimate indulgence. Paper plates, juice boxes and cartons of cold brew coffee.

AJ whistles through his teeth. 'Wow,' he tells her. 'You're not messing around.'

'No one ever told me how being a parent takes your snack skills next level.'

'Think my mum missed that lesson,' Jessie mutters, tearing open a flapjack wrapper with her teeth and devouring half of it in one bite.

'Good job you've got us then, eh?' Alice says, in an undertone, and at first Jessie only snorts a laugh through

139

her mouthful of flapjack, but then gives Alice a shy smile as she chews. Jessie still isn't sure about Alice, but up close her warmth and no-bullshit attitude are doing it for Jessie much more than the middle-class yummy-mummy impression she had of her at a distance.

'Cool ink,' she tells Alice, observing the tiger tattoo on Alice's shoulder becoming visible as Alice shucks off her cardi.

Alice gives Jessie a sly grin of her own, remembering being not much older than Jessie, near-crushing the bones in her best mate's hand as the tattoo artist moved the needle. 'Thanks.'

AJ is too distracted by the food to notice this exchange. 'None of us are gonna go hungry tonight with all this and the banquet that Levon's laid on.'

'Well, not quite,' he says, as he appears with a tinfoil-covered plate and a box of chocolates under his arm. 'But I made nougat,' he adds, removing the tinfoil to reveal pale sugar-dusted chunks with a sweet saffron scent. 'And the group that just left very kindly bought me some chocolates as a thank you for finding them time in the room hire schedule.' He deposits the ribbon-wrapped box of truffles on the table. 'I'm happy to contribute those to such a worthy cause.'

'Mollie is going to be bouncing off the walls with all this sugar,' Alice says, taking in their spread with a dawning look of horror. She glances over to the kids' corner, where the toddler is curled up in a beanbag, engrossed in a book and not paying any attention to the grown-ups.

'But while she's not bothered,' Alice continues. 'Any ideas on where we should start?'

AJ scrunches his face in thought. 'Divide and conquer?'

'The snacks or the archives?'

'Both?'

'Good call.'

They fix themselves a plate each, Levon giving them a gentle warning to keep all food and drinks away from the books. The archive is at one end of the library's main room – tall metal shelving units that reach from the faded grey carpet almost to the fluorescent tube lights overhead. The shelves are much more tightly packed here than in the other bookcases. There are back issues of newspapers, in piles and bound in bulging navy-blue folders, along with all sorts of other papers – maps and letters and photos collected by the local community, Levon explains. An ongoing, evolving record of the area. Incomplete but important nonetheless. Alice sucks a square of chocolate and wanders up and down the aisles, eyeballing how much information is collected on those shelves. *Don't get overwhelmed*, she orders herself. *Just start somewhere. Anywhere.*

'What do you need me to do?' Jessie asks, hanging back to watch as AJ and Alice pick a pile at random and get settled at the table.

'Come with me,' Levon says, and motions for her to follow.

'Cool. We going to see the ghost?'

'Pardon?'

'Nothing,' Jessie sing-songs, exchanging a grin with AJ as she lets Levon lead her to the other side of the room.

'Your mission,' he tells her, when they're out of earshot of the others, 'is to leave us to it and get your coursework finished.'

'No offence, Lev, but that's not happening.'

'I thought you said it was due in soon.'

Jessie makes an exasperated growling noise. 'It is,' she admits, not meeting his gaze. 'On Monday.'

'So you can't afford to get sidetracked by this. You've got more than enough to be focusing on.'

'But we're all in it together, aren't we? I want to help.'

'I know you do, Jessie. But that can't be at the expense of your education.'

'And you don't think it'll impact my education if I get made homeless next week?'

'If that happens, your teachers will understand. But you need to do your part in that. Didn't you tell me you were on your final warning with your history tutor?'

'Eurgh. I thought I'd won her over getting such a good grade on that last essay, but she said she's got to take track record into account. She's threatening to not submit my work to the exam board if I don't get this one in on time. Which means I might not even get a grade. After everything. All the work I've put in. How can that be fair?'

Levon stares her down, soft and sympathetic. Knowing he doesn't need to tell her how much about their situation isn't fair.

'Whatever,' Jessie replies to his silence. 'If she wants to punish me, she can. I'm sick of it. I'll never pass anyway, and definitely not if I have to move out next week. So it's pointless, isn't it?'

'I don't know about that. The college will have some process, I'm sure. Extenuating circumstances. And if it comes to it, I'll help you with that. But you know your history is against you here.'

Jessie narrows her eyes. 'That better not have been a pun.'

Levon holds up his hands. 'Coincidence, promise. But you need to get this thing done. Especially if it's due so soon. So why don't you stay here and keep us company, but work on your project for college? You'll be here, being part of things, but it won't take you away from what you need to do.'

'It's all bollocks, though. I'm wasting my time.'

'That's not true, Jessie. You've got so much to be proud of with how you've been turning things around.'

'Yuck. Gross. No.' Jessie pushes the heels of her hands against her eyes, twin blots of eyeliner imprinting on her skin when she drops her arms and finally meets Levon's eyes. She's been thinking about what he said about his time at school. About how she needs to see past this moment and focus on the future.

'You helped,' she says, in a begrudging tone. 'A lot.'

'So now help yourself,' he tells her. 'You've got the talent, and the skills.'

'Mate, you'd better not be about to tell me that all I need to do is believe.'

'Am I that predictable?'

Jessie widens her eyes and mimes zipping her mouth.

'What if I told you it's a cliché because it's true?'

'I'd say you were off your head. I'm a fuck-up, everyone knows it. And I've already missed the UCAS deadline, so even if I wanted to go to uni there'd be no chance for me now.'

'And is that what you want?' Levon's voice is low and gentle.

'I don't know.' Jessie's voice crackles with irritation and uncertainty. 'And it doesn't matter, does it? It's impossible. I've not got the grades, or the money, or anything. It's just a stupid fantasy.'

'If that's what you want, you'll find a way. You could go through clearing, or if this term's too soon you could defer.'

'And go next September?' She gives a sceptical scowl. 'That might as well be next century.'

'I'm just saying. If you want it, there are ways to make it happen.'

'Okay, mystical library genie.'

'I'm serious.'

'I don't even know if I want to go!' Jessie glances round, giving an exasperated arm wave that takes in the library, and the others, flipping through piles of documents in their respective corners, and Mollie snoozing on a beanbag with the *Funnybones* book open over her face. 'I don't want to have to move away and start all over again.'

And it's that, more than anything, that makes Levon's throat close. Because Jessie could be talking about going away to uni, and she could be talking about what might be on the cards for all of them next week. And even though it's hard to talk with the collapsing sensation in his chest, he forces a steadiness he doesn't feel into his voice.

'So stay in Leeds,' he tells her. 'And go to university here. Get your assignment done tonight, while we search for something that'll let us all stay on the street. And then whatever help you need when you start your course, I'll be there. We'll be there.'

Her voice cracks. 'But what if it doesn't work?'

Again, she could mean her studies and she could mean the demolition, but for the minute it doesn't matter. *She's just a kid. She needs reassuring.* So Levon squeezes Jessie's shoulder tight and says they'll cross that bridge when they need to. If they need to. Together.

Fine,' Jessie scowls. 'Whatever. I'll do my stupid coursework. But if I see you in need of my skills, I'm having a break so I can help.'

'As long as that applies the other way round as well.'

'Deal.'

They size each other up, postures mirrored in a serious stand-off, then Levon puts his hand out and they shake.

'Don't tell me you've been calling him a boomer too,' AJ pipes up, wandering over to look for Levon.

'AJ.' Jessie gives a theatrical, chest-clutching gasp. 'I would never disrespect my elders like that.'

'Also I'm incredibly young at heart and hip with the kids,' Levon announces.

'You saying I'm not?'

'I would never,' he reassures AJ, putting an arm around his shoulder and ushering him back towards the shelves. Jessie shakes her head and gives in, for now, booting up her laptop and crossing everything that the others find something in time.

Levon tries to be blasé about the exchange with Jessie, but he's distracted as he takes a seat at the table with the others and pulls a pile of papers towards him. Going to university was an important rite of passage for him; the first time he had access to other people like himself, people with mixed heritage and a ravenous appetite for learning, people trying to put all the disparate pieces of themselves together into one coherent identity. People who taught him about culture, music, protest, politics, lust, love. The list could go on for ever. He wants Jessie to have access to all that too, can see the potential for the person she could evolve into if she only had the chance. Wants it all for her: an education and a safe home. Knows all too well what having these things did for him, how they gave him the foundation he's leaned on ever since. Knows the thing Jessie needs most right now is the reminder to not give up.

Hours pass. Jessie moves between her laptop and the shelves, occasionally consulting with Levon to be directed to the research materials she needs for her essay. Outside, the snarling wind has whipped itself into a storm, the rain a drone on the library roof and the metal shutter over the front door rattling. It makes Alice appreciate the cosiness of it, being squirrelled away in secret with a good stash of snacks. *If this weren't so high stakes and stressful, it could be weirdly fun,* she thinks. Their common purpose is a thread that connects them even as they're each immersed in their own separate worlds, the sound of revellers leaving the pub after last orders at odds with their methodical page-turning, the muffled beat from Jessie's headphones and Mollie's pigletty snores.

But the pressure is mounting, and the smeary type of the old newspapers is making Alice's eyes blur. AJ's got his contacts out and glasses on, scrutinising a mammoth ledger of minutes from obscure, decades-ago council meetings, periodically swearing when he gets a papercut. 'Should've raided the hospital for some protective gloves.'

Levon's poring over old zines put out by a nearby housing co-op, diligently going back to the shelves to dig out even older documents when one of the zines mentions a 1930s rental strike by Leeds council tenants over poor conditions. He cracks his back and neck each time he gets up, but otherwise seems like he could keep going for ever. Alice isn't so sure.

*Just one more. One more year of back issues. One more month. One more week. One more day.* Alice keeps amending the bargain with herself, and it's made even more complicated by her sneaking suspicion that whatever they're searching for won't be front-page news. Council re-zoning or clues for legal loopholes aren't going to make headlines. So she's forcing herself to scan every single line of text, even the tiniest paragraphs, the one-sentence stories with only the scarcest details.

A few times, the words Leodis Street sparkle out of a page, snagging Alice's frazzled brain. Everything else has become a meaningless mush of words, but the name of their street still has enough power to make her freeze when she reads it. She's lost count now of the number of times it's happened, but each time it's been followed by a sick swoop of disappointment, reading announcements of births or deaths. Other times, it'd be another street name entirely that her exhausted wishful thinking had mangled and misread. She reads about a factory strike where workers – including several from the street – had campaigned for a pay rise. She reads about someone who lived on the street being Sun Goddess at the first ever Carnival. She reads about the opening of the nearby West Indian Centre in the early eighties, followed by sporadic reports of some of its most legendary raves. She scans headlines about the punk scene, Thatcher and the Yorkshire Ripper, national and local news all fusing together in Alice's head until she can't take any more.

'There's nothing here,' she growls, half to herself, lashing out at her current pile and sending papers skidding across the table. 'I'm done,' she adds, when the others look up. 'My brain is mashed. I need to get Mol to bed, and message Sam back, and I've had a ton of missed calls from Mum and Dad, and I just can't do it any more. I give up.' She swipes tears away from her eyes before they fall, a hot crawl of shame about her outburst giving way to a bruised slump of defeat.

'Alice,' AJ says. 'Chill. Take a breath.'

'You can go,' Levon adds. 'Get Mollie home. You must both be exhausted.'

From behind her laptop, Jessie sees the movement and pulls her headphones down from her ears.

'What's going on?'

Alice gives a sad shrug. 'Nothing. I'm being stupid. Didn't mean to disturb everyone with another existential crisis. Sorry.' She turns to Levon and AJ. Their kindness and the permission to go has re-energised her: just a scrap, but enough.

'Fuck it,' she says, pulling the pile of papers back towards her. 'Ignore me. If you're staying, I am too.'

Jessie slides her headphones back into place. She's used to her mum's tantrums, but she's begrudgingly impressed by how rapidly Alice shook hers off and got back down to business. *Stop stropping and find something useful.* Jessie beams the thought across the room to Alice, then realises she needs to do the same thing. She concentrates on her essay again: she's been beavering away on a section about the aftermath of the war, and she wants to include something about Leeds' history of protest and activism, but she can't quite find a way to tie it all together. She's been reading about the Yorkshire chapter of the CND and the Leeds Revolutionary Feminist Group, the ones who started the first Reclaim the Night march right here on their doorstep. But all the information Jessie's been devouring about both of those relates to events in the seventies. With everything she's read, Jessie reckons she could weave a narrative from the war right up to and through those surges of collective defiance and action, but she knows it's not what her teacher's looking for. So she bookmarks the websites for later and goes back to her Word document, rereading her last paragraph about the changes in the city in that first decade of peace after VE day. Decidedly not looking at AJ, Alice and Levon, Jessie slinks over to the shelves Lev showed her. Stretching on tiptoes, she peers at the top row – a neat series of navy binders, sticky labels on their spines revealing they contain special editions of the local paper from the 1950s. *Alriiiight. Mother lode. There's got to be something in here I can use.* Wobbling under the weight as she eases a folder off the high shelf, Jessie plops herself down on the carpet right there in the stacks and creaks the brittle cover open.

The first few pages are supplements from the *Yorkshire Evening Post*: headlines about a June 1953 heatwave followed by torrential downpours and storms. Jessie peers at a murky black-and-white photo of bedraggled circus tents on a flash-flooded Hyde Park, recollecting a rain-soaked sugar-crazed rampage around Woodhouse Moor funfair with her mum for her thirteenth birthday. She snorts at the memory, then turns the page. Bumper Queen's coronation issue, boasts the cover. Ten-page special edition pull-out inside. *The Royals never had to put up with this shit. Writing essays and being made homeless all at the same time.* She flicks past pages detailing the ceremony, wondering why it even got the coverage in a local paper like this, then realises the rest is pictures from the parties held all over Leeds.

*What am I even looking through this for?* She leans back against the wall, stretching her legs out and rubbing her eyes. But she keeps flicking through the pages. There's something nostalgic about seeing photographs of Leeds from so many decades ago; a familiarity to some of the architecture, the shape of the buildings in the background of the celebrations in Victoria Square. She can see the bones of the city's evolution, and wonders how many of the people in these photographs are still alive, if they even recognise it now. There's one with a more recognisable background in Roundhay Park: children clutching flags and mugging for the camera. Jessie's far too punk to be a royalist, but the kids' mile-wide grins and retro outfits are cute. Then she turns the next page, and time stops.

It's the street, *their* street: strings of bunting zigzagging from one lamp post to another, a mishmash of tables dragged into the middle of the road, laden with food and surrounded by families. She can tell from the angle that the photographer must have stood near what's now Levon's house. She kneels up and over the paper, bending her head to examine it more closely, looking for her own front door. There are puddles on the pavement, but the sun is blazing down onto what are now Bill's and Alice's gardens. *Families on Leodis Street celebrate*, the caption reads. Inset to that is another photo, three boys sat on a wall, the smallest one in the middle holding a slice of cake, his face smeared with what looks like jam, and the older two with their arms round his shoulders. They're wearing shorts and smart shirts, collars open and sleeves rolled up. One has a chipped tooth, the one in the middle has a plaster on his knee, but they're all wearing matching badges for the coronation. Though the littlest one has blonder hair than the others, their identical dark eyes and mischievous dimpled grins make it obvious they're brothers.

She imagines the boys ruling the street with the other kids that must've lived there, recollects her own upbringing before her and Donna's last few house moves: terrorising the local lads with her best mate Lianne who lived six doors down, necking blue WKDs outside the off-licence and never having to walk home alone. Realising she's disappeared inside her own head, Jessie forces herself to fight through her fatigue and concentrate. That's when she sees the caption below the photo of the three brothers on the wall. Pins and needles glitter up and down her arms.

'Levon?' He answers with a questioning glance and a tired half-smile. 'Do you know what Bill's last name is?'

He closes his eyes, clearly scanning his memory. 'Hang on, it'll come to me. Starts with a C.'

'Coates?'

'Yes! What made you ask?'

Jessie holds up the page she's been staring at, rereading the caption again.

> Let them eat cake: Edward, William and Alfred Coates
> (10, 8 and 12) enjoying Victoria sponge made by their
> mother at the Leodis Street coronation party.

'I think I've just found Bill.'

# CHAPTER SIXTEEN

Standing in his lounge on Monday morning, Levon listens to the repeating ring of the phone. His bare toes curl into the thick pile of the rug, and he glances around at his beloved bookshelves, the record player with the neat stack of LPs beside it, the glass amulet hung in the window, the turquoise eye casting its protective gaze across the room's rich terracotta walls. He listens to the ring echo for so long that it takes him by surprise when a voice comes on; a sore-throat smoker's rasp saying, 'Sabina Hanson speaking,' in a lilting Irish accent.

'Sabina, hello. This is Levon Amiri. You probably won't remember me, but we spoke last week. I live on Leodis Street, in Chapel Allerton, and—'

'The one they're trying to knock down?'

He gives a dark laugh. 'So you do remember.'

'Yeah, my auntie lives not far from there. She's pissed off about it as well. Someone at the local library told her about it and now she's convinced that if it goes ahead, her street's going to be next. Keeps sending me links to the petition.'

*That was probably me*, Levon thinks, casting his mind back

over the people he's spoken to over the past few days. He decides not to sidetrack the conversation by revealing this detail, but he does make a mental note to tell Jessie that whatever she did to make the petition more shareable seems to have done the trick.

'Well,' Levon continues, 'last time we spoke, you said you needed more of an angle. That it wasn't news on its own, but—'

The reporter sighs. 'Look, I'm sorry if that came off harsh. I know it must be a nightmare for you, but without more of a hook it's just not something I can cover.'

'That's just it. We think we might have something: we've just learnt that one of the street's residents has been here over seventy years. It's been his family home for at least three generations, maybe more. The only home he's ever known, and it's going to be taken from him this time next week.'

For a moment there's silence. 'This is one of your neighbours?'

'We found a photograph of him as a child, in an old newspaper about the Queen's coronation. That's seventy years ago. Almost to the day. Surely that's something you could work with?'

Levon recalls Jessie at the library the other night, gushing about the topic for her history coursework as she cued up the email to her tutor with her completed assignment. *Significance is personal as well as global. The personal is political.* Levon knows there must be a way to get Sabina on board, that this story could tap into some personal significance for her, if only he can find the right words to connect it. Elder care. Vulnerable people. Insecure housing. He doesn't want to treat the terms like cheap buzz words. Not when there are so many real people behind the news headlines, the numbers shared by politicians, the campaign slogans that make so many promises but never seem to lead to change.

Sabina asks whether Bill's got any family left.

'Not that we know about, no.'

'So he's on his own,' she says, tone thoughtful. 'That could play. People don't want to think of themselves being made homeless when they're old and vulnerable. And there's definitely an angle about the changing demographics of the city.' Sabina pauses.

'Anything you can do would be wonderful,' Levon tells her. 'We've got less than a week, and it's not looking good, for him or any of us.'

'So what are we talking in the way of footage? Can I come and interview him?'

Levon considers this. An invisible draught from the disintegrating wooden window frame sets the eye amulet slowly spinning, sending a blue lighthouse beam revolving round the room.

'Ah,' he says, not wanting to discourage Sabina or commit Bill to something without his consent. 'I'd have to ask him about that. He's not much of a talker.'

'I'll need him on camera.' Levon can hear her wanting him not to get overexcited, but it doesn't stop hope surging through him.

'I'll help however I can,' he promises her. 'Whatever you need.'

'How long have we got?'

'We're supposed to be out next Monday. That's when they're sending in the demolition team.'

'Shit. Okay. You said you've got photographs?'

'From the newspaper, that's right.'

'Leave it with me and I'll let you know. But listen, we'll

need him on camera. The way you've told it, he's the story. So talk to him and make sure he's up for it, yeah?'

'I will. I'm sure he will be,' Levon tells her, putting all the certainty and confidence he can into his voice. *I hope.* They say their goodbyes and hang up. *Well,* he thinks. *This is it, Bill. You're the story. Now how are we going to convince you to share it with the world?*

That night, they're at Alice's. Jessie sits on the floor with Mollie, who's ransacked Jessie's pencil case and found a stash of neon markers she's now using to draw on Jessie's skin. Jessie lets her do it, holding her arms out to be decorated with wobbly spots and spirals while listening to the others talk. AJ, Levon and Alice hunch forward, cups on their knees.

'You really think he'll listen to us?' AJ asks.

'Only one way to find out,' Levon says.

'Come on,' Alice says, smacking her knees and standing up. 'Let's go.'

'Now?' AJ stares up at her. 'Don't we need more of a plan?'

'Haven't got one,' Alice admits. 'But we need him on side. So let's go and talk to him. That's all we can do.'

'Got it,' AJ says. 'I'm right behind you.'

The three of them troop towards the door. 'You cool to stay here with Mol, Jessie?' Alice asks.

'So I'm getting left out again? Nice one.' Jessie's voice is joke-moody, but her tone is enough to make Alice turn back.

'What's up? You want to come with us? You know what Bill's like, he's not going to be a happy bunny if all of us including a feral toddler show up demanding a favour.'

Jessie crosses her neon-swirled arms over her chest. 'I'm just saying. We wouldn't even have that photo if it wasn't for

155

me. Might be cool if you treated me as one of the team and not just a babysitter.'

Alice summons all her TA-trained patience to stop herself from lashing back. *That was you, ten years ago. A kid pretending to be an adult.* Alice remembers being eighteen: playing bass guitar in her best friend's band, saving up her bar job wages for a Glasto ticket, blitzing through her French, English and History A Levels, the summer between college and uni a glorious no-responsibilities whirlwind of adventures and music and teenaged romance. Not like Jessie, who's had to grow up long before her time, who's been working hard to build a tentative future all by herself and who next week might see it demolished into rubble along with all their homes.

'I'm sorry, Jessie. I'm out of order just storming off and not even talking about who'd stay here. You're just so good with Mol, and I honestly don't know if Bill's even going to open the door to any of us, let alone everyone.'

'Just go.' Jessie flaps a long, rainbow-spotted arm, all the fight draining away now she's at least been acknowledged. 'I'd rather chill with Mollie anyway. You lot go and work your magic. Just do whatever it takes, okay?'

AJ and Levon wait at the end of the path, Levon giving Alice's shoulder a wordless pat when she joins them.

'We can do this, right?' AJ asks. 'Or do you really think he might not even answer?

'I don't know,' Alice says, steeling herself. 'But I'll knock all night if that's what it takes.'

They assemble on Bill's doorstep. The clunk of the door knocker echoes back from the bricks on both sides of the street. A cluster of pigeons squabble in the gutter. There's the distant thud and yells of a football match on the park. The downpour from the day before has evaporated; the night is

156

sticky with warmth and humidity. For a moment, Alice wishes she'd prepared more: washed her face, tied her hair up. *You did all that with the lawyer and look how that went.* Besides, it's only Bill. And it's too late to turn back now, anyway. Levon and AJ stand just behind her, shoulder to shoulder, and all three of them can hear the slow shuffle from inside, coming closer to the door.

There's a metallic scrabble of locks and chains before the door eases open a crack.

Bill's eyes narrow when he sees the three of them; the creases in his face furrowing further as he scowls.

'Can't get a minute of bloody peace,' he grumbles, leaning against the door frame like he expects an explanation.

'Hello, Bill,' Levon says, in his unflappable voice. 'We'd love to talk to you for a minute if you have time.'

'It's important,' Alice adds. 'Do you think we could come in?'

*No.* It's obvious that's what Bill wants to say. His knotty knuckles grip the door hard. He sighs, one that comes from deep down and deflates him even more. He tilts his head, sizing them up for a long moment that none of them breaks, then finally gives another huff, his face softening as he pushes the door further open with his walking stick. He's got Sal's voice in his head, saying *never turn neighbours away*, and although he's uncertain about inviting them in, he knows it's what she would've done.

'If you must,' he mutters, then turns away and starts making his way down the hall, leaving the others to follow. 'Not that I like it, mind,' he adds to himself, under his breath, as he leads them into the living room, but Alice is close enough behind him that she hears.

'I know you don't,' she tells him in a low tone, with a soft grateful touch to his back. The gentleness of it gives Bill that flash again, of how much Alice reminds him of Sally. *Must be going soft in my old age*, he thinks. He waits for the others to follow them into the room, then gestures with his stick towards the settee.

'Go on, then,' he says. 'Have a seat. Suppose I should offer you something, shouldn't I? Tea?'

He stomps back out before any of them can reply, leaving AJ, Alice and Levon to stare after him and around the room before they take a seat.

The room is cosier than Alice expected. She doesn't know what she'd pictured, really, but it was sadder and lonelier than this. Seeing Bill looking so old the other day had rattled her, and it'd been just one of the threads of worry keeping her awake at night, the idea of him being alone and elderly and vulnerable, not able to cope with the house he's in and definitely not with moving. Her mental picture of his house transforming over time, becoming bleaker and bleaker, colder and more shadowy, with cobwebbed corners and cracked plaster and an empty, mould-freckled fridge. But she sees now how wrong she's been. Bill's is a home that signposts loud and proud that it's been a container for care and love. There are photos and artwork everywhere, a mishmash of frames of all different shapes and sizes, none of them crooked, cracked or furred with dust. She doesn't want Bill to think she's nosing when he comes back, but Alice is fascinated. On the sofa, AJ and Levon are conferring in quiet whispers, and from the kitchen there's the clatter of cups and soon the shrieking whistle of an old-fashioned tea kettle. But Alice isn't paying attention. She's distracted by the bookshelves with their well-thumbed paperbacks, the photo of Bill and his bride on their wedding day, the other grinning faces in the other photographs. By what must be

158

Bill's armchair there's a circular side table; a battered paper-back book with a shadowy cover, a newspaper, a week's worth of tablets in a day-by-day dispenser, a bag of toffees, a metallic rainbow of wrinkled wrappers, the TV remote. A pair of wire-rimmed bifocals with a smudged fingerprint over one lens. The intimacy and anonymity of it makes her want to cry. She perches on the edge of the settee in the space Levon and AJ have left for her.

Bill comes creaking back into the room with a tea tray, stick wedged under his arm. The cups give a chattery-teeth rattle, and AJ jumps up to grab the tray from Bill's wobbly grip, setting it down on a patchwork-upholstered footstool and dishing out the drinks. There's an open packet of shortbread on the tray too, and they pass it round the room, each taking a biscuit while Bill gets settled.

'This best be important,' Bill grumbles, once he's in his armchair, mug cupped between his hands. 'Didn't even have my teeth in when you knocked.' In a move that makes Alice want to crack up laughing, he gives a comically huge cartoon-ish leer, flashing his teeth as if to tell them they're honoured he's gone to this much effort on his behalf.

'It is important,' she says, putting her tea down carefully and leaning forward, elbows on her knees. 'Bill, we've come to ask you something. How long have you lived here?'

'This again?' He scowls with suspicion. 'Weren't you asking me about this the other day?' He knows he didn't imagine that conversation. In the street, at the end of the path. The day before the bins. Which would've made it last Tuesday. He may get things mixed up sometimes, but he's not going bloody senile yet.

'I did ask you that,' Alice reassures him. 'But you know, Bill, you never really gave me an answer.'

'I think I did. Not a secret, is it? I may as well be part of the bloody furniture, I've been here that long.'

'The thing is,' Levon puts in. 'You've been here longer than any of us.' Bill grunts as if to question why he's stating the obvious. 'Which means none of us really knows how long you've been here.'

'Right,' Alice tells him, pulling out the folded copy of the newspaper cutting from the library. 'And then we found this.'

She crosses the room to show him, standing by his armchair as he holds out a hand for the paper.

'What is this? I already put my teeth in, don't tell me I need my specs too.'

He reaches up and angles the nearby lamp to give him more light, holding the paper near to his nose and peering at it intensely. Outside, dusk is just falling, bringing a soft gloom to the room. Alice wonders for a moment whether Bill's trying to save on his electricity by using the lamp rather than the overhead.

'Kids,' he says, with a dismissive grunt, looking up from the paper. 'Messy buggers 'n' all from the look of this one in the middle. What's that got to do with me?'

Alice retrieves his glasses from the detritus on the table. 'Put these on and have another look.'

'You're just like my Sal, you know.' Bill glances up at her, half-amused and half-irritated. 'Always bossing me about. Don't remember marrying *you*, though.'

'Just humour me,' she tells him, and passes them over. 'Please?'

'Fine, if it'll make you gi' over. Give them here.'

He lays the sheet of paper in his lap and puts the glasses on, tutting at the tremor in his hands.

They all watch as he bends to re-examine the newspaper

page. And slowly, so slowly that Alice can't tell to start with whether she's imagining it, one corner of Bill's mouth starts to curl. He keeps looking at the page, and his smile widens, his eyes crinkling at the corners.

'Me,' he says, voice papery with disbelief. 'Me and Alfie and Eddie. Where did you even get this?'

'We found it in the archives, at the library.'

'Me mam had a copy, when it came out. It's probably still around here somewhere. Threatened to give me a right good hiding, she did, for looking such a state when I was having me picture taken, but me dad said it was the best thing in the entire paper.' Bill finds a hanky down the side of his chair cushion and mops his leaking eyes. 'Aye, that's where it went, I remember it now. He pasted it into the lid of his work toolbox. That way he could see us with our cake while he had his butties each day. Tickled him pink, it did, that he'd come up with a way for us to all have our dinner together.'

'This was taken in 1953. Do you remember that?'

'Course I do, I'm not daft. Brilliant, it was. As many different types of cakes as houses on the street. And loads of it, as well. We were eating it for weeks.'

'The newspaper said you were eight years old when this picture was taken,' Alice says, retaking her place beside the others. 'So you must have been little when you moved here.'

'Moved here? What are you talking about, woman? I never moved here.'

'Bill,' Levon puts in. 'Are you saying this is the only place you've ever lived?'

'Course I am,' he tells them, as though it's obvious. 'Born upstairs, wasn't I? All of us were.' He gestures to the brothers in the newspaper. 'Alfie took for ever to come, all the other mams on the street wanted her to go to hospital, but she weren't having none of it. And he was fine, in the end, so she was even more stubborn when it came to me and Eddie. Determined to have us here, she was. Mind you, I was late, but then I didn't hang about. She was always laughing on my birthdays about how she nearly had me in the garden, and how no one on the street would have ever let her forget it if Dad hadn't got her up the stairs in time.'

He looks at Alice, Levon and AJ sitting side by side on the settee. His wheezy laugh rocks round the room, his careworn face transformed and crackling with character.

'You look like you were a right cheeky kid,' Alice chances, and Bill nods with a snort.

'Ah, you know what they say, though, don't you, lass?'

'What's that?'

'It takes one to know one.'

'Cheeky as a grown-up, too,' Alice deadpans, and AJ and Levon both chance sniggers at that, too.

'So, Bill,' Levon says. 'If your parents lived here since before you were born, do you know when they would have moved?'

'Ah, you're testing me now. We've always been Yorkshire, but Dad's family were from somewhere near Sheffield.' AJ makes a soft little hum at hearing this connection to his home town, but Bill continues like he hasn't heard. 'Mam moved in with them when they first got wed, but they were worried, you see, about the bombings. Back in the war, this was. Where they lived weren't far from a factory. Most of the locals worked there, and it made some machinery, I can't remember what it was, but it were summat needed for the war effort. Tank parts, summat like that. So it were obvious that sooner or later it was going to be a target, in the Blitz. My mam and dad weren't having that. Nowhere were safe, of course, look what happened here. But they wanted to be away from there.

162

They got the entire family to move, just before Alfie came along. Got me Nan and Grandad into a house in Meanwood, and Mam and Dad camped out in the living room there until they started renting here.'

'So sometime during the war,' Levon recaps. 'Bill, that's incredible. To think your family's been here at least eighty years.'

'Aye, suppose so. End-of-war baby, I was. There were a lot of us, you know. Everyone celebrating and feeling hopeful about the future. Lots of weddings. Lots of babies. Makes sense, doesn't it? After all that loss.'

'Do you still have any of the paperwork from when your folks moved in?' AJ asks. He's been making notes on his phone as Bill's been talking, but now he scooches forward to the edge of his seat. 'Anything that might have the dates on?'

'You having me on, lad? I don't even know where my specs are half the time, and I'm usually wearing them when that happens. There'll be summat somewhere, I can tell you that much. But I couldn't tell you where.'

'What about photographs? Anything that'd show how long they were here?'

'There's a picture of them up in the hallway. That were taken the day they moved in. Mam and Dad had been married a while by then, but renting this place was a proper milestone for them because it were just theirs. Proud as anything, they look. Suppose they'd been waiting a while, saving up for all the bits and bobs they needed to set up home together. All the uncertainty of the war didn't help that, I'm sure.'

'Can I go and have a look?' He gives Alice a nod and she slips out of the room, returning with the framed photo of the young couple on the doorstep. Even in black and white, their excitement shows: the man dapper and tall in shirtsleeves and waistcoat, the woman with shiny bobbed hair and a polka-dot tea dress. The man jangles a bunch of keys at the camera and the woman watches him, starry-eyed and laughing, one hand on the soft curve of her stomach.

'So what's all this in aid of, then?' Bill demands, as Alice shows Levon and AJ the picture. 'I know you didn't have me putting me teeth in at this time of night just for a trip down memory lane.'

Until this point, no one has mentioned the upcoming demolition. It's been a dark cloud hanging over the street for weeks and its shadowy return after the nostalgic sunshine of Bill's reflection seems to make the room smaller, almost claustrophobic. Like when the pressure of a nearing thunderstorm makes the sky feel too close to properly breathe.

'The thing is, Bill,' AJ says, 'we think you might be able to help us. All of us. With what's happening.'

'Eh?'

'There's a journalist we've been chatting to. Says she might do a story, about the street. Only she wants to talk about you, and how long you and your family have been here.'

'Don't be soft,' he scoffs. 'What does she want to do that for?'

'She reckons that there would be more impact to a story about them planning to demolish our houses if she can show what it means for the people involved. And who better to talk about that than you?'

'None of us want to leave the street,' Levon tells him. 'But you've been here your entire life. That's more compelling than anything any of us could say.'

'So I make a fool of meself on telly, and for what? What does that accomplish?'

'Maybe nothing,' Alice concedes. 'But we won't know until

164

we try. But we think there's a chance it could help. Maybe get more people on our side. Get them to complain to the council, or write to their MPs, or something. We don't know. But the clock's ticking, isn't it? We're almost out of options.' She meets Bill's grouchy gaze, willing him to soften. 'We want to take any chance we've got to stop it, no matter how long the odds.'

'I don't want some strange woman mithering me. I'm not used to talking to people. I'll say the wrong thing and sound stupid. Then I'll have done more harm than good.'

'She's not some strange woman,' AJ puts in. 'You'll have seen her on the news. Sabina Hanson, her name is. She's good, she's not going to be trying to trip you up. She won an award last year.'

'And we'll be right there with you,' Alice tells him.

'Give over,' Bill scolds her. 'No. Get yourselves another actor.'

'Bill, please. We need you. We can't take this shot without you.'

'I'm not letting strangers traipse through me house,' he insists, sounding aggravated. 'And I'm not showing meself up on telly.'

'Please just say you'll think about it,' Alice pleads. 'Whatever you decide, we'll respect your decision, but please don't say no just yet.'

'Do you know you're near enough the first people I've let in this house since my Sal passed?' Bill removes his glasses and scrubs his hands over his face before glaring at them. 'I'll not make that mistake twice.'

'We'll go,' Levon soothes, standing up. 'We didn't mean to upset you.'

'I'm not upset,' and even Bill doesn't look like he believes it. 'I just think you've got some bloody nerve, supping my brews and eating my biscuits and dredging up ancient history, and for what? To expect me to let the entire world in, nitpicking all my memories into nothing? You're daft.'

'I'm scared as well,' Alice tells Bill as he stumps with his stick into the hall, ready to show them out. 'All of us are.'

'Thank you for the tea, and the biscuits,' Levon says, taking Bill's cue and leading the others back through the front door. 'And for telling us about your family. Whatever happens, it's a privilege to learn more about the street's history.'

'And if you decide you're up for sharing it with the journalist, all you have to do is say the word,' AJ puts in. 'Just say the word, and we'll set it up.'

'I've said me piece,' Bill huffs, leaning heavily on the door frame. 'Now do as I ask and leave me alone.'

They traipse down Bill's path and back towards Alice's. Halfway to her own front door, Alice thinks she sees the curtains in the next door window move. Either she's imagining the shadow shifting behind them, or Bill's stood watching them go.

# CHAPTER SEVENTEEN

B ill lets the curtains fall back into place. Everything aches, but he doesn't want to sit back down, not with everything so stirred up in his head. He returns the tea things to the kitchen, realising how low he's running on food when he returns the last few pieces of shortbread to the tin. He's not bothered with shopping recently. He thought it'd make sense to use up what was left. Less to pack up or end up wasted when he has to move. The time's slipped by too fast. *That lad said there's only days left, didn't he? How can I have left it so long? Stupid of me, burying my head in the sand. Only got myself to blame, and who knows where I'm going to end up now?*

*Sod it*, he thinks, and changes his mind, retrieving the remaining biscuits from the packet and making another cup of tea to dunk them in. *No point saving them if I'm going to be out on my ear in a few days.* He adds a slug of whisky to the mug and returns to his armchair, thinking hard.

*What a mess, eh, duck?* he says to the photo of Sally. *Right enough, you'd have had words to say about me letting things get into this sorry state. And none of 'em good words, either. You'd have given me a right earful, and I'd have deserved it 'n' all.*

He glances down at the clipping of him and his brothers, where it's been left on the arm of the chair. They'd teased him something rotten when that picture came out, he remembers it now, but all of them had been so excited to see their picture in the paper, crowing to the other kids on the street on the walk to school about their claim to fame. And when Bill looks at the photo it's like he can feel their arms round his shoulders again, that weight and warmth and protectiveness that came from Alfie and Eddie always having his back. He never had a new pair of trousers or a second helping of pudding, not with those two around, but he never went short of unsolicited advice or sneaked sips of beer or unexpected interventions in the few scuffles he found himself in. Eddie driving their mam mad with his quiffed hair and Byron quotes, wooing all the girls on the estate with his poetry, and Alfie always brawling, a perpetually broken nose or black eye, but always looking out for Bill, ready to batter anyone if they looked the wrong way at his kid brother.

He'd not have been the same after losing them if it hadn't been for Sally. But then when it became clear he was going to lose her too, that's when things started slipping. It came on fast, her cancer. Bill had always told himself that was for the best, that she didn't have to live too long with the poison doom and terror of it. But sometimes he wondered if there had been anything either of them could have done differently. Whether it could've been identified earlier, whether there was a way to stop its relentless cruel advance. If he should have insisted on the doctors doing more tests, back when the two of them were first talking about babies. *That couldn't have been anything to do with it, could it?* Even now he doesn't really

168

understand how it happened, where it started, how it spread. Only that Sally had been fighting what seemed like a bug for near enough a month. Bill had been fussing her through it as best he could, taking her tea and toast in bed each morning, griping at her to do as she was bloody told and rest. But she'd just pull the blankets back and insist on him getting back in bed beside her to share the breakfast he'd made, then get on with things like nothing was wrong.

Then there was that day that she fainted: just for a second, but it was enough for her to stumble and fall. They were at their cafe just off the Headrow for their weekly treat of scones with cream and jam. Bill came back from the bathroom to find Sally on the floor in a mess of crumbs and cream blobs, the teapot in wet pieces beside her and the cafe owner, a sweet hairy wolf of a man, bending over Sally and asking if she was okay.

'Love? What happened?'

'Nothing, nothing.' She tried to wave away his concern. 'My pride's bruised but nowt else is.' She turned to the cafe owner then. 'I'm so sorry, Matty, I'll pay for the breakages. I don't know what happened. I tried to stand up and just went dizzy. Then here I am, feeling silly for making such a fuss.'

'You're fine, doll, don't worry,' he told her. 'Just stay there a minute, catch your breath. I'll get these bits out your way. Don't want you cutting yourself on top of that bruised pride, do we?'

Matty bustled round her, clearing the broken crockery and mopping up the spilt tea with kind efficiency while Bill crouched by Sally's side, reassuring her it was probably low blood pressure, low blood sugar or something equally innocent, claiming they'd just have to eat more cakes if she was so starved she was going to start fainting on him. But he'd been upset, he remembers that, to see Sally injured and disorientated, though he did his best to keep it hidden.

When Sally's cheeks had turned from ghost-pale back to their usual pink, he and Matty hooked her under the elbows and helped move her from the floor into a seat.

'I've called an ambulance,' the cafe owner told Bill in a near-apologetic tone, once Sally was settled. 'I don't think she hit her head, but concussion's not anything to mess about with. Best to get checked over, I reckon. Just in case.'

The hospital was a blur of tests, but Bill remembers waiting in the curtained cubicle, a slightly out-of-tune radio somewhere nearby playing a static-fuzzed schmaltzy ballad, his too-tight socks cutting into his ankles, the oversize poster with a photo of a serious doctor in white coat and stethoscope with the slogan, YOUR HEALTH IS IMPORTANT TO US.

'Not long now, love,' he told Sally, attempting to convince himself as much as her. The doctor arrived not long after, hair knotted up in a crown of elaborate braids and her eyes the colour of black coffee. He only remembers some of that conversation. Words like ovarian, and cervical. All the hidden, invisible places inside Sally's body where cells had been secretly, undetectably multiplying.

'Let's not get ahead of ourselves,' the doctor said. 'We need more tests first, then we can give you a full diagnosis. Once we've got that we can come up with a treatment or management plan.

'Treatment,' Bill had echoed. 'Or management?' And the world had fallen away from underneath him as he put together what the doctor meant.

Somehow, they made it through the tests and to the next appointment.

'Come on,' Sally had said, when the time came to leave

for the hospital. 'Let's get this show on the road. No point worrying until we know more, is there?'

He looked at her brave face and wanted to bawl. 'You know you don't have to pretend with me, don't you? You're allowed to be scared.'

Sally was having none of it. 'I'm scared of what you'll do without me,' she said.

'So am I,' he told her. 'Bloody terrified.'

'So let's cross that bridge when we come to it, eh?'

But as Sally put on her scarf to leave the house, he noticed the silver glint of the chain around her neck – a necklace he'd bought her years ago, a silly souvenir from a weekend away in Ireland with its shamrock charm. Sally was superstitious about it, said it always gave her luck, and was only to be worn on special occasions when she really needed its magic powers. She was calm, on the outside, but she kept a tight grip of his hand in the waiting room, only letting go when the nurse called her name.

Afterwards, they went to the pub, sat shell-shocked in a corner, surrounded by dark wood and glinting brass plates. It was a weekday afternoon, the bar only just opened, only them and a couple of students playing a hangover-slow game of pool, balls thudding on felt and the occasional zing of sound effects from the waiting fruit machine.

In their usual booth in the far corner, Sally unwound her scarf, a loose thread snagging on the necklace until she pulled it loose.

Bill waited, still in his coat. 'Right then, love,' he heard himself ask. 'What'll it be?'

'Gin and tonic,' she answered. 'Double.'

She glanced at Bill, then gave the saddest, darkest half-smirk twist of her lips. 'No point holding back now, is there?'

He brought over the drinks and they sat in near-silence for a while. When his pint was just froth webbing the sides of the glass, he put his arm around her and pulled her into his chest, hiding his face in her hair so no one in the pub would see his shaking sobs.

After that, things happened in a too-fast blur that was also torturously slow. He'd done everything he could – cleaned, cooked, collected the prescriptions of painkillers and nausea medication, tried to make her comfortable. There were a few more months where Sally was almost herself, just weaker and more tired than before. Then it devolved. She was sick every time she ate. She lost so much weight that her bones showed through and ached no matter what configuration he put the cushions in.

'You can't leave me,' he told her, one night. By then the nurses were doing daily visits, and although Bill was thankful for the things they could do that he couldn't, like administering morphine and somehow managing to get the sheets changed without disturbing Sally too much, having them in the house still put him on edge. Their kind and capable matter-of-factness seemed completely irreconcilable with how fast his entire world was rocketing towards oblivion. It always gave him a shameful tug of relief when the door closed behind them and it was just him and Sally again. He pulled the armchair closer to the bed.

'I know,' she told him, her dark eyes still shrewd and beautiful. 'But I'm going to. Can't keep dancing around it, can we?'

'But what am I going to do without you?'

'Keep living, you daft sod.'

He huffed and squeezed his eyes shut, and Sally reached up to stroke a finger against the whiskery scruff of his cheek until he opened them again.

'You can keep loving me,' she added. 'But you have to keep living, too.'

'I don't know how to do that.'

'Well, Bill Coates. You'd better figure it out, hadn't you?'

'Still bossing me about,' he cracked, smile small and bittersweet. 'You can't be feeling that bad.'

But they both knew how much pain she was in by then. He did his best to make it less frightening for her, but it was selfish too. He knew that by now they were on borrowed time, and that every single smile she gave him was counting down towards the last one he'd see. He wanted to up that allowance in whatever way he could, stack the numbers, play the system, eke out as many sweet moments as possible, like he could bottle them and save them for later, so he wouldn't ever have to go without.

Bill still can't explain how he got through the funeral. The day passed in snatches. Sitting on their bed, doing his tie in the mirror. The ride to the crematorium. The weight of the coffin on his shoulder as he and the other pallbearers carried her in. Recognising the faces of all the former foster kids who'd turned up, but not trusting himself to speak to them beyond gruff thanks for coming, the looming horror of realising he couldn't remember everyone's names.

And then they all went home. Bill sent himself to bed. The days after that were the hardest. But it wasn't until much later, when the thick grey fog of grief had started to thin, just the tiniest bit, that Bill realised how alone he was without Sal. She was the one who'd done the Christmas letters every year, sitting first on the floor then later at one end of the sofa with the card table propped over her knee, glitter on her fingertips and then in her hair or freckling the end of her nose as she penned individual updates to each person in her address book. Sally was the reliable author of the annual birthday cards for every foster kid who'd ever stayed under their roof, a tradition she continued even for the ones who'd been and gone decades before. Most of their friends from the street had moved on by then, and the ones who were still alive had already traded in the houses' steep steps and cantankerous Victorian plumbing for more comfortable options; care homes or families, bedsits or seaside bungalows.

A few of the kids had attempted to stay in touch, after Sally died. But Bill didn't want pity, or to be forced to face the crushing reality of everything he'd lost. He had no idea what to say, didn't even know where to start. So he let their phone calls, cards and letters go unanswered, and when they stopped coming it was a strange relief to let the guilt of not replying go. It was more comfortable being left to his own devices. But he hadn't ever intended to let his world get so small, or for this much time to trickle away without him really being here. He thought it'd hurt less, over time. That's how it had been with his folks.

The whisky-dosed tea burns the back of his throat, and he follows it with a chunk of shortbread, chewing thoughtfully. Those other griefs had ebbed with time because he'd been living despite them. The losses hadn't gone away, but there had been other things happening. He still had sudden heartbreak pangs, or out-of-nowhere stray recollections. Like Alfie's ridiculous falsetto singing voice that sent his mam into hysterics, Eddie and Dad taking over the cooking when Mam had done her ankle in, the roast potatoes burnt to cinders but the pineapple upside-down cake they'd laboured over for afters turning out to be the best Bill had ever had. He'd shared all of those anecdotes with Sally, and that had been part of how he'd moved through those losses. But he has so many of her that he's never shared with anyone. They'd told their first-date story, over the years. But their second date was one he'd never shared: the muggy August night they took the train to Marsden, euphoric with their freedom after each having given their respective parents some concocted excuse for the evening. The relief of being by the river after the clammy heat of the carriage. The grey haze of midges over the dark water. The stickiness of the blackberries plucked from the riot of brambles by the path. Blackberry-stained lips and blackberry-sweet kisses as they reached the moonlit reservoir, Sally staring him down like a challenge as she unbuttoned her dress. Scooping her curls into a topknot, hissing as her bare feet touched the wet stones of the bank. Then the blistering shock of the cold water setting their skin alight. The way their nerve endings stayed alight after, seal-wet and shivering.

All these memories are with him still, and sometimes it gets so much he can't tell if he's remembering or re-living somehow: he'll come down the stairs and half-expect to find them, all of them, like nothing had ever happened. Sally, the kids, his brothers, his parents.

He hates the thought of Sally only existing in his memories now, the way that when he goes she'll vanish altogether, and there'll only be photographs and bric-a-brac left. Not being able to share her with others keeps the pain of it so sore; that's what he's putting together as he thinks back to how they supported each other through the decades and all their different joys and sorrows. He's been wallowing for ten bloody years, and it's done him far more harm than good. And he's been letting Sal down, that's the bitterest part, because he'd made her a promise that he hasn't kept. Bill fumbles for the clipping again, wondering what his brothers would say if they could see him now, summoning up the vision of them at every age he'd known them, in various positions round this very room. Long-limbed Alfie perching on the clanking radiator, Eddie on a cushion by the record player. Of the three of them, he'd been the baby. Hadn't needed to be as brave, because his brothers were always there to defend and protect him, until they weren't, and by then he had Sal by his side to help him be brave when it was hard.

He could help, his neighbours had said. And they'd help him. But it still seems too hard, and too exhausting, and Bill doesn't even realise what's happening until his tears start mottling the newspaper page. It's late. He knows he'll pay for it tomorrow if he goes to sleep in his chair, but he's not sure he can make it up the stairs to bed. He swallows the last of his whisky and tea and lets his eyes blink closed. *Just for a minute*, he swears to himself. *Then I'll go.*

# CHAPTER EIGHTEEN

Alices shuts the front door after AJ, Levon and Jessie, the flat click of the lock an echo of Bill's earlier. They'd decamped back to Alice's afterwards, brainstorming alternative plans with increasing desperation until Lev stretched and said he'd have to call it a night. The others had concurred, trooping out in a sombre mood that was all the more gutting to Alice for its stark comparison to their wild delight and hope when Jessie found the photograph.

*I'm fuming he won't help. I know it's a long shot. I know he's scared. But for god's sake, that journalist is throwing us a lifeline, and Bill would rather we all drown than risk looking a twat on camera or whatever he's worried about.*

She knows she's being harsh, that her rage isn't really about Bill, or at least not entirely. But it feels good to have somewhere to aim her anger. Alice glares at the wall between their houses, not caring how much noise she makes as she slams around the kitchen, turning on the tap to do the pots and for once embracing the shuddery racket as the boiler lurches into action. The scalding suds round her wrists bring her back to herself enough to realise she's in way too much of a mood to soothe Mol back to sleep if she wakes, so Alice adjusts the volume for the rest of the kitchen clean-up. But she's too on edge to sit still. Alice can feel a bottomless pool of despair under her anger, and she won't let herself sink into it and drown. *So come on. Channel that energy into something useful. God knows you've got an endless list of things to do. Use this to power you through.* Taking her own advice, Alice storms into the living room, casting round the room for where to start. Bill was their last chance, and it's gone. *This is it. Game over. This time next week, you're out of here. So you'd better face it and get packing.*

The smart knock on the door jangles her out of her daze. *That better not be him coming to get on my case about the noise. I was too soft on him earlier. He doesn't need sympathy. He needs his head looking at. Can't be good for him spending so much time on his own.* Alice knows she's being nasty but she's got no capacity left to care.

The knock comes again. Irritated that Bill – or whoever it is – is just bashing away without a thought for the sleeping toddler upstairs, Alice stomps towards the sound to at least shut them up before Mollie kicks off as well. In the hallway, another possibility suddenly flickers through her head. *What if Bill's changed his mind? What if he's come round to apologise about before and say he'll help? What if it's not too late?*

She wrenches open the door, too churned up to even work out what she'll say to Bill if she finds him on the step. But it's not Bill. It's Paul Buchanan.

'What the . . . ?' Alice's voice goes high-pitched and Scouse with the shock, and she trails off, placing Paul immediately but still none the wiser about what he's doing here. He looks like he's come incognito: the sharp suit he wore last time is nowhere to be seen but the 'casual' dark jeans and shirt he wears instead still scream status and money.

'Hello, Alice. Mind if I come in?' His tone is pleasant but it transports Alice back to the meeting in his offices, and Paul's blandly smug face when he told them there was nothing they could do.

'Come in? Are you kidding?' She puts a hand on the door frame to steady herself, fury rocketing her heart rate. 'What are you even doing here? Come to check my house out before you smash it to bits?'

'Far from it, Alice, I promise.' On the step, he shifts his weight from one foot to the other. 'I'm happy to explain why I'm here, but it might be better done inside than on your doorstep.'

'Whatever you've got to say to me, you can say where you are.'

He holds his hands out in a placating gesture. 'I understand you're upset with me.'

'Hun, that's the understatement of the year.' Alice bites out the sarcasm. 'You're lucky you've still got bollocks left.'

He laughs like he's impressed. 'I probably deserve that,' he says, with a shrug, and the admission disorients Alice even further.

'Yeah, you do deserve it. You realise you're making me and my kid homeless next week?'

'Well,' he says, and makes a gesture like he's smoothing a tie even though he's not wearing one. 'That's what I'm here to talk to you about.'

*What if he's here to back down about the evictions? What if the petition got the attention of someone important? What if that journalist already did something about the street while we've been wasting time trying to convince Bill? What if Paul's here to tell me something's*

179

*happened and their plans have changed? Imagine I ruin everything for all of us because I'm in too much of a state to hear him out.*

'I'll give you two minutes,' Alice tells him, stepping back to let him into her hall.

In the kitchen, Paul glances round at the bright colours everywhere, the plants, Mollie's artwork and toys. An unreadable expression crosses his face. *That's right*, Alice thinks. *It's not just property, is it? It's a home. Is it weird for you to see it like this? Or are you just pissed off to see I'm not packed? Well, good luck with that, mate. If you even try to give me any grief about it, you won't like what happens.*

She sits at her table, arms folded hard over her chest. 'So, you've smarmed your way in.' *Isn't it vampires who can't cross your threshold without an invitation? Seems about right*, she thinks, assessing Paul's buffed loafers and his slicked-back hair. 'Start talking. Now.'

'Alice, I really mean it when I say I understand how upset you are.' The tone of his voice has changed to a gravelly pleading, and it takes Alice a moment of scrutinising him to pinpoint that, for the first time, Paul actually sounds sincere.

'You've been on my mind a lot since our last meeting,' he continues. 'The past few weeks must have been a nightmare for you.'

Alice's reply is menacingly monotone. 'You have no idea.'

'I know. I haven't got a clue what it's like to be in your situation, but I regret that you're in it, and that I've been part of it. I know you won't believe me, but I mean it.'

'If you've come here for forgiveness, you're not going to get it. Tell it to your hundred-quid-an-hour therapist. Or your coke dealer. Whoever. Just not me.'

'I'm not telling you for sympathy. I'm telling you because I want to help.'

Alice has a fleeting thrill of hope. *Maybe it* is *good news. Stop having a pissing contest with him and see what he's got to say. Don't inadvertently talk him into bulldozing the entire street tonight because he doesn't like women answering back.*

She moderates her tone but keeps the sceptical scowl. 'You want to help me? What does that mean?'

He gestures to Mollie's drawings on the fridge. 'Your little girl,' he says. 'She's three, isn't she?'

'What about her?'

'I've got a lad who's not much older. I'm a single parent too, you know. And I'd hate to think of me and Ben not having somewhere to call our own.'

The absolute privilege of it only ever being hypothetical. Alice doesn't trust herself to answer, so she just gives a *keep-talking* grunt.

'Look, I know you won't believe me, but I *have* actually got a heart. I don't want to see you and your kid being in this situation, and it doesn't have to be that way.' He reaches round to the back pocket of his jeans and pulls out a wedge of papers, which he smooths out on the table between them.

'What's this?'

'This is the answer to your predicament. It's a contract for your new home.'

'What?'

'It's all above aboard,' he promises, pushing the paperwork towards her as if encouraging her to look. 'This place is perfect for you. I had a word with a landlord friend of mine and got you a lease for an apartment in his latest development. It's not long since been completed, but there were a couple of properties left. This one is yours, if you want it.'

'You know I can't afford that.'

'You can.' He taps the contract. 'Same rental rate as you're paying now, locked in for the duration of your tenancy. In a property that's far better for you both than this place.'

He tries hard to hide it, but his distaste reveals itself in the tone of those last two words, and his snobbishness about her current home irritates Alice even more.

'I know you probably think anywhere would be better than this,' she tells him. 'But, as you might have guessed, I'm pretty attached to it. You want me to upheave my entire life by moving, you'd better explain what "better" means.'

'No upheaval, for one thing. This place isn't even ten minutes away. You can keep working at the school, Mollie can stay at the same nursery. It's bigger, and more modern. It's closer to the park, and the crime stats are much lower. And there's a back garden. Think about it, Alice. A safe place for Mollie to play. I know how important it is to me that my Benji has that. I want that for you, too.'

Alice is too sideswiped by his offer to properly process what he's said. Her brain snags on something else.

'How do you know my daughter's name?'

Paul gives a sheepish half-smile, half-sigh. 'It's not on, I know, but like I said, I've been worried. I wanted to reassure myself that you'd be fine, so I had my assistant look you up online. She briefed me about your job, and your daughter.'

'So what's in it for you?'

He meets her hard stare with his own cool calm gaze. 'I get to go ahead with this development knowing that you've got a good home. You asked me about morals when we last met, and that's what I've been thinking about. There's got to be a way to do this where everybody wins.' He gestures again towards the contract between them. 'This is it.'

Alice pictures it. A back garden with a swing set for

Mollie, maybe a hammock she could lie in and read on the days she gets all her lesson planning done. Central heating that doesn't cause migraines or third-degree burns. Enough room. And then she pictures the manky rain-logged mattress dumped in the alleyway six months ago that the council still haven't moved. She pictures the ever-present constellations of smashed glass from the teens that drink on the park, the silver gleam of crushed empty nitrous canisters like spent bullets in the gutter. She pictures Mollie's grazed, gravel-studded palms the last time the toddler tripped and fell on the cracked pavement outside.

'What about the others?'

'The others?' Paul echoes her question with a confused crinkling of his forehead.

'You know who I'm talking about. The other residents. My neighbours. Are they all getting a visit like this too?'

'Alice, work with me here. This is an opportunity for *you*. It's not one I can extend to everyone, but I've come to you because you're the one who needs the most support.'

*Is that even true?* She thinks of Bill, not even any attempt made towards packing or leaving, apparently in denial that anything's even happening. And none of the others have anything else sorted.

Paul sees her sceptical expression. 'Jessie Cassidy's name isn't even on the tenancy agreement. Technically the council could have evicted her before now just for that. I know she's got the option of living with her mum. So does Mr Campbell – he has family in Sheffield he could live with if he chooses not to find other accommodation in Leeds. Levon Amiri is well connected to the local community, with access to housing co-ops and other options and, besides, not having dependents means he's far more flexible in terms of where he lives. Same goes for William Coates, who I believe is going to be offered alternative housing by the council anyway.'

He makes it sound so neat and tidy.

Alice leans forward. 'So it's not everyone wins, is it? You win, and no one else.'

'Except for you, if you sign. I know you've been collecting signatures for your little petition, and I know you've been trying to get the media on side.'

*How does he know that? Did that journalist contact him after all? Has someone tipped him off, or has he been paying more attention than we thought?*

Paul's still talking. 'What are you doing it all for? So you and your daughter have somewhere to live. You won. Here it is. There's no glory in being a martyr, Alice. I'm offering you a lifeline here.'

Alice recoils. 'I'd rather drown than get rescued by you,' she spits.

Paul's eyes widen, a muscle jumping in his jaw. 'You can't mean that.'

Alice thinks of Sam telling her that her best and worst trait is being a fighter. Sometimes you fight just for the sake of it, he'd say. *Is that what I'm doing right now? What are we going to do if I don't sign?*

'Come on, Alice. Please. Do the smart thing.' He holds out a swanky fountain pen. 'Stop dragging our name through the mud, and all this nonsense with the petition, and just focus on what's important. A home for you and Mollie.'

For a moment, Alice is tempted. *I've been doing everything possible these past few weeks, and what has it got me? Nothing. I thought I was making connections here, but he's right, isn't he? I'm the only one with a dependant. I have to think about her. In less than a week's time this is all going to be razed to rubble and then we'll all have to go our separate ways anyway. There's nothing for me here if people like Bill won't even help when everything is desperate. I've been fooling myself to think otherwise.*

Alice's pulse is thudding in her ears. *Don't you* dare *start sobbing your guts out in front of him.* Summoning up every crumb of strength she's got, Alice fights the tears back. And then she zeroes in on Paul's last point. *He wants us to stop campaigning. Which means even if no one else cares, he's worried about it. Never mind all that cry-me-a-river stuff about his conscience. He's getting grief about us from someone, and he wants to shut us up.*

'I'm not taking anything from you,' she tells Paul, exhaustion washing over her. 'So you may as well just get out. I said you could have two minutes, and you've had way more than that. I've listened to all I can take.'

'Fine.' Paul stands, pushing the chair back over the lino with a juddery shriek. He waves the contract at her again before dropping it onto the table. 'But I'm leaving this with you. Maybe once you've calmed down you'll look over it properly and see sense.'

Alice puts her head in her hands and listens to Paul's footsteps thudding down the hall, followed by the quiet snick of the front lock. He's gone. Once she's alone, she eyes the contract from across the table with suspicion. *It's probably not even real. I should ask that lawyer to read it, see what ridiculous small print is in there just waiting to fuck me over. I'm not going to sign it, am I? I can't. I should rip that thing into a million pieces right now.*

But Alice doesn't tear the contract up. She can't bring herself even to touch it. Instead, she stares at it for a long, long time, her brain whizzing in every direction at once then glitching out every time it careens smack-bang into their upcoming deadline. Night falls and the kitchen goes dark around her. Leaving the papers where they are, Alice drags herself up from the table and up the stairs to bed.

# CHAPTER NINETEEN

Jessie takes the bus into the city centre, then another one out to Holbeck. She follows the map on her phone to the pub, soaking up the warmth of the sun on her bare arms and the almost-eerie quiet of everyone else still being at work. It's only early afternoon so the pub is quiet too, its few drinkers at tables in the beer garden rather than the cool shade of indoors. Jessie double-checks the crossed keys on the sign against her mum's message, then scans the pub's various alcoves to make sure Donna's not already there. Not a chance. Jessie slides into a leather-buttoned booth and boots up her laptop. After submitting her final piece of history essay on Monday, she can finally stop stressing about coursework. But it still doesn't feel real, even when she connects to the pub wi-fi and rereads the submissions receipt. All that's left now are the exams in a few weeks. *Who knows where I'll be then*, Jessie thinks. But at least the threat of not being allowed to take them has been lifted. That's one less stress. Giving a surreptitious glance around the room to make sure her mum's not coming and no one else is looking, Jessie pulls up a bookmarked page: an undergraduate course listing at Leeds Uni. History of Art with Cultural Studies. 'Study art with a cultural focus on theories of language, image, identity, gender, race, sexuality and class.' She deliberately doesn't click through to the fees breakdown, but her attention snags on the 'typical entry requirements', and below that the letters AAB. *I'm fucked.*

'Jessie-boo! Sorry, I'm late.' Donna pounces on Jessie from out of nowhere in a honey-musk cloud of knock-off Dior Poison, diving into her side of the booth and squeezing her so hard Jessie pictures her ribs bending almost to breaking point.

Jessie slams the computer shut, disentangling herself from Donna's arms and scooches backward on the seat to put some distance between them, taking in her mum's paisley-patterned maxi-dress and glowing suntan.

'Mum, what the hell? Have you been away?'

'Oh, babe, I told you about me and Nate going to the Canaries. For our six-month anniversary? I must have done.'

'You definitely didn't.'

'Well, I meant to. It was stunning, you should've seen it . . . '

Jessie only manages to interrupt the subsequent mono-logue about beaches, scuba-diving and all-inclusive buffets by asking her mum what she wants from the bar. Returning with their drinks, she slides her mum's lager into place then retakes her seat, rattling the ice cubes in her own glass of alcoholic ginger beer.

Donna must pick up on the frosty vibes, because she leans forward as soon as Jessie's settled, placing both hands on the table between them.

'Listen, Jess, I'm sorry I've not been there for you. You may be all grown up now, but you are still my little girl. You're so independent I forget that sometimes. But look, I want to make it up to you, and—'

'What,' Jessie cuts her off, gesturing to the huge glittering ring on her mum's left hand. 'Is that?'

'That's what I'm trying to tell you. Nathan proposed. While we were on holiday. It was so romantic, honestly ... ' Donna's voice goes gooey and breathless but Jessie interrupts again.

'Lovely,' Jessie monotones, squiggling with a finger in the condensation on the side of her glass. 'Congratulations. I'm thrilled for you. What's that got to do with me?'

'Wow, Jessie. Really?' Donna is incredulous. 'I'm doing my best to be civil. Do me a favour and do your part, won't you? Please?'

'Mum.' Jessie gives her best attempt at a level tone. 'I've barely heard from you in ages. I'm used to you doing your own thing, but doing it when I'm about to get evicted from what's supposed to be *our* house is a whole new level, even for you.'

'Well, I didn't want to tell you until it was definite, but now it's official ... ' She waggles the finger with the engagement ring and Jessie thinks she might be sick. 'Nate's getting a house. He spent most of his bonus from work on the holiday and the ring.' She stifles her giggle by taking a sip from her pint. 'But the rest plus his savings went on his new place. Our new place, if you want to come.'

Donna goes on to explain about the house: a three-bed semi-detached on an avenue close to Hunger Hills Woods in Horsforth. Jessie sips from her glass, listening. Waiting. But Donna's ramble goes on and on, and there's still no acknowledgement of what they'd be leaving behind in Leodis Street, or what Jessie might want for the future.

'So what about me? And the house?'

'Onwards and upwards, baby. We're moving onto bigger and better things.'

'But I don't want to move.'

'Oh, boo, grow up. We don't always get what we want, you know.'

'You seem to.' Jessie's words come out in a tear-wet growl as she snatches up her things and bolts towards the door.

The journey back to Leodis Street passes in a blur, but by then Jessie's changed her mind. She doesn't want to be home alone, confronting everything she'll be losing soon. *Should've got off at the library*, she thinks, regretting her spaced-out bus ride. *Now what am I going to do?* Levon will be in work, AJ will be in work or bed. Her sightline lands on Alice's front door, the sun-frazzled plants in pots at the edge of the path and the sparkly kids' wellies on the top step. Open windows in the front lounge the sign that they're back from school. *Fuck's sake*, she thinks. *Here goes nothing.*

Alice's house is chaos. She keeps going back and forth on packing, so there are half-full boxes and suitcases everywhere and every room is a bizarre mess. Dresses hung over the bannister, books stacked on the landing, and abandoned scraps of bubble wrap everywhere which originally had Alice's assorted ornaments nested inside them before being unwrapped and the bubbles popped by Mollie. She's volunteered to host another street meeting later, a last-ditch attempt to come up with a plan or have one more crack at convincing Bill, though Alice suspects the journalist's probably moved on to her next story by now. Alice reckons she'll just about be ready for the others by then, if she can whirl through her to-do list in the time in between. So she's not expecting the knock at the door, when it comes. For a moment, she panics it might be Paul back again, but finding Jessie on the front step is just as confusing.

'I know I'm early,' the teenager blurts, her expression shifty and her voice subdued. 'Like, really early. But is it cool if I crash here for a bit beforehand? My internet's down again and ... ' Jessie trails off but Alice is too distracted by everything else to dig any deeper.

'Come on,' she says, standing back to let her in. 'Join the mad house.'

Jessie doesn't even get as far as turning on her computer and pretending to do college work: Mollie's on her demanding to play a game before she can sit down. Grateful for a moment to herself, Alice leaves them to it in the lounge, disappearing into the kitchen to make tea and dig out her emergency packet of pink wafers, which she brings through with the brews.

Half-absorbed in building a precarious tower of blocks with Mollie, Jessie ends up explaining to Alice what had happened with her mum. Alice listens but keeps her attention on the books she's moving from the shelf to a suitcase, instincts telling her that giving Jessie her full focus will only make her clam up. But she makes all the right commiserating noises and even confides some details of her own sometimes-turbulent childhood. Gradually, as they talk more and finish the biscuits, the wound-up jitteriness of Jessie's movements relaxes into something looser. The teenager lolls on the floor, propped up on a cushion, Mol curling up beside her with a picture book.

Seeing the toddler so uncharacteristically chill prompts Alice to check the time on her phone.

'God, Lev and AJ will be round any minute, and I need to get this one sorted for bed. Can you entertain yourself for a bit while I take her upstairs?'

'Sure thing.' Jessie shoots finger-guns, then collects her empty cup from the side of the settee. 'Shall I put the kettle on again?'

'Read my mind. Yes, please.'

Supervising Mollie brushing her teeth and then wrestling her into her pyjamas, Alice feels weirdly content knowing Jessie's downstairs. It's calmed her down having company for the afternoon, and it's been good to finally start building a connection to the spiky teenager who's been so bristly with her so far. Gritting her teeth against the wave of grief that comes when Alice thinks about how little time they've got left for moments like this, she kisses Mollie good night and heads back downstairs.

She finds Jessie in the kitchen, the kettle bubbling. But Jessie isn't making tea. She's bending over the kitchen table. Alice's blood turns to ice. 'Jessie, what are you—?'

Jessie spins round, face pale and eyes blazing. She's holding up the contract, turned to Paul's looping signature on the last page. 'Alice, what the *fuck*?'

# CHAPTER TWENTY

'I can explain,' Alice takes a tentative step forward, hands up in surrender. 'Take a breath, Jessie. It's not what it looks like.'

'Wow. Really? Got any more clichés you wanna chuck my way, or shall we just go back to you lying right to my face?'

'I haven't lied.' Alice comes closer. Her voice wobbles but she's trying hard to keep calm, doing everything she can not to freak Jessie out even further. 'I haven't lied about anything.'

'I've been here all afternoon and you never thought to mention you've got another place lined up? Or that you've been having secret meetings with that shady twat who's about to knock down our entire street? Seems like a pretty important omission.'

'Jessie. Calm down, okay?' Alice makes a half-hearted motion towards the kettle. 'Let me make this tea, we'll sit down and I'll tell you everything.'

'Get lost,' Jessie hurls back. 'There's nothing you can say that can make this better. *Nothing*. You're just as shady as he is. I knew you couldn't be trusted.'

Alice reels back. 'What's *that* supposed to mean?'

'I had a feeling about you, you know. And now look what's happened.' Jessie waves the contract in Alice's face, smacking the papers with her other hand. 'You've stabbed every single one of us in the back.'

'I haven't, Jessie. Please just listen to me.'

'No. I'm sick of listening to you. You've had the entire street listening to you for weeks and look where it's got us. Nearly homeless and fucked over by a backstabbing *traitor*.'

Alice's fists clench at the viciousness of Jessie's words, but she forces herself to speak calmly. She uncurls her hands and shoves them into her pockets. 'I know you're upset. I get it, okay? I get it. You've had a bad day, and this feels like one thing too many, but if you just stop for a minute and let me explain—'

'Woah, what's going on?' AJ demands, coming down the hall and into the room.

'We heard raised voices from the bottom of the path,' Levon adds, peering over AJ's shoulder. 'I'm sure we can resolve it if things have got a little heated. Why don't the two of you take a moment and tell us what the matter is?'

'Ask *her*,' Jessie says, with a violent motion towards Alice. 'Or actually don't bother, because all you'll get back is lies.'

'Alice? What's she talking about?'

But Jessie cuts her off before she can answer. 'She's done a deal. With Paul fucking Buchanan. She's got a signed contract from him promising her a new house.'

'That is *not* true,' Alice lashes back, and the kitchen suddenly feels too full, too hot. Everything's escalated way too fast.

'Oh, yeah?' Jessie demands, brandishing the contract again. 'So what's this doing on your kitchen table?'

'He came round to see me the other day, okay?' Alice's words tumble out in a desperate rush, and she cringes at the crestfallen looks that crash across Levon and AJ's faces.

Jessie sneers sarcastically at Alice's upset expression. 'Finally, some truth! S'pose I shouldn't be too shocked it took this long when everything else she does is so goddamn *fake*.'

'Alice, it sounds like you'd better tell us what's gone on.' The seriousness of Levon's tone cuts through Jessie's ranting and makes Alice's skin prickle with shame.

'I will. I'll tell you everything.'

Jessie does a fake cough that sounds a lot like *traitor* and Alice wheels back to face her. 'I mean it, Jessie, that's *enough*. Just let me get a word in edgeways, will you?'

'Hey,' AJ puts in, hooking an arm round Jessie's shoulders. 'Don't snap at her like that.'

Levon clears his throat. 'Perhaps everyone should take a breath, hm? No need for anyone to say anything they'll regret.'

'I'm not going to regret calling her a traitor, because it's the truth. What's the point listening to her when all she does is lie?' Jessie lobs the contract at Alice, the bundle of papers spinning towards her face, making her step back and knock into one of the kitchen chairs.

It crashes to the floor with a bang. There's a heart-beat of silence, then a loud woeful wail starts up from Mollie's bedroom.

Alice squeezes her eyes shut so hard she sees stars, then opens them again.

'Paul came to see me,' she admits again, through gritted teeth. 'And he gave me that contract. But it's not how it sounds. So just let me go and sort Mol out, and then we can talk. Good?'

'I'm not staying here another minute,' Jessie spits. She

ducks out from under AJ's arm, hurtling down the hall and out of the still-open front door.

Mollie's screams get louder. The others stare at each other.

AJ dithers for a moment, then announces he's going after her. 'Jessie, wait up,' he calls from the doorway, then all they hear are his footsteps, a slammed door and Mollie's ear-splitting bawling.

'I think I'd better go too,' Levon murmurs, then slips out of the kitchen.

Alice scrabbles up the stairs, almost falling as she gets to the landing. She scoops Mollie up in a blur of tears, holding the toddler over her shoulder so her daughter won't see how upset she is.

'Shush-shush, baby. It's okay. No need to cry.' In the soft peachy glow from Mollie's unicorn night-light, Alice flumps into a cross-legged position on the carpet to rock Mollie back to sleep. Her heart is thundering inside her chest, panic threatening to overtake her any moment. She rubs the toddler's back in circles to keep her shaking hands occupied.

'No need to cry,' Alice whispers, over and over, rocking them both back and forth. But the words don't stop either of their tears from falling.

# CHAPTER TWENTY-ONE

A lice's night goes on for ever. Once Mollie's settled, she retreats to her own bedroom, where she sits cross-legged on her bed, cuddling a pillow to her chest. How can things have deteriorated this far? She doesn't even want to go back downstairs, to face the chair lying sadly in the kitchen, the contract scattered on the floor where Jessie flung it, the half-packed suitcases and boxes strewn everywhere. She wants to hide. She wants someone to rescue her. She wants to wake up to Mollie burrowing into bed beside her, the entire ordeal relegated to a vivid but unreal anxiety dream. Unlocking her phone, Alice scrolls through her contacts, but who can she message? *No one's coming to save you, lady. You'd better get your shit together yourself.*

Eventually, she steels herself and descends the stairs to return order to the kitchen, then the lounge. She considers a bath. Candles lit, bath bomb fizzing, face mask on. *No point saving your fancy toiletries for a special occasion any more.* But Alice knows none of her usual tricks will bring her back to equilibrium tonight. *Desperate times call for desperate measures*, she thinks, and flicks the switch on the kettle for more coffee.

She takes her mug to her usual perch on the front step, inhaling the fumes and gazing down on the sleeping street, thinking hard. The nearest street lamp is buzzing, its septic yellow glare flickering on and off in a halo of moths, but otherwise the scene is peaceful: the sky a deep-blue velvet, the only sound the occasional low growl of traffic passing on the main road. *We can't lose this. We can't.* Alice wonders how many of her neighbours are still awake. Probably everyone.

Alice stays there until her bum turns numb on the cold stone step, her slipper-booted feet dead from being tucked under her body. She doesn't know how much time's passed until she realises with alarm that the section of sky she's been staring at has started to shift from night-dark to dawn-pale. The deadline of eviction day is looming large but her mind can't comprehend it. It's murky and blank. Alice doesn't know where they're going. She doesn't know what will happen. But she knows she can't bring herself just to leave the house that last time the way she's been told. *Do you even lock the door behind you when your house is about to be smashed to bits? Why do I even need to think about that?*

Alice has read, in amongst all their research, about other properties that were bought by developers. Other residents evicted. Then shady money things happened with investors and markets – all those words Alice could never fully get her head around, but the upshot was stark enough. The houses stood empty and abandoned, sometimes for years, before the demolition finally happened. That's what happened with Valley House, a huge Victorian building just off Cardigan Road split into council flats. The council had tried to sell to a property developer who only wanted the land, but the residents revolted. They managed to get all the local businesses to voice objections, so the council backed out of the sale and instead just left the building to rot, hoping the other nearby neighbours would come around, that they'd rather have luxury apartments than spooky boarded-up dereliction. That wretchedly slow, pointless decay is even more gutting a prospect for Alice to contemplate than the abrupt noisy violence of their homes being destroyed the minute they leave. She doesn't want to picture their little house dark and cold without them: steel bolted over the doors and windows to stop it being squatted, the star-spangled sky mural in Mollie's bedroom mottled with messy graffiti, the uneven floors blackened by local kids' fires. And the prospect of it not existing at all is just static in Alice's mind. She doesn't want to imagine the demolition, but she can't stop picturing it; twisted metal, smashed glass, cratered concrete. The grind and crunch of the machines. She doesn't want to be there when it happens, but she knows she won't believe it's happened unless she sees it with her own eyes. And before that, she needs to know she's done everything possible, right down to the last possible second.

Alice collects her long-empty cup and retreats indoors, sitting down at the kitchen table with a refilled mug and one of the yellow lined pads she uses at school. By the time she's finished, the page is full of scribbles and crossings-out, but the words that remain convey everything that Alice has been fumbling for. Using her sleeve, she scrubs away the tears that fell while she concentrated on writing. Sunrise is coming, and Alice races against it as she copies out four clean versions of the letter, then seals them into envelopes. Leaving the front door open so she'll be able to hear Mollie if she wakes, Alice emerges out into the street, the sky now glowing pale pink and shimmering gold. Fingertips trembling with adrenaline and exhaustion, she fumbles an envelope through each of her neighbours' letterboxes – one each for Bill, Levon, AJ and Jessie. Mission complete, Alice returns to her kitchen. She retrieves the contract from the table and stands over the bin. Page by page, she shreds each page into confetti, then slops the spent coffee grounds on top. *No coming back from* that.

# CHAPTER TWENTY-TWO

Dear Neighbour

These past few weeks have done a number on us all. I know they have on me! We can only take so much stress and fear before we start behaving erratically: lashing out and making mistakes, and I've done a lot of that lately. For that I can only ask for your forgiveness.

But that's not the reason I'm writing to you. I'm writing to say thank you. The past few weeks have been hard, but they've also been incredibly important to me. They've shown me what connection and community can mean.

The past few years since moving to the street were some of my loneliest. I've never admitted that before, not even to myself. And I hope I'm not over the line in speculating that each of you, in your different ways, might be able to understand that. But for all their stresses and challenges, these past few weeks haven't been lonely. They've shown me what a special place this street is. It breaks my heart to think that soon that'll be taken away from us, too. Not just our homes, but our connections to each other, and everything those could grow to be if we had more time together. I don't want our time together to end yet. Things seem hopeless right now, but I still believe this street, and all of you — all of us — are worth fighting for.

So this morning, I decided that's what I'm going to do. Keep fighting. On eviction day on Monday, I won't be leaving my house. I'm going to stay put, for as long as I possibly can. I'm not giving up on everything I've built here, and that includes my connections to all of you. They can drag me out by my hair if they want to, but I can't just walk away.

I'll understand if you don't want to do the same. But if recent events have shown me anything, it's that we're stronger together than alone. So if you want to fight too, I'd love us to fight together. Maybe united we can make a difference. And if not, at least we'll know that we gave it everything we've got — together.

I hope you'll join me at mine tomorrow to make a plan. But if not, thank you for everything. It's been an honour to have you as my neighbours. And I truly hope, for all our sake's, that this isn't the end.

All my love,
Alice x

# CHAPTER TWENTY-THREE

Overturning all of Alice's expectations, Jessie arrives first. 'I'm still mad at you,' she glowers from the doorstep, but her face transforms when Mollie barrels into the hall at the sound of Jessie's voice. Mol takes Jessie by the hand and leads her inside, and all Alice can do is follow.

'You've got every right to be upset,' she tells the teenager, once they're back in the kitchen. 'I should've been more honest.'

'Yeah, you should have,' Jessie echoes, leaning against the counter. 'But whatever.' She bends to pull a loose thread from the hole at the knee of her jeans, then stands and focuses properly on Alice for the first time since coming in. 'Are you really going to refuse to leave?'

Her face is sceptical, but there's a hunger underneath. Alice thinks again about how young Jessie is. She takes a big breath, and nods. 'Yeah. I think so. It'll be scary, but I've got to see this through until the bitter end. I don't want to feel there's anything else I could've done.'

'Hardcore,' Jessie mumbles, in an approving voice. 'I'm

doing it too. All of us should. We can livestream it. They've made things hard enough for us these past few weeks. Why should we make this bit any less hard for them?'

Alice has been worried about this. She doesn't want to exclude Jessie, or clash with her again. But she's apprehensive about what could happen, and she's on the edge of voicing those concerns when AJ and Levon come in.

'So the band's getting back together?' AJ cracks, with a wary glance between Alice and Jessie.

'Something like that,' Alice says. 'Thank you both for coming.'

'Wouldn't miss it,' Levon replies, sliding another tinfoil-lidded plate onto the counter. 'Like you said in your letter, miscommunications and mistakes are bound to happen when we're navigating such adversity. Let's give each other some grace. We're together. That's what matters.'

Alice makes tea, and they each take one of Levon's muffins – he's adapted a traditional recipe to a vegan-friendly version in the hope Jessie would be here – before going over Alice's suggestion of staying in their homes as long as they can. Levon's immediately on side. He's been there the longest, after Bill, and so Alice supposes it makes sense he'd want to stick it out however he can.

AJ seems conflicted at first.

'I'm up for it,' he says. 'I am. But I'm worried about work. I can probably swap my shifts for Monday, but I'm not sure how long I'd be able to stay put without telling them what's going on.'

'Me too,' Alice admits. 'I can't afford to lose my job. And I don't expect anyone to do anything they're not comfortable with.'

'What about that reporter you spoke to, Lev?' AJ asks,

thoughtful. 'What did she say when you told her Bill didn't want to be interviewed?'

'Didn't get back to me,' he admits, face twisted in disappointment. 'I left her a voicemail, but sadly no response. What are you thinking?'

'Might be worth another go,' AJ suggests. 'If we're doing this, we want media attention, right?'

'You know, that's a good idea,' Levon says, thinking. 'Perhaps she could interview us about our plans not to leave. Or she could be here, when it comes to it. The more people watching, the less the property company's security team is going to want to come across heavy-handed.'

The words *heavy-handed* make Alice flinch, just a bit. She knows too many stories of protesters who've been hurt during actions, by private security or police. *This won't be like that*, she tells herself, but the thought of it still burrows into her brain, an invasive internal film reel of violent imagery. Those fears make her all the more concerned about Jessie.

'You sure this is something you want?' she asks the teenager, her uncertainty echoed by Levon and AJ.

'No chance.' Jessie foresees where they're going and shoots them down before they can suggest she think twice. 'Don't even bother. I'm doing it, and you can't stop me. I'm eighteen, I'm an adult. I'm going to do my part.'

'It's not just about you being the youngest,' Levon puts in. 'It's just … it's not even your name on the council tenancy agreement, is it, Jessie? It's your mum's. So if anyone stays put in your house, it should be her. Not you.'

'I've spent way more time there than her,' Jessie says, her voice close to cracking, her back sliding down the kitchen cabinets so that she's sitting on the floor. 'Why should I be penalised for her leaving me on my own? Just because we moved in before my last birthday. So what? I'm not a kid. That place is far more mine than hers.'

'We're not disputing that, babe,' Alice says, nudging Jessie's foot with hers. 'We're just saying it might be an idea to have your mum be part of this conversation, too. Especially if you want to stay once the deadline passes.'

Jessie skids her phone across the kitchen linoleum, sending it spinning in Alice's direction.

'You want to talk to her? Good luck. You'll need it, though. She didn't even reply to my last messages.'

'It's just ... ' Alice tries again. 'We don't know what they'll do. If we don't leave. They said it'd be considered trespassing, didn't they, in that original letter? And I don't want you getting arrested.'

'Wouldn't be the first time,' Jessie mumbles, under her breath.

'You have?' AJ asks. 'What for?'

'Shoplifting,' Jessie mutters, with a small smirk. 'I was only fourteen, though, so all they did was caution me. And then at a protest, last summer. Obstruction of a highway. What a joke. The road was closed, so we weren't obstructing anything. But I know how it works. I'm not scared.'

'Okay,' says Alice. 'Like you said, you're an adult. It's your call. But if that was before your birthday, it might be different now. Being charged as an adult might have different consequences.'

'What about university?' Levon puts in. 'Some courses ask about criminal records, you know. You need to think about your future here.'

'Well, seeing as I missed the deadline to apply to uni, I think having a house is a bit more important right now.'

'Don't be impulsive, Jessie,' Levon tells her. 'Just think it over. That's all I'm saying.'

Jessie folds her arms, a stubborn glint in her eye. AJ shimmies from the counter to sit next to her on the floor. Doesn't say anything, doesn't touch her. Just sits close by, their knees almost knocking but not quite. A stalemate stretches and then Alice breaks the tense silence.

'Look, I've been arrested before, too. Also shoplifting,' she explains, with a sheepish eye roll, in response to Jessie's incredulous look. 'But I've got Mollie now, haven't I? And I work at a school. So I'm just saying: we all need to think carefully about potential consequences.'

'All they'd have on us is trespass,' Levon says. 'If it even comes to police, which hopefully it won't. Trespass, or resisting arrest.'

'They can arrest you for resisting arrest? That's some meta shit right there.'

'I know. That one's not so bad, though. You'd usually be released without being charged. But trespass can be charged as a criminal offence. So up to a year, or an unlimited fine.'

'Unlimited,' Alice echoes, her voice hollow with fear.

'Whatever we do,' Levon says, 'it's important everyone goes in with their eyes open. I don't think it'll come to being charged, but there's a chance.'

'How do you know all that, Lev?' AJ asks, pretending not to notice that Jessie's slumped in her sitting position so that her head's resting on his shoulder.

Levon gives a coy smile. 'I was quite . . . ah, political in my youth. And not always through the proper channels. But I did check this out more recently. Went through the zines in the library archive, did some online research. Just in case, you know. To make sure my knowledge is up to date.'

'It's a chance worth taking,' Alice says, now trying to push the words *unlimited fine* as well as unwanted images of police brutality out of her head. 'For anyone that wants to, I mean.'

'And here was me thinking my anarchist days were behind me,' says Levon, with a wink.

'I can do that first day,' AJ repeats. 'If it ends up being some epic stand-off I might have to think again.'

'I'm gonna buy Pop-Tarts and peanut butter and charge all my devices. I'll outlast all you bitches.'

'It's not a competition, Jessie.'

'Whatever,' the teenager replies, snuggling into AJ's shoulder with a smug expression. 'I'm gonna win.'

'I'm not having Mollie here,' Alice says, when they've toasted to their collective decision. 'I don't think it'll be dangerous. Not physically, anyway. Like I don't actually think they're going to demolish our houses with us inside them. But if there's even a microscopic chance of me getting arrested, she can't be here. And I don't need her having a meltdown in the middle of everything.'

'Where will you take her?'

'I'm going to ask Sam. His mum's more stable now, he's back in Leeds. Hopefully he can have her.'

For a moment Alice gets a flicker of self-consciousness about how often she seems to have been mentioning Sam lately. But she dismisses it. He's Mollie's dad. It's relevant. 'It's his weekend with her, anyway,' she adds, questioning why she feels the need to explain. 'So if he can have her Sunday night and take her to school from there on Monday morning, that should work out.'

'Then you're free this weekend?' Jessie asks, from the floor.

'If you can call grappling with existential doom and impending homelessness free, then yeah. Why?'

'We could make banners,' she suggests. 'Hang them from our windows and take photos?'

Alice, Levon and AJ had had a similar idea, back in that

first meeting that Jessie wasn't there for. They'd discarded the plan when they realised no one but each other would see them. Alice's expression must betray her confusion, because Jessie's staring at her like she's stupid. 'Hello? Earth to Alice. It's a brilliant idea. We get some spray paint, go wild on some bedsheets, do a photoshoot then put everything online and explain that we're not leaving.'

'Won't that just tip off the property developers and mean they come prepared for a fight?'

Jessie shrugs. 'So we do it just before they come. That's what this is about, right? Staying until the end, making them confront what they're doing? This could be part of that.'

'If we're going down,' Alice says, putting every ounce of conviction she's got into her voice. 'I'm going down fighting.'

'Yeahhhh,' Jessie growls, waggling her tongue. 'Maybe you *are* a bad bitch after all.'

But Alice isn't entertained. She's scared. And as she stares off into space, some of Jessie's irreverence seems to drain away and get replaced by melancholy too.

'I wish we could all be together for it,' Jessie announces to the room.

'I know,' AJ says. 'But we need someone in each house, don't we? United stand and all that.'

'All for one,' Levon puts in, with a grim gallows grin.

'One for all,' Alice finishes, blinking fast.

Later that night, after everyone's gone, Alice is still awake. The noise that worms its way into her bedroom is so strange that at first she thinks she must have dozed off, dreamed a violent grinding that echoes off the terraces and distorts down the street. But she sits upright and the noise still comes. She crosses to the window, pulls back the curtain and cranes her neck to see up and down the road. The street is quiet, not even any sign of the usual cats and foxes slinking from shadow to shadow. But the noise is still there. She goes downstairs, threading her bare feet into her unlaced boots and pulling on a baggy mohair jumper over the camisole and shorts she's been attempting to sleep in. The May night is humid, sticky and still. A half-moon hangs low. Peering out of the open front door, Alice still can't tell where the noise is coming from.

She shuffles forward in her undone boots, searching for the source of the sound. She starts nearly out of her skin when she sees the dark shape of Levon at the end of his path, dressed in pyjama pants and his denim jacket, a mug held to his chest. He wasn't there when she looked out of the window. He must have just slipped outside, same as her. They stare at each other for a long moment, and then Levon gestures with his cup.

Alice's house isn't at the same angle as his, but when she comes to the end of her own path, she can see what he's pointing towards. On the scrap of grass near the playground, a makeshift camp is being assembled. Temporary floodlights illuminate a fenced-off rectangle of land, into which several bulldozers are being manoeuvred. As they watch, a scurrying team of hard-hatted workers move huge hoardings into position, hiding the machinery behind them. The moon is as yellow as the street lamps, half-obscured by tatty rags of grey cloud, but it's enough for both Alice and Levon to see the logo and company name on the hoardings: GATSBY LUXURY APARTMENTS.

They stay out there for a long, long time, not moving or speaking.

When everything seems to be still and the flood lamps

behind the fences go dark, Alice and Levon retreat to their separate houses.

Alice makes herself tea and peanut butter toast, taking it through to the living room. She flicks the switch for the fairy lights, so the room comes awake with a soft firefly glow. Then she sits on the floor on one of Mollie's fluffy unicorn cushions and methodically starts unpacking the half-filled boxes.

Her phone blips, pulling her out of her reverie. She swipes tears from her eyes before thumbing open the message, pushing away the thought of Sam before it can even form. It's not from him. It's a text from Jessie: I saw them too.

# CHAPTER TWENTY-FOUR

When AJ's shift is finally over, he gets straight in his little gold car and drives home on autopilot. The Saturday morning sky is paper-pale but bright, sun hidden behind a thick bank of cloud. He barely notices the never-ending roadworks that have disrupted every commute for the past six months, or the hoardings sectioning off the park. He doesn't even hit the stereo for Whitney to sing him home. It's been another night that's made him question whether he's even got it in him to be a nurse. It's all too much sometimes. The scrambling to save someone, and all the adrenaline of that, then nowhere for it to go when the worst happens, leaving paperwork and family members to phone and the bed to strip as though nobody was ever there.

As he pulls up at home it's like coming round from hypnosis, and it takes him three attempts to get his key to turn in the sticky temperamental lock. He kicks off his shoes, puts the kettle on, excavates his dead phone from his jacket pocket and plugs it into charge. It pulses into animation, notifications pinging through. AJ ignores them at first, concentrating on one

212

thing at a time. Tea. Sugar. Milk. Bowl. Cereal. Spoon. He stands at the counter with his breakfast. He's got that hollow, exhausted sensation that comes from being famished for sleep as well as food. His shift flashed in such a blur that he can't remember whether he's eaten anything proper since Levon's baking at Alice's last night.

He wolfs down his cocoa puffs, knowing his mam would do her nut if she could see him eating something so sugary before bed. And then, like the very thought of his mam has manifested her presence, he glances down at his charging phone and sees six missed calls. But it's not like his mam to phone more than once, especially when he's working; she'll message and send a voice note if she doesn't get him first time. Concern creeping through him, he fumbles for his messages, finding the icon for the voicemail and clicking through. He holds the phone tight and tells himself the rising panic is just leftover adrenaline from work, that there's no need for him to worry.

'What am I going to do with you, AJ? I can't believe you didn't tell me what was happening! Why don't you talk to your old mum any more? I can't believe you kept this a secret from me! You are in serious trouble when I get my hands on you, let me tell you.'

Her voice fills the kitchen, the comically shrill tone transporting him back in time and making him suddenly nostalgic for his teen days of being told off for scuffing the trainers he'd begged for so relentlessly, or hanging out with the cousins she considered a bad influence. Her Jamaican accent is always stronger when she's in a flap, and he can picture her pacing about and fluffing her hair in her agitation, ready to activate the aunties network and dissipate her energy through repeated retellings of his misdeeds to every single one of her friends.

Confused, AJ searches his exhausted brain for an explanation as to what he could have done to incur this wrath. He can't come up with an answer, but he does realise there's another voice message from her, sent immediately after the first. Bracing himself for more, he hits play.

'The thing cut me off, but you're not getting away that easily! Listen, you ring me back as soon as you get this and explain yourself. I already went on the internet and found the petition, and I've sent it to everyone.' AJ groans, picturing her frantically messaging her colleagues, her friends, people from church and book club, his entire extended family. 'But there must be more I can do, so you phone me back fast and we will get this fixed. I will come up there and have words with whoever it takes. I'm in shock you let things get this far. You should have come to me, AJ. You should have come to us. I know how hard you've worked. I don't want to see you lose your home.'

Her voice gets choked up towards the end, her tone shifting from manic determination to sorrow, with the edge of wheeziness she gets when she's trying hard to keep tears back. AJ winces at the sound. The message ends. And AJ is left staring blankly at his bowl of cereal, more baffled after this message than the first.

*She knows. She knows about what's happening on the street. But how did she find out?*

Then he sees the link she's sent. When he clicks through to that and the video plays, his mug slips from his fingers and shatters on the kitchen floor, sending ceramic shards and the last of his brew everywhere.

But AJ has already snatched up his keys and his phone, scrambling out the door still in his socks, dashing over the road to Alice's.

They're all there again. *Have they been there all night?* Jessie is cross-legged on the counter this time, while Levon and Alice sit at the kitchen table.

'AJ, what the hell?' Jessie cocks her head at his sudden appearance. 'How come you've got no shoes on? Did all those people coming into A&E with Barbies up their bums or whatever finally make you crack?'

Alice bites back a laugh, hurling an exasperated glare towards the teenager and then a concerned one over at Mollie, hoping she hasn't heard.

'Better than that,' AJ tells them, motioning for them to come closer. 'You seen this?'

'What?'

'You'll see,' he says, and plays the clip. Clustered close together around him so they can all see his phone, they watch a sequence that starts out cutting between images of their street. First it's black-and-white photographs, like the ones they found in the archives. Then it's colour shots. Then film footage, up to date this time, they can tell from the chalk drawings outside Alice's and AJ's dented gold car just at the edge of the shot.

*This street was built in the Victorian era, and has been part of Leeds for over a century,* a smooth voiceover announces. *In just two days' time, it's scheduled for demolition. As concerns about gentrification rise, we spoke to one of the street's residents, a man who's lived here his entire life.*

Jessie grabs at AJ's arm as the visual cuts to Bill, sitting in his armchair in his living room, pictures arrayed behind him. They just have time to glimpse how he's smartened himself up, with his usually unkempt eyebrows smoothed into neatness and his ever-present flat cap conspicuously absent, when AJ's screen blinks into blackness as his battery gives up again.

Alice wails in frustration, but Jessie is already on her laptop and searching.

'Got it,' she shouts, doing a wiggly victory dance as she stands at the counter, her eyes widening when she sees the page that's loading is from the local news site. The video starts buffering, and she passes the computer across to Levon, who places it in the centre of the table so they can all circle around it as the same montage of photos plays. On repeat viewing, Alice realises they're not the ones they found in the newspaper article. They must have come directly from Bill.

'He did it,' Alice mutters, almost to herself, as Bill comes on-screen again. 'He talked.'

'I'm here with seventy-eight-year-old William Coates, who's lived on this street since he was born in 1945. Mr Coates, can you tell us a bit more about your time living on this street?'

'Aye, I can. I lived here with my mam and dad, and my brothers, then me and my wife took the house over after they died. Now it's just me. And I know I'm old now and don't do much. But I've always paid the rent, never been late with a single payment. I've been part of this community for decades; I've been here the longest of anyone who lives here now. And I don't think I deserve to be chucked out with only a few weeks' notice just so some rich so-and-sos can get even richer.'

'And what has it been like for you, living here all this time?'

'I can't pretend it's always been perfect. I've had hard times, like anyone.' He falters, voice cracking. 'But the people on this street have always been there for me when I've needed them. Always in and out of each other's houses we were, when I were a nipper. And my wife knew everyone's names, and all the kids' names. Our house had the same open-door policy.'

On-screen, another montage of faces: Bill and Sally on their doorstep. Bill and his brothers as gap-toothed grinning kids, holding up pans of home-grown tomatoes. Other children none of them recognise, posing in roller skates or with water pistols. Then it's back to Bill's face. 'It's old fashioned now, to know your neighbours, isn't it? And there've been years when I haven't always wanted to. Streets change over time, and some of the people who've lived here over the years haven't always wanted to bother with each other. It's been a lonely time for me here since my wife died.'

'And what about your neighbours now?'

Bill squints at the reporter, a wry grin crossing his face. 'Well, they won't let an old man live in peace, I can tell you that.'

Alice closes her eyes and re-opens them, willing herself not to laugh hysterically as the reporter asks Bill what he means.

'That they've been better to me than I've deserved, and I'm grateful to them for it. My neighbours now are the best I've ever had; they barely know me, and they care about me even so. They looked out for me even before those blasted notices came, and they've done even more since. They're the ones who told me to get in touch with you, and they're the ones giving this fight everything they've got, to make sure we don't all lose our homes.'

Levon sniffs. Alice reaches down and laces her hand into his.

'Mr Coates, I hope it's not insensitive for me to share with our viewers that while Leeds Housing Federation declined to comment, when we contacted Gatsby Luxury Apartments, they said they have no intention of cancelling the scheduled demolition of your house and the others on this street. What would you tell those viewers about that?'

'Aye, it looks pretty hopeless, I'll admit it. But I wanted to talk to you anyway. What good does it do to hide away and pretend it's not happening?' Bill's voice wavers, but he steels himself and continues. 'At least this way I can hold my head high and know I did my bit. I know my Sal would have been proud of that.'

'So what will you and your neighbours do once you've been evicted?'

Bill gives a huffing shrug. 'No clue. Can't imagine being anywhere else. And if me making a show of myself accomplishes nowt else, I want people to think about what they'd do, if they got a letter like that on the doormat one day. Old codgers like me, we know how vulnerable we are. Nowt you can do to avoid knowing it, at my age. But young 'uns like to think they're invincible. I know I did when I were younger. And then something like this, it's devastating. My neighbours don't deserve it. Not in any case, but especially not with all the good they do in the world.'

'What do you mean?'

'There's my next-door neighbour. Alice, her name is.' Alice yelps when she hears her name said. 'Oh god,' she mumbles, 'here we go.'

But Bill is still speaking: 'She's a single mum to a lovely wee bairn *and* she works in a school. She's got her hands full, I can tell you, but she's still always offering to help me.' He pauses and then adds, 'Not that I take her up on it anywhere near as much as I should.'

'No, you don't, you cranky old git,' Alice heckles the laptop, her smile making her cheeks ache.

'Then there's Levon,' Bill continues, warming up now he's built his confidence. 'He works at the library, and he knows everything about the local community round here. Helps everyone, and never asks for owt in return.'

Levon squeezes Alice's hand tight and doesn't stop.

'And AJ, he works at the hospital, sorting people out when

they're poorly and in pain. And there's a young lass, Jessie, she's studying. Can't be doing any of them any good, can it, to be facing all this stress and uncertainty?'

Jessie hip-bumps AJ and he chucks his arm around her shoulders, pulling her into his side.

'So,' the reporter says, a devil's-advocate archness creeping into their tone. 'What's your response to those who say investment and redevelopment is a necessary process for areas like this?'

'Necessary?' Bill's impressive eyebrows meet in the middle, scandalised by the suggestion. For a moment, Alice sees his face crumpling, almost in slow motion, and thinks again how certain angles and moments make him look so old. But then he rallies, his voice staying calm and level and his emotions written all over his face.

'What's necessary is having a roof over your head. Our houses have stood here long enough. Nothing to stop them standing decades more, other than pure greed. Who benefits from that? A few people whose wallets get fatter. And who gets hurt?' His voice cracks again, and a tear trickles down his cheek. 'Me and my neighbours, and all the other people in every house and every street that they decide to do this to once they've got away with doing it to ours.'

The camera cuts away. *William Coates there, resident of Leodis Street, scheduled for demolition on Monday*, the voice-over summarises. The shot pans down their street, holding on each of their front doors in turn, then zooms in on the hoardings around the bulldozers assembled at the end of the street. Fadeout.

For a moment, they all continue staring at the laptop screen. None of them wants to break the spell by speaking first. But then Jessie whistles, long and loud.

'Why did none of you tell me that grumpy old mofo was such a *player*?' AJ puts her in a headlock and ruffles her spiky hair until it's a chaotic mess.

'Why are you always so inappropriate?'

'Shut up,' she cackles, fighting him off. 'You love it.'

Alice is still gazing blankly ahead. Levon nudges his shoulder into hers. 'Alice? You okay?'

'We have to go,' she says, and even though the words come out soft, they make the kitchen go quiet. 'We have to go next door and tell him how amazing he was.' *If I don't do it right this instant*, she thinks, *I'll start crying and never stop.*

'Absolutely,' Levon concurs. 'That was incredibly brave.'

'It was baller,' Jessie confirms, ducking out of the way before a snickering AJ can mess her hair up again.

They move towards the door.

'You think he'll want to talk to us this time?' AJ asks.

'He will,' Alice says, scooping Mollie up and onto her hip.

They troop round, a strange procession with Mollie in her unicorn onesie and AJ still without shoes. Mollie demands to be the one to knock on the door.

There's the same shuffle-clunk as before, and this time Bill doesn't give his usual suspicious peer through a narrow gap.

'Oh aye,' he mumbles, leaning on the door to ease it back wide as it'll go. 'Here they are, then.'

'We saw you on the news.'

'You were amazing.'

'That was so brave, Bill, honestly.'

'It. Was. Epic.'

He blushes so hard even the tips of his ears turn pink.

'Gi' over,' he says, with a shadow of his former scowl. 'It were nothing. I should have done it before now, when there might have actually been time for it to help.'

'Don't say that,' Levon reprimands. 'You told your story, and all of ours. That was the most any of us could have done.'

'Well, my Sally would've given me what for if she'd been here to see me moping. Couldn't carry on letting her down like that, and letting all of you down 'n' all.'

From the doorstep, Alice pushes forward to give him a one-armed hug. She's still holding Mollie, who squeals in delight and strokes Bill's bald head with the utmost gentleness, like he's a beloved but skittish pet. Bill's arm hovers, then closes round Alice's back, holding her a moment then patting between her shoulder blades as Alice disentangles the three of them.

'She'd be really proud of you, Bill. I know she would. You did us all proud.'

'Behave,' he grouses, but there's a pleased gruffness to his voice. 'Just wanted to do me bit.' He meets Alice's gaze. 'S'pose I should be grateful to you, lass. That letter you wrote really helped me see sense. It's been a long time since I was around anyone who cared that much, about anything. Didn't realise I were missing it so much. S'pose sometimes it hurts more to care, but it's worth it, isn't? Some things are worth caring about.'

'Amen,' AJ chips in, when Alice only nods like she doesn't trust herself to speak. AJ's so tired he's swaying where he stands, arms hugged round himself but a giant grin on his face. Jessie hangs back, half-hidden behind Levon and semi-shy now they've done their initial gushing. Now she's meeting him properly, Bill reminds her of her long-gone grandad, a barely remembered figure who comes to her in a swirl of recollections about sitting on his knee to watch *Only Fools and Horses* reruns, terrible knock-knock jokes and caterwauling along to the Pogues in the kitchen at Christmas.

Bill's grouchy tortoise face is even more endearing in real life than on-screen, and Jessie finds herself wanting to sit him down and ply him with toffees and tea and get him to tell her all his stories. Of all the reading she's been doing for her history coursework, the bits she's loved most are the personal accounts: the oral histories recorded on radio, the interview transcripts. Real people sharing their memories of how things were, in their real voices, with none of the mumbles or slang or sarcastic asides taken out. *He's definitely got some anecdotes in him*, Jessie thinks, and when she wonders about all the things he's experienced during his decades on the street, the synapses in her brain start sparking. She wants him to tell her any stories his parents had, about the war and its aftermath. What he remembers of the rubble and ruins left behind in the city centre after the Blitz. She wants to know Bill's take on the Chapeltown riots in the eighties, whether he knew anyone involved in what happened then or in the miners' strikes. Whether he was ever a mod, a rocker or a punk. It makes it more real, to know someone who's lived through so much change in one place, seen culture shapeshift round him through the decades. *He might be up for it*, she thinks. *He's agreed to be interviewed once already, hasn't he? I could interview all of them, about their time on the street and the other places they've lived. So those memories don't disappear, even if the places and people do.* And the thought gives her a sense of what it might be like if she gets into university. Things that she could do on her own but probably wouldn't, but if she could do them as part of a project, with support and structure, and other people in her corner, that could be another story. Could be possible. Could be good.

She comes back to herself to find that Mollie's wriggled down from Alice's hold and is knocking on one of Jessie's legs like she's banging on a door. Jessie picks her up and Mollie gets comfortable in her arms, her head against Jessie's collarbones. Alice glances towards them, giving a relieved nod to see Mollie's not causing chaos, then turns back to Bill, who's been confiding about how he'd had to work up himself up to making the phone call to set up the interview.

'How did you even get in touch with the reporter?' AJ asks. 'No wonder she didn't ring us back. Not when she had the star attraction all lined up.'

'Aye,' Bill mumbles. 'She said you'd been phoning. You told me her name when you were here, didn't you? And then the next time the news were on, I saw her. Knew who you meant. You were right, I had seen her before. So I wrote the name down, then rang up directory enquiries. They got me through to reception, at the news station. I said who I wanted and that were that.'

'You should have told us,' Alice says. 'We'd have helped.'

'I know you would. But I were being a coward. Didn't want you to know till it was done. Didn't want to let you down last minute if me nerves got the better of me or I mucked it up somehow.'

'And have you seen it? On the news?'

'Oh aye,' he says, flushing again and gesturing indoors. 'Had to check they weren't just having me on, didn't I? Had the news on with me breakfast, just in case, but I didn't want to get my hopes up, you know. They did warn me they couldn't guarantee it was going to make it on. "You never know what's going to happen, with news." That's what she said. And I thought that might've been her way of letting me down gently, that maybe I hadn't done a good enough job.' He recalls it with a snort, as though irritated with himself for having been so unsure. 'She said she were pleased, when they were going, but she could have just been humouring me, couldn't she? So I told myself it probably weren't going to be on, that I was just watching to make sure. But I suppose there were nowt more important happening today.' Bill's face crinkles, proud but bashful. 'So they were stuck with me after all. Just like you lot have been.'

There's a ripple of rueful low laughs. And Levon, of course, wants to reassure Bill, saying how they've all been stuck with each other, how he should have tried harder, earlier, to get to know everyone, to form stronger connections from the start.

'It took me a while to get myself settled in Leeds,' he says. 'I think I'd got used to being an outsider, first by coming to England and then later by choice. I just assumed I'd always be on my own. And then the library was my gateway to the local community here, and I started putting down roots. So I shouldn't have left it so long to get to know my own neighbours. I was foolish to leave it as long as I did.'

'Not your fault,' Bill chips in. 'I've played me part in that 'n' all. It's not always been my cup of tea, living here. There's been some over the years who've made me want to move. But this –' he lifts his stick and gestures to them '– this is the best it's been in a long time. You've made it better. You've made me want to be better. I never thought I'd know my neighbours' names again. Didn't even realise I did until that camera was filming. Houses are just bricks and mortar and memories, but this is real. That's worth saving. And I'm not going to my grave knowing I didn't do what I could.'

'Great minds think alike,' Alice says, and expands on the plan from her letter about staying put as long as possible on demolition day.

'Good for you,' he says. 'I'm staying put too. They can pull it down on top of me if it comes to that. Wouldn't be the worst fate, going out in the same place I came in.'

'It won't come to that,' Levon soothes.

'Even if it does,' Bill says, 'this is my home and I'm going nowhere.' And he raps his walking stick on the door frame as if to say *that's that*.

# CHAPTER TWENTY-FIVE

When they get back from their visit to Bill's, Alice's emotions are all churned up. The hope and warmth from watching his interview is a precious bright bubble she doesn't want to burst, but she's still terrified about Monday. She makes herself concentrate on getting ready. Mol's buzzing with excitement about getting to spend an entire weekend with her dad again, and so selecting the correct toys, books and outfit for the occasion takes some time. Mollie packs and repacks the ladybird rucksack she uses for nursery, then steals a tote bag from Alice's room and fills that with other essentials, before donning shiny purple leggings decorated with silver cobwebs. Alice has a sneaking suspicion this new-found obsession with the macabre is somehow Jessie's fault, but whatever. *The kid's due a goth phase sooner or later.* She can't face one of Mollie's meltdowns today. Alice stands on the landing, listening to the toddler chattering away to herself, hoping hard that this isn't the last time Mollie gets to roam through these rooms. That this won't be her last memory of the time they spent together here.

It gives Alice a wrench to remember all the child development textbooks she's read, whether for work or back when
she was pregnant, devouring every scrap of info she could
that might help her feel ready for what was to come. Now,
she recalls phrases like *attachment object* and realises that
while it might seem ridiculous for Mollie to need six books,
four teddies, a pair of sunglasses and glittery wellies to go to
her dad's for the weekend, a place where Sam definitely has
all the essentials covered, Mol probably just wants to have
things with her that remind her of Alice, of home. Alice has
to grip tight to the door frame, remembering Mollie snoozing in a soft warm bundle against her chest when she finally
got the keys from the council and worked out how to jiggle
the lock just right to get inside the damp-warped front door.
She knows it's for the best not to have Mollie with her on
Monday, but she wishes it didn't have to be that way. Mol
makes her braver. That's how it's always been. And the possibility that she'll have to explain to Mollie later that the only
real home she's ever known has gone, that Alice never gave
her a chance to say goodbye to the building where she grew
from a peaceful silver-eyed baby into a proper tiny human –
that feels too big to even comprehend. *I really hope you don't
have to go through this in therapy later*, she thinks, as Mollie
pirouettes into her bedroom doorway, announcing that she's
ready to go. *I hope I'm not explaining it in therapy later, either*,
she snorts to herself, and then ducks into her own bedroom
and looks in the mirror. Black jeans with rips in both knees, a
faded racerback vest with the Aerosmith insignia and scuffed
but comfy silver trainers. Alice brushes three thick coats of
black mascara onto her upper and lower lashes, then paints
on liquid eyeliner in fat swoops that flick out at the corners
of her eyelids. *There*, she thinks, stepping back and checking

over her reflection again. *You look tough, you coordinate with your unseasonably goth kid, and now you've got a really good reason not to cry.*

'Okay,' she calls to Mollie, who's bidding a dignified good-bye to the teddies that didn't make the final line-up and the snake plant Levon brought to that first meeting, now living on Mollie's sunny windowsill. 'Let's get this show on the road.' They walk the long way round to the bus stop, not passing the hoardings on the park.

'There she is!' Sam opens the door to Mollie's knock with all the energy of a coked-up children's TV presenter. She squeals, leaps into his outstretched arms and he spins her around on the doorstep then lowers her and lets her scurry off into his house.

Once Mollie's inside, the performance slips. When he turns back to Alice, she can see he's not his usual self.

'No offence, Sam,' she says, as he gestures for her to follow their daughter inside. 'But you look like shit. What's going on?'

'You look like Helena Bonham Carter,' he retorts, eyeing Alice's wild hair that's been given one of Mollie's 'makeovers' on the bus ride over. 'Is this the reason my daughter looks like she's on her way to audition for a Tim Burton film?'

Alice drops Mollie's bag onto Sam's charcoal-grey settee. His living room has cool blue walls, dark varnished floorboards and a giant yucca tree taking up one corner. It's zen enough that it brings Alice's heartbeat back to a tolerable tempo, and makes her curious about whether Sam's sporadic attempts at getting into meditation have finally stuck. His Headingley flat is in a converted mansion; it's got a massive stained-glass window and a balcony that looks over a communal garden. It's beautiful, but more anonymous than it should be given he's lived here since their split.

Sam always said Alice was too much of a nester, that they'd go to parties, lose track of each other for hours and then whenever he finally found her, she'd be settled in some corner as though she'd never been anywhere else. Sipping mushroom tea from jewel-bright Moroccan glasses on a beanbag in someone's bedroom, a new best friend she'd met that night braiding her hair or reading her tarot cards.

'Why is it,' he'd asked once, as they made their way home through the Hyde Park dawn, 'that everywhere I find you ends up looking like an illustration from an arthouse film or a really strange children's book?'

She'd tucked herself into his side. 'I have no idea what that means.'

He slid an arm round her waist, brushed a kiss to her hair. 'Adorable, but weird.'

'Thank you?'

'You're welcome.'

Standing in Sam's lounge, Alice remembers that exchange, and recognises that it's a skill, her ability to make anywhere magical. Not everyone's got it, she sees that in Sam's flat. She can tell he's done his best to make this place a home; the mantelpiece has several framed photos of Mollie, and the home cinema and gaming system show how he spends his time in this room. But it isn't loved the way their place is.

The kitchen is messier, in a comforting way, and Alice examines the chaotic overlap of photos stuck to the fridge while Sam fills the kettle. She sees Sam and his siblings, dressed up for someone's wedding, holding champagne flutes and beaming. There's his parents, in fancy dress as Gomez and Morticia Addams, his dad suave and moustachioed in a pinstripe suit, his mum in a long black wig and vampy dress. There are tons of Mollie, growing up across the jumbled collage, from the shadowy ultrasound printout to blowing out candles on her last birthday, glitter face paint turning the toddler's puffed-out cheeks into sparkling butterfly wings. There's none of Alice. *Why would there be?* She focuses on Sam instead of this absence.

'So you're sure you don't mind having her?' she asks.

'You kidding? I've missed her.'

'But what if something happens with your mum?'

'She's sound now,' Sam tells her, a shadow flitting over his face before he meets her gaze and smiles. 'Honest. Or out of the woods, anyway.'

'But what if there's an emergency?'

Sam stares her down. 'I'll take Mol with me.'

'You can phone me, you know. If anything happens.'

He snorts, turning from the cupboard with cups in both hands. 'Aren't you going to be chained to a radiator or something?'

Alice sighs. 'Not unless things take an unexpected turn.'

She'd told Sam everything, in the end. She needed to explain why he had to take Mollie, and she felt she owed him the truth. He'd taken it in stride more than she'd expected, but at the time she'd written it off as him having been too distracted recently to properly process anything else. But now Sam's watching her and Alice can't tell what he's thinking.

'What are you going to do?' he asks, 'if they find a way to force you out?'

Alice zips the pendant on her necklace back and forth on its chain and makes herself meet Sam's gaze. 'Sort something out.'

He puts the mugs on the counter. 'Like what?'

'Stay with Mum and Dad for a bit.'

'In France, you mean?'

Alice grimaces and shrugs.

'No way.' He points a spoon at her in accusation. 'We have to be in the same city.'

She laughs, confused by the intensity of this reaction. 'For Mol, I mean,' he adds, and turns away to pour the water.

*Change the subject*, Alice thinks. 'You're sticking here for now, then?' They'd had a brief exchange, over text message, at one point, when things with his mum were looking bad. About whether Sam might have to move back home to help out his dad. But the conversation was all speculation, and Sam pulls a face now at this reference to it.

'I reckon we're past the danger point, so I'm staying put. And honestly, Lish, you've been a star. I know you've been juggling a lot and shit's been hitting the fan, but you've still checked in on me. Not many people have done that.'

Alice narrows her eyes. 'Who else have you told?'

He pulls a face, opens the fridge for milk and makes a non-committal noise from behind its door. Suspicions confirmed.

'Still shit at asking for help, then?'

'Pot. Kettle. Black.'

'What about Yulia?' Alice says his girlfriend's name as casually as she can, not wanting any accidental tone to start an argument.

Sam rakes a hand through his hair. 'She's staying with her cousin in Hebden Bridge. She got hardcore into Extinction Rebellion, and then things spiralled a bit. She's not sure what she wants or where she sees herself. She says I'm a "typical beige man" –' he clowns the air quotes, one hand still holding the spoon '– and I need to think about that.'

Alice chews her bottom lip to stop herself from laughing. 'Wow,' she deadpans.

Sam sees right through it and pulls a face in reply. 'I know.'

'So have you?'

'What?'

'Thought about it.'

He stirs the tea and doesn't meet her eyes. 'I've had other things on my mind.'

'Me too.'

'You know –' Sam passes her the mug, their fingers just brushing on the handle of the cup '– you could always move in here.'

'Get lost.' The words fall out of Alice's mouth on instinct, before she even has time to think of a reply.

'Could be good,' he says. 'The three of us.'

For a moment, she imagines it. Someone to share things with at the end of the day. Someone to split chores and bills with. Someone to be there for Mollie, on more than just alternate weekends. But the vision of it doesn't do anything. Doesn't connect.

'We were kids, last time we tried this,' Sam continues. 'We're not kids any more.'

'I still feel like a little kid.' Alice puts down her mug. 'And about a million years old. At the same time. That shouldn't be possible, should it? It's messed up.'

Sam grins and slurps his tea. 'Everything's messed up,' he mumbles, into his cup.

'Like us when we were together,' Alice snarks back. She keeps her tone as light as she can but she wants to deflect, alleviate some of the pressure that's building up in her chest. Even as she says it, she knows it's not true. Things between them were mostly glorious, that's what made its ending so heartbreaking. Her body and brain irreversibly changed by pregnancy and birth, their relationship collateral damage of the post-natal depression that eclipsed everything, the long shadow it left even once they'd decided to separate. They did the right thing. Alice knows that. But she grieved so hard for it at the time that even the idea of getting back together makes panic start to crackle through her veins.

Sam keeps his gaze locked on Alice. 'So that's a no, then?'

*Remember that conversation we had in the mirror about not crying? You don't want to walk out of here looking like the Joker, do you?* 'Sam, come on.' Alice's voice comes out sad and tired round the lump in her throat. 'I can't think about this now. My head's way too mashed.'

Then Sam pushes himself forward from the counter he's been leaning on with sudden purpose.

*Please don't try to kiss me.* The thought zips through Alice's brain too fast for her to even process, and her body floods with adrenaline, unsure what to do. But Sam's not coming towards her. He's grabbing for the fridge door handle.

'You're right,' he says, face hidden from her again. 'Fuck that. Beer?'

Alice slumps against the cooker and lets a hysterical laugh bubble up. 'Fine. Whatever. Why not?'

They leave their tea to go cold on the counter and let Mollie lead the way down into the garden, where she inspects every corner for fairies and frogs and Alice and Sam sit on the flagstones, backs against the sun-warmed wall, drinking their bottles of beer.

Alice watches ants clamber over each other in a frantic black seam between the paving slabs, then tips her head back against the bricks and lets the sunshine come through her closed eyes.

'I'd better go,' she says, not moving. 'You two gonna be good?'

'Pizza and ice-cream sleepover? Hell yeah.'

'What about tomorrow?'

'There's a fair in Meanwood Park. Rides, music, petting zoo. We're going to get absolutely off our tits on candyfloss.'

Alice cocks one eyebrow but doesn't rise to this bait. 'And Monday?'

'No plans yet.'

'You're not working?'

He shakes his head. 'Took some time off between contracts when Mum was ill. Got another week till the next one starts.'

'So you'll be okay?'

'Alice,' he says, sighing with exasperated affection. 'Babe. Please trust me, okay? I got this. I got you. Whatever you need.'

She scrunches her face up but doesn't argue.

'So you've booked Monday off work?' Sam prompts.

'Yeah. Not sure what I'll do from there. See what happens, I suppose.'

'Have you even told them what's going on?'

'No.'

Sam looks sidelong at her as he tips the last gold drops into his mouth.

'Shut up,' Alice tells him, before he can answer.

'They might know by now, anyway.'

Alice whips her head round. 'What?'

'I mean, I saw your neighbour, that old guy. On the news. And online. You don't think someone from school might have seen it too?'

'Even if they have. How would they know it's my street he's talking about?'

'They might.'

'It's not like I've lied about anything. I'm taking a personal day. Probably to watch my house getting demolished from inside a police van.'

Sam snorts. 'Pretty solid excuse for a day off. Better than going the dentist.'

'Thanks. Wish it weren't true, though.'

'Keep in touch, yeah, Lish? You need us, we can be there.'

'I don't want Mollie in the middle of things.'

'I get that. But if you change your mind, just say the word.'

'Cheers.'

She calls Mollie over, gives her approval to each of the toddler's newly found treasures (a pearly-pink snail shell, a leaf she claims is an entrance ticket to a goblin castle in the nearby oak, and a mouldy cork with a shiny fat beetle clinging onto one end), then kisses her goodbye.

She leaves them in the garden and makes her way out of Sam's avenue, onto the main road. Revelling in the rare opportunity for a long walk without Mollie's little legs to contend with, Alice ignores the exhausted drag in her limbs and stomps straight past the bus stop and the nearby parade of shops, only stopping to thread in her headphones and turn the music up, loud. It's hot, and even though it's not long past noon, every beer garden she passes is full. In a typically British response to the sunshine, everyone she passes on the pavements is wearing next to nothing. Alice weaves past two topless lads carrying a case of lager towards the park, passing the post office, the Oxfam bookshop and a series of cocktail bars before turning off Otley Road onto Wood Lane. The quiet road is bordered by low sandstone walls and trees with lush, low-hanging branches that cast the lane in a shifting lace of shadow and sun. Alice slows her pace, enjoying the cool breeze on her bare arms and the thundering drums in the song she's listening to, grateful for the chance to turn her brain off for a while.

Halfway home and wishing she'd thought to put on sun cream, Alice turns onto Potternewton Road and ducks into a corner shop, intending to grab a bottle of water. Inside, it's blissfully cold, her skin goosebumped but relieved after the relentless heat. Trance-like, she mooches up and down aisles of cut-price booze and snacks: gooey cakes in plastic packets, boxes of crisps, bottles of fruity cider and punnets of strawberries in a humming fluoro-lit chiller. The lad behind the counter ignores her; he's battling long rolls of lottery scratchcards into their dispenser, clingfilm wrapped round his forearm, its wrinkled layers hiding the details of what must be a brand new tattoo. As she queues at the till, she hears the news coming from a small paint-spattered radio wedged into the behind-the-counter rack of cigarettes and painkillers. The few words she hears are about the vegan weekender at the market, and the punk festival taking over Temple Newsam at the start of June. Alice wonders briefly if the TV channel that put Bill on has syndicated their interview with him to radio too, whether there's a chance of his voice reaching people while they grab their snacks and supplies for a sunny Saturday. For a moment, she thinks about asking the lad who's ringing up her can of G&T and salted caramel Magnum, but before she can work out how to explain her question he's already handing over her change.

Back at home, Alice paces round her house, unable to settle. *This is limbo*, she thinks to herself. *And it's weird*. On the ten o'clock news that night, she watches Bill's segment get repeated, his interview followed this time by one with Paul Buchanan, a brash statement from behind the desk of his swanky office. 'We regret the impact on the residents of

236

Leodis Street,' he'd said, in a bored, irritated tone. 'But we have no intentions to delay or cancel this project. We will be moving forward with the development as planned.'

*Fuck you*, Alice thinks, nausea and fury swirling through her system as she turns off the TV. *No you won't.*

And that's when there's a knock at the front door.

# CHAPTER TWENTY-SIX

'Jessie?' Alice asks. 'What's wrong?'

'Couldn't sleep,' the teenager says, shrugging apologetically on Alice's doorstep. 'And I saw your light was on. But I can go if . . . ' She trails off.

'Shut up,' Alice says. 'Come in.'

Jessie's wearing pyjama bottoms printed with grinning ice-cream cones and cartoon suns, and a T-shirt for a band that look like heavy-metal bondage ballerinas, the sleeves hacked off and trailing loose threads. Alice ushers her into the lounge. After being alone with her brain eating itself for the past few hours, she's relieved to have some company.

'Have you eaten?'

'Sort of,' Jessie replies, folding herself into a ball on the sofa and hugging her knees. 'Not really.'

'What does that mean?'

'Made another attempt at meeting up with Mum. She said she wanted to buy me lunch. You know, as a sorry for not being around. But we just ended up arguing again. I walked out halfway through my pizza.'

'Babe, I'm sorry.'

''S okay,' Jessie wipes her nose with the back of her hand, reminding Alice of Mollie. 'Levon knocked on before, he gave me some pastries he's made.'

'He did?'

'I've got some for you too,' Jessie says, gesturing to her rucksack. 'He made a shit-ton, from the sound of it. Wanted to use up all his ingredients, he said.'

The impact of that is all the louder for staying unsaid.

'We can talk about it, if you want,' Alice offers. 'Things with your mum. But I reckon we should order food first. You only getting to eat half your pizza is one tragedy too many.'

Jessie is instantly cheered by this suggestion, unravelling her long limbs to take over the entire sofa. 'Sounds like a plan.'

They find a local pizzeria that has a vegan option Jessie deems acceptable and an obnoxiously cheesy one for Alice. Order placed, Jessie excavates the plastic container of pastries from Levon and then digs in her rucksack again.

'Drink?' she asks, and unveils an amber glass bottle.

From her armchair, Alice squints at the label. 'What even is that? Tequila?'

Jessie holds it up to the light. 'Another peace offering from Mum. She went to Tenerife with her boyfriend, brought me this back from duty-free.'

'Sadly, Jessie, I think my days of tequila shots might be behind me.'

'Such a grown-up,' Jessie snarks, with a roll of her eyes.

'I seem to remember *someone* standing in my kitchen yesterday going on about being an adult.'

Jessie waves this away. 'Barely,' she scoffs. 'Not like you.'

'We're all faking it, though. You know that, right?'

Jessie scrunches her face in disbelief. 'Not you.'

'Definitely me,' Alice tells her, recalling her earlier chat with Sam. 'Making it up as I go along, all the time.'

'Nah.'

'It's true. I still feel like a teenager inside. And you've had to face way more than most teenagers. You should give yourself some credit for that. You're smart, and resilient, and creative. Those three things will see you far.'

Jessie folds her knees up, resting her face against them, and huffs a massive sigh. 'Not if they bulldoze my house with me inside it.'

'So dramatic. That's not going to happen.'

'It might.'

'In that case, maybe we do need a drink.'

Alice grabs the bottle of tequila from beside the settee and takes it into the kitchen, fixing Kahlúa over ice for herself and a tequila and orange juice for Jessie. She leaves the bottle in the kitchen when she takes the drinks through. This tentative ceasefire with Jessie is fragile but sweet, and Alice doesn't want it sabotaged by either of them getting too pissed.

When their food comes, they wolf the pizzas straight from the boxes. Then they devour Levon's baking as dessert. After that, Jessie empties the rest of her cavernous rucksack: a folded bundle of fabric and a rattling selection of luminous spray-paint cans.

'I know we didn't really reach a conclusion on this, before,' she says, going coy and then defiant. 'But I brought the stuff to make banners. You know, if we want.'

Alice yawns, stretching out on the rug and surveying the supplies. 'That's amazing. You had all this to hand?'

Jessie shrugs. 'I went to the art shop on my way home. Needed some retail therapy after seeing my mother, and this has the potential to be pleasingly cathartic and therapeutic.'

'You're brilliant. But I think I might be in too much of a carb coma to be artistic tonight. Can we make them tomorrow?'

'We don't have to,' Jessie blurts, scrabbling to collect the paints.

'No,' Alice tells her. 'We should. We will. But it's been a long day. So let's do it when I'm more awake, okay?'

Jessie nods. They put a film on, settle in their respective corners of the room. Calmed by the background noise, the company and her carb-heavy stomach, Alice lets the day's tensions slip away, dozing off then waking with a start to a dark room. Jessie's turned the lamps off, so the room's lit only by the fairy lights and the glow from the muted TV screen. Alice sits upright, a blanket that definitely wasn't there before slipping from her shoulders.

'Hey,' Jessie acknowledges, from the sofa, removing her headphones. 'Sorry. I didn't want to leave without you being awake to lock up behind me.'

'No,' Alice tells her. 'It's fine.' She nods to Jessie's phone, which she's been watching so as not to disturb Alice. 'What are you watching?'

Jessie pulls a face. 'It's stupid.'

'Well, now you have to tell me.'

'I went down a rabbit hole of activist occupation strategies. Stuff they do to avoid getting moved.'

'Like what?'

'Locking on, they call it. When they bolt themselves to things that are hard to move. Or glue, that's another one.'

'Is this for Monday?'

A shadow crosses Jessie's face. 'I don't know. Maybe. Knowledge is power, right? Isn't that what Lev says?'

'So what's that one you're watching now?'

Jessie's face darkens even more. 'Like I said, I went down

that rabbit hole. And now I'm just watching highlight reels of different demolitions. It's, like, a thing. That people get all excited about. I don't know why I clicked the first one. Morbid curiosity, maybe? And now I'm like an hour in and I can't seem to stop.'

'An hour in? How long have I been asleep?'

Alice digs between the cushions for her phone to check the time, then gives a snort of disbelief. 'Right,' she says. 'Definitely my bedtime. You staying over?'

'Can I?' Surprise curls through Jessie's answer, like it's strange to even be offered.

'Course,' Alice tells her. 'On one condition.'

'What?'

'You stop watching those,' she says, pointing to Jessie's phone, and balls the blanket Jessie had draped over her, dropping it over the teenager's head as she leaves the room.

# CHAPTER TWENTY-SEVEN

'Oi. Alice. Wake up.'

'What?'

'It's me. Jessie.'

'I know that.' Alice's voice is groggy, muffled by her pillow. 'Why are you here?'

'You let me stay, remember? But I can go if that's not cool, I—'

'I meant why are you here? In my bedroom. On the one day Mol isn't here and I can have a lie-in.'

'Bollocks,' Jessie mumbles. 'I never thought of that. It can wait. Sorry.'

'No. I'm awake now. What is it?'

'Um, something's happening. Online.'

'What is it?' Alice asks again.

'Can I come in?'

Alice puts a pillow over her head. One arm waves from behind it, beckoning Jessie further into the room.

Jessie comes closer. 'You know,' she says. 'You are *not* how I expected you to be in the mornings.'

'Neither are you,' Alice groans from under the pillow.

'I like mornings. That's when it stops being just me. I never sleep, and some nights just disappear, you know. I get sucked into something, then I look up and it's getting light. But other nights last for ever. And morning means it's over. So I'm not on my own any more.'

Alice pulls the pillow down and gives Jessie a look through bleary, mascara-smudged eyes.

'I mean, I am a dark and evil denizen of the night,' Jessie amends, to detract from this uncharacteristic sincerity. 'Sunlight flees before me. *Muahaha.*'

'Can the denizen of the night make coffee?'

Jessie gives a thoughtful hum. 'Yeah. But only if it's dark and evil coffee.'

'Sounds glorious. Almond milk and two sugars please.'

By the time Jessie returns, Alice is marginally more conscious, sitting on top of the covers in her pyjamas, still tangle-haired but teeth brushed, curtains and window open to let the sunshine in.

'What did you say before?' she asks, as she takes the mug from Jessie. 'About something happening?'

'Oh yeah. It's Bill.'

'What do you mean?' Alice sits up straighter, looking panicked. 'Is he okay?'

'See for yourself,' Jessie says, and slides her phone across the duvet cover towards Alice's fluffy-socked feet.

@BBCLeeds: VIDEO: Pensioner Bill Coates speaks about his upcoming eviction from his lifelong home in Leodis Street, Chapel Allerton: bit.ly/LeodisSt

1758 retweets, 312 replies

Alice boggles at the numbers, then clicks into the replies.

@ZenBen1973: I remember Bill! Lived on Leodis Street 1973-1986. Smashed my knee up coming off my bike outside his house when I was 10. Bill patched me up AND gave me a massive slice of the best carrot cake I've ever had. Total. Legend.

@YogiSuzie: @ZenBen1973 RU Ben w/ the blue bike?! I was three doors down, 1968-1978, think I used to babysit you sometimes! My Dad knew Bill, do you remember the Xmas he dressed up as Santa?

@ClaireBear5000: @YogiSuzie My Auntie Sue was good mates with Bill's wife Sally – when Sue got laid off one December Sal sent Bill round in a Father Christmas outfit with a sack of presents and a tin of mince pies. My cousins went on about it for YEARS, think it started a tradition!

@Robbo_B: We used to go trick or treating round Leodis Street at Halloween. One house always WENT FOR IT; dunno if it's the same guy but I can picture this Bill in a Frankenstein mask, top hat and tails, giving out toffee apples! Brings back memories!

@ShelleysSalon: Lodged with my Dad on Leodis Street when I was a student. Party animal phase, got halfway home one night before passing out on the playground. Sure this is the same bloke who found me on his walk to work and gave me a piggyback home!

@Stevie_LUFC: Remember Bill well from my landlording days at @WhiteHorseTavern, so glad to see he's still alive + kicking! Disgraceful action from local council, wouldn't you agree @MayorofLeeds?

@LeedsRollerDolls: Sad to see this. This guy seems like a class act! He deserves better than being hurled out of his house after so many years. #LeaveLeodisStStanding #LeaveBillAlone

@SalfordAllotmentPunks: Just spoken to our founder Baz who remembers being given food from Bill's folks' veg patch way back when! Totally outrageous the way he's been treated after such generosity!

@HydeParkBookClub: Breaks my heart to think of someone my grandad's age being treated this way. @MayorofLeeds sort it out hun! #JusticeForBill

@HousingAnarchyNow: Average rent increase over last year was higher in Leeds than London. Current housing system is unsustainable. WE NEED REVOLUTION.

@BlackHoneyGallery: Knew there was a reason everyone's moving out to Saltaire and Todmorden. No soul left in Leeds if these developers have their way. #RIPLeeds

@OldKeysTapHouse: Drinks on the house for Bill and anyone else living on Leodis Street! This area has changed so much since we took over the pub + we don't want to see real residents priced out!

@ChapelALibrary: Standing in solidarity with our library colleague Levon who is one of Bill's neighbours and also risking eviction. Sign the petition against the Leodis Street demolition: bit.ly/LeodisStPetition

There's a series of tweets from blue-ticked names that Alice doesn't recognise, but when she clicks through to their bios, she finds out that there are soap stars, musicians, artists and all sorts of other local celebrities, all coming out to voice their support for Bill. Alice's hands and feet start to prickle with pins and needles: she knows there's another storm in a teacup every day on Twitter, but after weeks feeling like it's just her and her neighbours against the world, having other people even know what's happening is a bittersweet relief. But then she sees something else.

'Jessie,' she says in a warning tone, still tunnel-visioned into the screen, scrolling and reading. 'What did you do?'

Alice holds up the phone, demanding an answer.

'Oh yeah,' Jessie shrugs, faux-casual but with a wicked gleam underneath. 'I took a photo of your letter and uploaded it. So people know we're not giving in.'

She takes the phone back from Alice, swipes through, then hands it back. Overnight, the letter has been shared thousands of times, the #DearNeighbour hashtag a constantly refreshing stream as more and more people comment. Some calling them all sorts, saying they're naive and stupid and living in a dream world, or tagging @WestYorksPolice. Those ones make Alice wince. But more, far more, are on their side, leaving hearts, raised fists, gifs of superheroes and people marching in the streets. Comments that say they're doing the right thing. Alice is torn between shocked joy at this flood of support, and her deep discomfort at the idea of so many people reading words she wrote in such a desperate, sleep-deprived haze. Words she never intended for anyone but her neighbours to see.

She drops the phone onto the duvet, meeting Jessie's gaze again, the teenager chewing a thumbnail and waiting for Alice's reaction.

'You should have told me you were going to do that.'

'Never lied though, did I, babe?' Jessie's sarcastic tone is an echo of Alice's words in their kitchen stand-off the other day, sucker-punching Alice in the gut. She grappled with her guilt for a long time that night: her lie by omission about what had happened with Paul *had* been misleading, and it nearly ruined all the tentative connections they'd been building.

'Suppose I deserve that,' she mutters to Jessie, whose smirk transforms into an adorable grin.

'Besides, you did make me promise to stop watching the demolition videos. Had to do something else instead, didn't I?'

Alice gives her a grouchy joke-glare.

'That's not all.' Jessie takes the phone from Alice's hand, taps on the screen a couple more times, then hands it back. 'Look at this.'

Alice presses play on the video Jessie's cued up. It's a clip from the local news studio, a robotically glamorous presenter in front of a panoramic backdrop of Leeds city skyline: the Dalek-looking tower of Bridgewater Place, the Sky Plaza student halls and the rust-coloured Jenga blocks of Broadcasting House.

'Yesterday,' the presenter announces, 'we brought you the story of Bill Coates, a lifelong resident of Leodis Street, which is scheduled for demolition tomorrow. Following our interview, we were contacted by many former Leodis Street residents keen to share their experiences, including Kyle Wallace, who joins us live now from Manchester.' The presenter cocks her head, listening to an earpiece, and the screen divides in half to show a man with a kind face, smart shirt and scruffy beard, beaming into the camera.

'Kyle, good morning. Thanks for joining us. Can you tell us what prompted you to get in touch?'

'Thanks, Angelina. I saw Bill on the news yesterday and just wanted to share my experience, really. I lived with Bill and his amazing wife Sally for eight years. Foster parents, you know. I was only eight when they first took me in, and I stayed until I was sixteen. My sister, she was a few years older than me, and when she was stable enough to have her own place, I moved out to live with her. But I wish I'd stayed, to be honest.' He breaks off, then continues. 'Because I never lived anywhere before or since that was as loving as with them. Things were all over the place for me for a long time after that, but I got myself sorted, got my own place. I work for a non-profit here in Manchester now, organising emergency housing for people that need it most. Because I'll never forget what a difference it made to me, having a safe place like that. That house has been that for so many people, it deserves a blue plaque or historic landmark status or something. Not just being torn down like it's nothing.'

'So when were you last in contact with Bill?'

'I've been sending letters the past few years, since his wife Sally died. Wanting to see how he is, you know. See if he needed anything. But Bill never answered. I thought maybe he'd passed away. But I kept trying. Just in case. I'd love to be back in touch with him. To be able to thank him properly for everything he did for me. To be able to have a pint with him and tell him everything I've done since, where I live and what I do. It's because of Bill I'm who I am. I'd love Bill to have the chance to get to know who that is, if he wants.'

'Despite having lived on the street his entire lifetime, Bill's house is one of several on the street scheduled for demolition next week. What do you think of that?'

Kyle gives his head a soft shake of disbelief. 'It's heart-breaking, honestly. I'm not against things changing, but it's got to be done responsibly. And I can't imagine Bill being anywhere else.'

The clip credits and ident flash up on the screen, with a line of text encouraging people to get involved in the discussion online. Alice looks up at Jessie.

'Wow,' she says. 'I never knew about that. Did you?'

Jessie shakes her head. 'But he's not the only one. Look at this.' She retrieves her phone from Alice's grip, cues another video and passes it back.

'What's this? Another news interview?'

'No. Someone recorded this themselves and put it straight online. It was an Instagram live, but they uploaded the video after. It's everywhere now.'

The video shows the head and shoulders of a tanned woman at a table, talking into a phone. The background is a chaotic, colourful room, with large paintings stacked against the wall behind her, hanging baskets of plants and at least three cats chilling in various positions. The speaker has a sweet but well-worn face: sea-green eyes framed by dyed blonde wavy hair and dangling earrings shaped like seashells that chime against the woman's cheeks as she speaks.

'Hello,' she says, then laughs, like she's been caught out by the sound of her own voice. 'It's Kiki, for anyone not already following. I don't usually do videos like this, but today I've got something I wanted to say. Some of you have probably seen an interview on the news with a man called Bill Coates, who's in danger of losing his house. Well, I lived with Bill and Sally for seven years, from age eleven until eighteen. They were my longest-term foster parents, and the best. By a long, long way. And you know what?' Kiki hesitates, then steels herself, her blonde curls and earrings bouncing with the resolute nod of her head. 'I made it really difficult for them. I'm not proud of it, but I put them *through* it. That's part of being a foster kid. You get in the habit of pushing the boundaries. By the time you've bounced round the system a bit, it gets hard to believe you're going to stay anywhere long-term. So you have to test people, find out what you can get away with. Where the lines are. Then at least you know where you're up to, you know?' A white cat walks in front of the camera and Kiki scoops it onto her lap and continues. 'I was eleven going on eleven hundred. Thought I knew *everything*. Always in trouble at school. And out of school. Fighting, stealing, you name it, I did it. Didn't take long for people to have had enough of me, and honestly, I can't blame them. But Sally and Bill, they were kind right from the start. They gave me my space. I didn't even talk to them for about a month when I moved in, but they weren't fazed. And when I got in trouble, they fought my corner. No one had ever done that for me before. So bit by bit, I started to settle in. And when I turned eighteen, they said I could stay, long as I wanted. They wouldn't have even got paid for that, unless they charged me rent, but they never asked for money. They wanted me to have a home. But I had all these ideas, about getting back in touch with my birth mum and buying this banged-up double-decker bus with my friend and fixing it up so we could go all round the world in it, and well ... ' She trails off, then comes back to herself. 'Short version is, I left. But I'd still get a birthday card from them every year. Usually months late by the time it got to me, not that that was their fault. I moved around a lot, sofa-surfing and staying with

251

mates. And not always with the sort of friends who are reliable about sending post on.' Kiki gives a snorty belly chuckle and widens her eyes, as if to tell her viewers they can infer what they want from that.

'Then one year,' she continues. 'The card didn't come. And I knew something must have happened.' She pauses again, gives a deep, sad sigh. 'By the time I got the invitation to the funeral, it had already been and gone.'

Kiki strokes the cat on her knee, her expression far away and then returning.

'Anyway,' she continues. 'I'm a foster mum myself now. Most of you know that already, that's probably why you're on my page. But I haven't talked much about my first experiences in fostering. That first time was a nightmare. They almost burnt the house down, and it *wasn't* an accident. Thought I'd made a huge mistake. But Bill and Sally never gave up on me. So I stuck it out. And now I have Alisha, who came when she was two years old. She's five now. We finalised her adoption paperwork last month.' Kiki ducks out down for a moment, showing that one of the canvases behind her is an in-progress painting, a portrait of her and a young girl. A half-completed background of vivid abstract swirls radiates energy and joy even though it's unfinished. Then Kiki retakes her previous position, addressing the phone camera once more.

'I never thought I'd have a proper family. But Bill and Sally showed me family can be so much more than blood. I'll always be grateful for that. When my letters didn't get answered, I thought Bill must have died too. I'm so happy to see he's still alive. And maybe he doesn't want anything to do with me, but even so. He's the closest thing to a dad I ever had.'

She takes a deep breath. 'So,' she starts, and then her voice breaks a bit before recovering. 'Dad.' Kiki gives another laugh at the unfamiliarity of addressing someone this way. 'I really hope you get to keep your house. But if you need it, there's always room for you here. You gave me a bed and so much more when I needed it. I can't ever repay everything you and Sally did for me. But it'd be a good start if I could do the same for you in return.'

Alice lowers the phone, eyes shimmery with tears, and looks at Jessie, who's curled her knees up, resting her face on them. 'Do you think he's seen those?'

'I don't know. Does he even have the internet? Or a mobile?'

'No clue. We have to show him, though.'

Jessie nods, but seems apprehensive. As though she's already had enough emotion for the day. 'Can we have more coffee first?'

'Did you even sleep?'

Jessie scrunches her mouth into a lopsided *not-really* expression. 'I was reading the anarchist Reddit. And the comments on your letter. Then I started refreshing the numbers on the petition. They've gone up, you know. By a lot.'

'Do you think it'll do anything?'

'I don't know.'

Once they're ready, they go next door to Bill's. There's no answer. Alice wonders where he'd have gone at this time on a Sunday morning, or if he's in but just ignoring them. They retreat to Alice's, where she makes more coffee and granola for breakfast while Jessie devours the last slices of yesterday's pizza.

It's weird without Mollie. It's weird being in her house for what might be the last entire day. Alice can't stop herself from touching everything as she moves from room to room. The walls. The light switches. The whistling bathroom tap that always spins round too far, unleashing a symphony of clanks from the pipes. It's all become impossibly precious, time slow-ing down and distorting, heightening everything.

*Come on*, she tells herself. *Snap out of it.* She clears the breakfast things away and tells Jessie to message AJ and Levon. 'If they're around and want to help us, tell them to come over whenever. Let's get your materials out and make these banners.'

After bickering about the joys and dangers of inhaling the spray paint fumes, they decamp to Alice's front garden. The sun has evaporated the morning dew, so they spread the fabric out onto the grass, debating slogans and designs.

It takes most of the day.

Jessie is a brilliant artist, but she keeps getting distracted by what's going on online: disappearing into a deep scroll then coming up with updated petition figures and the latest highlights of who's been sharing Bill's story and Alice's letter. Local politicians, punk bands, community groups. Everyone knows they're planning to stay in their homes until they're forcibly removed, and apparently everyone's got something to say about it. By lunchtime, Alice demands a phone amnesty, the constant drip-feed reminder of the outside world making her too anxious to concentrate. They sit on the steps and eat an improvised salad cobbled together after raiding their fridges. Half a packet of cashew nuts, an avocado, slices of apple. Pearl-sized baby tomatoes from Alice's windowsill, some heroically edible spinach leaves rescued from a soggy half-blackened bag. Levon emerges to give his oversight, claiming his back won't thank him for kneeling over the in-progress banners himself. He talks at length about what he knows about housing crises in other places, the way different groups have banded together to form alliances and resist. He quietly discourages Jessie from adding Satanic symbols to her design. AJ joins after work, sitting on the garden wall in his scrubs and teasing Jessie about having kept her artistic skills so well hidden until now.

By the time the sky has shifted from hard bright blue to dreamy red-gold, they're done.

'We don't want to leave tomorrow, right?' Jessie asks, standing back to admire the finished banners. 'Until we get dragged out? That means we need to do the photos now.'

Carefully manoeuvring the still-damp sheets of fabric, they each manage to get them into position, draping the banners from their upstairs windows, securing them between the windowpane and sill. Her own sign in place, Jessie returns to the street to direct the others. Using her phone, she snaps individual photos of each house, then walks to the corner to get as much of the street as she can in one shot. They reconvene in the road.

'I'll edit these to get the lighting better, then send them to the group chat,' Jessie tells them.

'Brilliant,' Alice says. 'Thank you.'

AJ and Levon echo the praise. Jessie rolls her eyes, blushing.

'No offence, everyone,' AJ says, as they continue to stare around the street, the sunset lengthening their shadows, 'but I'm gonna call it a night. I just shifted back from nights to days, and that always knocks me on my arse. And I probably don't wanna sleep through the stormtroopers breaking in to drag me out tomorrow, eh?'

Alice cringes at this image, then the surrealness of it gets to her again and she gives a dark laugh. 'Wouldn't be ideal,' she says. 'We should all get our rest. Whatever happens, we're going to need it.'

'Let's keep in touch,' Levon says. 'Jessie's idea for a group chat was a good one. Anyone needs anything, tonight or tomorrow, we've got each other. Even from separate houses, we can give moral support and help each other. We're in it together, right?'

'Together,' AJ echoes, and Jessie and Alice murmur the same. Alice glances back towards Bill's, but there are no lights on and no movement to be seen.

They say their goodbyes and head back indoors. Not long after, Alice's phone buzzes. It's the photos Jessie took: she's adjusted the colour, the contrast and the saturation, deepening the red brick of their houses so the banners are even more striking, the white fabric a glowing background to the bold, sharp-lettered words.

## PEOPLE NOT PROFITS

## WE SHALL NOT BE MOVED

## HOUSING IS A HUMAN RIGHT

And Alice's favourite, hanging from her bedroom window:

## SAVE OUR STREET

# CHAPTER TWENTY-EIGHT

Alice wakes up to the custom notification chime she still has for messages from Sam. The blue glow from her bedside clock says 6.17 a.m. She fumbles for the phone, her insides a storm of panic. Something's happened. With Mollie, with Sam's mum. She swipes the screen unlocked to a photo of Mol on Sam's balcony with the dawn coming up all technicolour and glorious. She's got a blanket hooded over her head like a shawled fairy-tale crone, hands emerging from the fabric folds to hold a pint tankard of what looks, from its sickly pink colour, to be strawberry milkshake. Mollie gazes out at the sunrise with a sleepy calm.

Remember when we used to be up this early bc we hadn't gone to bed? Those were the days! Good luck today Lish, thinking of you xxx

She flumps back into bed.

*This is it. Today's the day.* Ever since Alice wrote the letter swearing she'd stay put until the last possible moment, she's hoped it wouldn't come to this. She's not ready. If she has to do this, she wants to be like Tank Girl or Joan of Arc, all guns blazing and facing down destiny with bravery. *Never let 'em see you sweat.* That's what her dad used to say. She's not sweating now, but it's not because she feels invincible or righteous or any of those things. Everything is unreal. One of those vivid dreams where everything is almost like real life, but not quite, and it's difficult to pinpoint the differences. But there's an unsettled, foreboding atmosphere all the same. It reminds Alice too much of her time with PND, when even having a bath or getting dressed was like clawing through an invisible but noxious grey mist. And underneath the numb nightmare fog, Alice is *scared.* She can't shake the feeling she's made a mistake. She could get out now, pack the essentials in a suitcase, grab Mollie from Sam's and book a flight to France. Let her house be crushed into nothing and never look back. Find a new house, a new job. If she gets charged with trespassing like they threatened, that could be a nightmare turned into reality. Sam's told her anecdotes about his girlfriend's friends: climate-change activists who've been put in prison for trumped-up charges that should have never even got to court. She doesn't want to have to disclose any kind of criminal record to school, or have to meet with the safeguarding officer to decide if it'll cost her her job. Alice is even uneasy about the conversation with Sam yesterday. *What if he wants to punish me, for rejecting him? He could fight me for custody of Mol. If it came to a custody battle, couldn't an arrest record be twisted against me?* There's no end to the terrifying hypothetical futures she might be moving towards.

Alice decides to make the most of being up, scoffing at Jessie's judgement of her yesterday and wondering whether the teenager is already awake. She decides against messaging her to find out; with only hours left, every minute has become more precious than ever before. She stretches in bed, luxuriating in the cool silky texture of the sheets, the sunrise kaleidoscoping through the glass beads that hang from the curtain rail over her window. She takes a long bath, then makes herself breakfast. After yesterday, the fridge is bare, but she's got a few slices of bread left, and eggs. She makes French toast, filling the kitchen with the comforting smell of sugar and cinnamon. It takes her a long time to eat it, but she keeps going even once it's gone cold. *You'd better fuel up, bub. Going to be a long day.* She's talking to herself like a child, making her recall conversations with the school counsellor. 'Every child needs parenting, even our inner child.' *Fuck's sake.* It's exhausting, working so hard to do things right. To give herself gentleness or tough love in turns. She knows she should be practising mindfulness and self-compassion, that she should probably meditate or write down all the million thoughts spinning through her head. She should have meal-prepped healthy snacks or at least bought cereal bars so she doesn't pass out if they end up in some stand-off with the demolition crew all day and into the night. Should have bought bike locks to attach herself to the radiator pipe like in the activist tutorials Jessie showed her. She could have gone to the hardware shop on the high street, bought a bike chain. *Even a sex shop would probably have sold handcuffs.* She bites back a laugh at this train of thought. *Get a grip, Alice. No time to get hysterical.* She pushes away the plate. *Fuck it*, she thinks, and retrieves the half-empty bottle of tequila Jessie left behind. Alice does a shot, then another. The booze burns its way down her throat, curdling in her stomach. She tips the rest down the sink before she can change her mind, then heads back upstairs to get dressed.

Alice opts for the same denim pinafore she wore when she went to see the lawyer. *Not that it brought me much luck then*, she snorts to herself. But she wants to be comfortable. She does her make-up, in part because it's a soothing routine she can perform on autopilot and in part because there's a squirm of worry in her gut that with all the attention Bill's been getting online, some of the local press might send photographers.

That in itself doesn't bother Alice too much. She wants the world to see them, to see what they've been put through. But she doesn't want to look a mess. If she's going to get arrested and have it on camera, a photo that'll come up every time someone searches her name, haunt every job application or other attempt she makes to carve out a new future, she doesn't want the additional disgrace of looking shit. So she goes full Scouse, pencilling in her eyebrows, painting on thick eyeliner and threading the biggest hoops she owns into her ears.

Nine comes and goes and nothing happens, except Jessie messaging on the group chat to say she's posted the pictures of their banners. Perhaps it's the association with school, but Alice expected things to be underway by this time, and the waiting is driving her crazy. She doesn't want to go to the door. Adrenaline floods through her and pins her feet in place each time she flashes to the mental image of bulldozers grumbling towards the street. *I'll hear them coming. I don't need to see them. I'll know when it starts.* She stays in her bedroom like that's safer somehow, that anyone coming to drag her out will have to get through the bolted front door and then search each of the downstairs rooms for her before they venture this far. There's a strange nostalgia to it, too, like being back in her teenage bedroom, the walls decorated with posters, Polaroids and art, fairy lights on every surface, a rainbow of silk roses glued round the edges of her mirror. She'd spent so many hours in there rejecting the outside world entirely, wanting only to read or listen to music, ripping up charity-shop clothes and stitching them back together in ever-increasingly bizarre but brilliant configurations. Even during the times when she was banned from going out, when she'd broken the rules, stayed out past curfew or let her grades slip, the punishment of being confined to her room was no punishment at all, as long as she had her books, her laptop, her bass guitar and her sewing machine.

That bedroom was her sacred shine, with all its precious objects that would just be junk to anyone but her. And that's how she feels in her adult bedroom now: there's a heightened sense of meaning to everything. Everything in there is significant. The soap dish on her bedside table where she leaves her jewellery each night. Mollie's drawings tucked into the frame of the mirror. The ridiculous iridescent platform heels she'll probably never wear again but loves too much to get rid of. She tries to imagine these items, abandoned in the ruins, like TV footage in the aftermath of earthquakes, sifting through the rubble. One boot and a bent earring, left behind like relics. *Surely they can't. Surely they won't.* Alice tries to stop her thoughts from spiralling, but it's impossible. The end is here, it's happening, and Alice wants to appreciate every second she's got left.

*You're not dying*, she tells herself. *You'll survive. People live through worse every day.* But the idea of it still freezes her sobs in her throat. She can't get past it. She can't summon a vision of herself living anywhere but here. It's this or black nothingness, and that's scarier than all the other possibilities that keep whirling through her head. Alice doesn't know how long she's in this daze, but she comes to when she sees a couple she doesn't recognise walking, hand in hand, down the street. They're younger than Alice but not by much, and one of them heel-toes along the kerb like they're on a tightrope while the other one laughs, hip-bumping them off balance then grabbing them round the waist before they fall. The tightrope walker wears a polka-dot dress and has copper hair in perfect rockabilly rolls, while her partner is more androgynous, in combat pants and biker boots, their dark skin set off by close-shaved lime-green hair and matching metallic eyeliner so vivid Alice can see it from her upstairs window. They stop while the woman takes a photo of the broken street name sign on her phone, then continue down the road. They get closer to Alice's front door, pausing and conferring in low voices, spinning round to admire the banners and snap more pictures. As she watches, the two of them sit down on the pavement, their backs resting against the low wall at the bottom of Bill's path. From that angle, they're mostly hidden from Alice's view; all she can see is the tops of their heads, nestled close like they could be kissing, and the ends of their stretched-out legs.

Alice remembers the videos Jessie's been watching, of demolitions in all sorts of different places. *Have they come to watch? Is that a thing?* She'd prepared herself for the possibility of press, but she hadn't expected spectators too and the thought makes her feel sick. She moves away from the window.

Over the next half-hour, things escalate. A man who looks like a geography teacher wanders up like he's lost, then sits down beside the couple and starts to roll a cigarette. Three women in beautiful church clothes and head-wraps emerge from a taxi, and lean against the wall, bangles jangling as they talk. Soon after, they're followed by two lads on bikes. One wears a T-shirt that says EAT THE RICH in swirly glitter text, the other has dragon tattoos adorning both muscled arms and a dachshund puppy in the basket of his bike. They sit on the opposite pavement to the others, passing a can of energy drink back and forth, the dog racing round in circles on the end of its lead. *Surely they're not here to watch our houses getting destroyed? What sort of sick pleasure could they possibly get from that?*

A trio of women Alice vaguely recognises from the local roller derby league are next, although she might just be making that association because one has a pair of sleek black roller skates knotted by the laces to her rucksack. They know the boys with the dog, one of them diving across both boys' laps, followed by the puppy piling on top.

Over the next half hour, another dozen people turn up, in ones and twos and threes. Some seem to know each other, while others keep to themselves, finding space on the garden walls or the pavements, like the busker Alice saw near the library, saxophone case on his back. He loiters on his own, bopping his head like he's listening to music, though Alice can't see any headphones.

No one comes to the door.

Are you all seeing this? She texts the group thread. What are they doing here?

Then before any of the others can answer, Alice sends another message. I'm going out to ask.

Alice's fingers fumble and slip on the bolt, then the lock, but one by one she gets them into position, wrenches open the door and makes her way down the path.

The hubbub of voices quietens as she comes closer, and every face turns in her direction at once. Alice gets a sudden bizarre vision of where she should be today: in the classroom at school. She shakes the image away, keeps her focus on that first couple she saw and directs her question to them.

'Can I just ask ... I mean. What are you. What are you doing here?'

Polka-dots grins. 'We're here to stop the street being demolished.'

Alice's mouth falls open. 'What?'

'We heard about it,' Polka-dots' partner puts in. 'Wanted to help.'

'More of us there are, the better,' calls one of the women leaning against the wall, and her two friends nod and click their fingers in agreement. 'Strength in numbers, right?'

'We thought they'd have a harder job knocking the houses down if we're here, in the middle of things. Making a nuisance of ourselves.'

'But what made you want to do that?' Alice asks, confused. 'No offence, but none of you live here, and—'

'Could be our street tomorrow,' calls one of the punky roller derby collective that's settled on the opposite pavement.

'Besides,' Polka-dots speaks up again, 'this street deserves protecting. All those stories online. That beautiful letter you wrote. There's so much history here. We can't stand by and let it be destroyed.'

'No way,' grunts the busker. 'Not happening. Not on my watch.'

Realisation starts to creep over Alice. 'So you're protesting? For us?'

'For all of us,' the lad in the EAT THE RICH T-shirt corrects her. 'Symbolic, innit? But yeah, for you as well. All of you, and all of us.'

'That's ... that's amazing. But what are you going to do when the demolition crew comes?'

'Fuck 'em up,' mutters Dragon Tattoos, just as one of the glamorous church ladies says, 'Why don't we cross that bridge when we come to it?'

'What can I do?' Alice asks.

'I'm getting a numb arse on this concrete,' says the man who looks like a geography teacher. 'Can I come and sit in your garden?'

Alice clamps down a hysterical laugh and says he definitely can.

'Thank you,' she says. 'All of you.'

'There'll be more,' someone says.

Alice starts fumbling through her pockets for her phone. 'Excuse me a minute, will you? This is just ... we didn't expect it, and ... well, I'd better tell my neighbours.'

'Hey, darlin',' calls the busker, as Alice heads back up her path. 'You couldn't put the kettle on while you're at it, could you?'

She gets inside and leans back against the door.

There's a message in the chat from Levon: What did they say?

They're here to help us, she types, and describes her conversation.

I knew it, Jessie types back. I think a couple of them are from the comic shop. And someone from college asked me for my address, so they might be coming over.

Someone from the library just messaged me, Levon adds. They said a couple of the community groups might have members coming down too.

Alice's Northern working-class conditioning kicks in: Anyone up for helping me make tea?

I'm your man, Levon says. Kettle's on.

AJ says he can contribute biscuits.

Pass on being tea bitch, Jessie sends. I'm going to take some more pictures and do a livestream of what's happening.

They get to work.

The numbers are bigger by the time Alice next goes

outside. Some people have decamped to the grassy sections of their front gardens, but the pavements are even fuller than before. The W.I. branch from Levon's library has shown up in style: their contingent features several adorable but ferocious grandmas and numerous heavily tattooed women between the ages of eighteen and eighty, equipped with camping chairs, sun parasols and knitting projects. They boss everyone into shuffling up so they can claim a sunny stretch of pavement, and soon get settled, setting out picnic blankets and flasks and peeling back the lids from plastic tubs to reveal gooey chocolate brownies and pastel-yellow lemon squares. Before long, the singing starts: protest songs and folk songs and ones that combine the two, a not-quite harmony of beautiful clear voices despite not all of them being in tune.

Alice makes as many cuppas as she can, retrieving her collection of teapots and setting them all to brew. She passes out mugs and collects the empties to be refilled, glimpsing familiar faces with each trip. Afshan, the lawyer, is there, and someone Alice thinks she might recognise from her first-year uni elective. She only goes to the end of the path and back, leaving people to disseminate the tea themselves from there. It's wild, what's happening. She still can't believe it. And strange as it might seem, Alice still isn't entirely convinced that the whole thing isn't some sort of elaborate trap. Can't shake the suspicion that there could be someone from Paul Buchanan's company in amongst everyone else who's shown up. Someone from Gatsby, or the council, or the police. She's scared she's going to get lulled into a false sense of security: bring out the brews and then turn round to find someone's slipped through her open front door and locked her out. So she shuttles between the garden and the kitchen, keeping her mind and hands focused on her task to keep the fears at bay.

There are hundreds of people gathered in the street by the time a gleaming powder-blue VW Beetle slowly crawls as close as it can, coming to a halt at the edge of the crowd.

'Bloody hell,' AJ says, stopping dead in his collection of empty cups, the tray almost slipping from his hands.

'What is it?' Alice asks, the surprised tone of his voice enough to make panic claw at her chest.

'You see that car that just pulled up?'

'Yeah?'

'That's my mam.'

# CHAPTER TWENTY-NINE

A J shoves the tray at Alice, then weaves his way over. His mum emerges from the car like royalty, and stands there, hands on hips, surveying the scene. She's a tall woman, and wide, the sort of stature that could be wielded for intimidation when necessary. Her skin's darker than AJ's, but they've got the same bone structure and the same hypnotic eyes. She's wearing billowy palazzo pants and a silky tunic, hair knotted in a gold and turquoise headwrap.

'Mam? What are you doing here?'

'Sweetheart, are you kidding? Wasn't going to miss it, was I?'

She folds him into a crushing hug. His nose squished against her collarbones, AJ inhales her familiar jasmine perfume and tries hard not to cry. By the time his mum lets him go, his dad's by their side too, shorter than both of them. AJ gives him a joyous squeeze and an exaggerated smacking kiss on the top of his bald head.

'Your mum saw a video of the street on Twitter an hour ago,' his dad explains, gesturing to the banners and the crowds.

'Bundled me straight in the car and got me to burn rubber all the way here.'

'I just need a minute,' Alice mutters, passing the tea tray AJ shoved at her to someone nearby. It makes her sway on the spot, seeing AJ being embraced by his parents; she feels her Docs creaking where they encase her ankles, has this heady moment where the heat and the noise all combine to make her feel like she might faint. *There's no one coming for you*, she thinks. No friends from work or uni. Her parents are over a thousand miles away, oblivious to everything. Sam would be here, if she asked, but that thought is a bruise she doesn't want to press. She's facing this day alone, or as alone as anyone can be when there are hundreds of other people there.

In everything that's going on, it takes a while before anyone realises Bill's door has opened. There's a hush that ripples out, from the people on Bill's path to those furthest away. And then, before the hush has even taken hold, the closest protesters start clapping. The lad with the dachshund puts two fingers in his mouth and gives a long and loud wolf-whistle. That cuts through all the other faltering murmurs and everyone starts cheering.

Bill leans on the door frame, taking it in. Then he makes his way down the path, slow even with his stick.

'You reet, lass?' he asks Alice, in a concerned mumble. 'Saw you having a moment there.'

She links her arm through his. 'Now who's fussing who?'

'Bill,' someone shouts across from Alice's front garden. 'What made you come out?'

Bill glances at Alice, fights back a smirk, then nods to the end of the street, where a van has just grumbled to a stop. The driver gets out, hefting a camera bag over one shoulder and tucking a tripod under their arm. The passenger angles the rear-view mirror to check her lipstick and fluff her hair.

'That reporter phoned me,' Bill explains. 'Wanted to do another interview. Couldn't go letting my adoring public down, could I?'

There's a queue of people who want to shake Bill's hand, take selfies with him, talk to him. Sabina can't even get close, but she's happy enough directing the cameraman to capture the crowd, pointing at the sun and the shadows and making him get footage from every possible angle of the masses packing out the street, the banners on the houses and the additional signs brought by some of the protesters.

AJ is on full charm offensive, thanking the reporter for taking a chance on them, and for doing the original interview with Bill. AJ's mum is even more charismatic than her son, introducing herself to the reporter, lavishing praise on AJ and – without really meaning to – somehow talking herself into the entire family being interviewed together. The reporter stages them on AJ's step, first asking AJ's parents to describe what's going on.

'We're here because it's not right that my son is being threatened with losing his home,' his mum tells the camera sternly, her arm round his shoulders like a vice.

'AJ, what's going on here on Leodis Street has become something of a lightning rod around the issue of gentrification in the city, and nationwide. How does that feel?'

'If people are talking about our street, and that makes them think about where else this might be happening, then maybe all this stress will have been worth it,' AJ replies. 'Because if this can just happen and everyone rolls over, what then? It's only going to keep happening, isn't it? And the people involved get richer and richer, and more powerful, and what happens to the rest of us? No offence to my mam and dad here, they're amazing. But I don't want to end up living on their couch. But if things carry on the way they are, I might have to. It'll be all I'll be able to afford.'

'AJ knows he can come back to us any time he needs,' his mum puts in. 'But not everyone has that option. And it's not what he wants. He's a brilliant boy, a hard worker. And he's single!' she adds, with a devilish grin. AJ's dad cracks up and AJ, standing between them, just bugs out his eyes at the camera, like *she did not just say that*.

The cameraman gives them the all-clear wave.

AJ turns to his mum. 'Why are you so mortifying?' he groans.

'Oh, sweetheart, come on,' she twinkles, clearly not sorry at all. 'I didn't say anything that wasn't true.'

'You were all brilliant,' Sabina tells them, and then turns to confer with her cameraman.

'I'll upload that and send it to the studio now,' he says. 'Then we can do whoever's next.'

'Is it really going to be on TV?' AJ's mum coos. 'Maybe your future husband will see it, AJ.'

AJ groans and looks to his dad for help, who creases up again. Jessie, who's been watching the entire production from nearby and filming her own video on her phone, looks delighted to have captured this moment.

'We'll submit it for broadcast,' the cameraman explains to AJ's mum. 'The producer decides what goes in the segment. But it'll get edited and packaged for online, radio and social as well. This story's been getting so much traction, we need the content.'

Jessie overhears this and huffs.

'Yeah, and then tomorrow the news cycle moves on, and

we get forgotten about. These are our homes. Our lives. Not just content.'

'You seem like you've got a lot to say,' Sabina chimes in. 'You want to be interviewed next?'

'Not sure why I should give you more free *content*,' Jessie enunciates the word with a withering look towards the cameraman. 'When I could just film and post it myself.'

'Your call,' Sabina shrugs. 'But news can change things, you know. And sharing stories is how it happens. Always.'

'You'd better not edit me to make me look like a dickhead,' Jessie warns, then ducks into her house to check her make-up, coming back out in a biker jacket covered in badges.

'No swear words on any of those, right?' the cameraman asks, shifting the tripod to face Jessie's front door.

'Nah,' Jessie calls, and holds the lapels up so he can read. DEAD MEN CAN'T CATCALL, says one. PIZZA ROLLS NOT GENDER ROLES. PUNKS RESPECT PRONOUNS.

'Fine,' he says, with a wry smirking head-shake, disappearing behind his camera. 'Sabina, ready when you are.'

Jessie's interview goes better than any of them could have anticipated.

'This is nothing new,' Jessie tells the camera, her voice and gaze both hard and clear. 'This has been happening for decades, but never more so than now. This is happening at an unprecedented scale, and it's unsustainable. Whatever happens today, this is *not* over. Not for us, not for anyone. This will always happen, and we will *always* need to fight. If we don't learn from history, all we do is repeat it.' She deliberately doesn't look at Levon. 'We need housing reform, better contracts that protect our rights, and an end to prioritising profits over people.'

The moment the cameraman gives her the signal that he's

stopped filming, the lads with the dog give a whooping victory cheer.

'That's *right*,' one shouts, snapping his fingers. 'You get 'em *told*.'

'Was that okay?' Jessie asks, hiding under her fringe once more and looking to Levon and Alice for reassurance.

'Incredible,' Levon says, as Alice gives her a squeeze.

Levon goes next, talking about his experience of being an immigrant. 'A lot of people in this area probably have an experience that parallels mine in some way. If not in their generation, then further back. And that diversity, if you ask me, is one of this area's greatest strengths. But if you've got experience of displacement, putting down roots can be hard. It can be lonely. But the kindness I've received in my life has outweighed the cruelty. It's made the bad times bearable. I try to reciprocate that as much as I can. And that's what we've been asking for, with our homes. Some kindness and understanding. I believe in those things. We all do. And when you believe in something, you show up for it. Like we have by not vacating, and like everyone else has done who's come here today to show us their support.'

'I'm not sure what I can add that the others haven't already said,' Alice says, when it's her turn. 'Only that I wish my daughter Mollie was here.' She waves and blows a kiss, just in case Mol gets to see this later. 'But the reason she isn't is because we were all so uncertain about what would happen today. And that hasn't changed. I am so grateful for everyone who's come out to support us, and I truly hope it makes a difference. We still have no idea if and when they're coming to knock down our homes. We don't know. They've not shown up so far, and that's brilliant. Maybe that means they've decided they don't want the drama of doing it today. But that

273

doesn't mean they won't try tomorrow, or the next day. Next week, next month. Who knows? None of us can stay in our houses indefinitely. And I know everyone who's come here today has lives and commitments they'll need to return to too. They can't stay here for ever.'

'Well, one person's already set some records for staying here way longer than anyone else,' Sabina says, once Alice's interview has been concluded. The reporter nods towards Bill, who's finally made his way out of the hordes of people wanting handshakes and pictures. 'Reckon we can grab a few minutes with him now?'

During his interview, Bill's initially a little gruff, hiding his emotions. But he warms up once he's asked what he thinks about the crowds who've gathered on the street.

'Listen,' he says. 'I've seen this place gather together before. Seen it full of life. But that was always for celebrations. Parties, you know. Not people coming together for a common purpose, like this. I've spoken to so many people just now. More than I've probably spoken to in the last ten years, if I'm honest with you.' He gives a soft chuckle as he hears himself say this sentence and realises it's true. 'A couple of them stayed here, with me and Sally, years ago.' He gestures towards a cluster of people on the wall at the edge of his garden. Alice recognises Kyle from his TV interview. Kiki with Alisha on her lap. A couple of others she doesn't know. 'Foster kids,' he explains, with a disbelieving shake of his head that they're here. 'Well, not kids any more. They're all grown up now, but they've shown up today because they wanted to be here. For me. For all of us. Suppose everyone else who's turned up wants the same.' Bill stares around the street, a dazzled, near-tears expression on his face.

'How does that feel?' Sabina prompts.

'It's been a long time since I felt I had anyone in my corner,' Bill tells her, voice trembling for a moment. 'I've no one to blame for that but meself, because I retreated and hid meself away when I should've been letting people in. But between my neighbours, and the kids, and everyone else who's shown up here today, I don't feel like that now.'

'We love you, Bill!' Kiki calls.

'There you go,' he summarises to the camera, tilting his head to acknowledge her words. 'That's how I feel.' He doesn't say the word love but it comes across anyway. 'You can love a place,' he continues. 'And I have. But it can't love you back. But the people can. And whatever happens with our houses, I'm grateful for that.'

Alice presses her face into Levon's shoulder. Her face aches from beaming but the intensity of all the heightened emotions has left her raw and near-overwhelmed, scared she might break down into sobs any second. The vertigo has returned, and she keeps expecting to wake up and be back in bed, a wrecking ball looming outside her window. *This can't be real.*

She doesn't realise she's said it out loud until Levon squeezes her hand and tells her that it is.

'You know what else is real?' Jessie asks. She points to a gleaming black BMW that's just pulled up at the end of the street, a murderous-looking Paul Buchanan climbing out from the driver's seat. 'We've got company.'

# CHAPTER THIRTY

P aul picks his way through the crowds with obvious distaste. His sleeves are rolled up and his hair slicked back
with gel. He's had work done since their last meeting: his
forehead is suspiciously smooth given the dark set to his face.

'Afternoon,' he says, his slimy smile more strained than at
their last meeting. 'Can I have a word?'

'What is it, Mr Buchanan?' Levon's voice is polite but cold.
'As you might have guessed, we've no intention of leaving. So
if you're here to persuade us, it's not going to work. Might as
well send in the heavies. But they'll have their work cut out
for them.'

The people nearest this conversation overhear them talking, and mutters start moving from group to group as people
piece together who Paul is.

' . . . that dickhead from the property developers . . . '

'Who does he think he is?'

' . . . can't believe he'd show his face, after everything he's
put these poor people through . . . '

Paul pretends not to hear and focuses again on the street's

residents. They've instinctively clustered closer together, as though their proximity will give them some protection.

'I'm here to invite you to a meeting at my office. So we can talk properly, away from all these ... distractions.'

'Is he gonna offer us money? Or murder us? No way, man, I'm not going to your creepy office to get assassinated.'

Jessie's mumble is more to herself than Paul but AJ elbows her into being quiet anyway.

Alice glances at the waiting car, and at the masses around them.

'No offence, Mr Buchanan, but I'm not sure I trust this offer, either. How can we know you're not just trying to get us out of our houses so you can change our locks, then move your demolition crew in?'

Paul gives what he obviously thinks is a winning smile. It comes off lizardy and insincere. 'Come on, now,' he says. 'No need for that. No harm in talking, is there?'

'There will be if you knock my house down while we're at it,' Bill grouches, and the rest of them concur.

'Our last little chat caused a lot of drama,' Alice tells Paul, arms folded. 'But I suppose I should thank you for it. Without that, we might not have rallied together and decided to stay put. But I'm still not up for going anywhere with you.'

'Fine! The office isn't important. I just wanted to talk somewhere more discreet.'

'With fewer cameras and people watching, you mean,' Jessie mutters. 'Which means it's something shady.'

'All I want to do is talk. In private. If you won't come with me, let's find another option. This stalemate can't last. You all know that as well as I do. So let's talk.'

'We can go in mine,' Alice says, after a pause. 'As long as everyone else is up for it. But there better not be any funny business while we're in there.'

'There won't be,' Jessie says. 'I've got an idea.'

She darts around the street, recruiting and orchestrating people into position. AJ's mum takes a seat on the steps of AJ's house, somehow making it look as grand as a throne, his dad being bossed into taking pictures. The punky lads with the puppy take up the same position at Jessie's. The saxophone player does the same for Levon. Kyle, Kiki and Alisha squeeze onto Bill's front step.

'There,' she says, returning to the group. 'No one's getting in, changing the locks or doing anything. They've all got my number, and if anyone approaches any of them while we're inside, they're going to kick up enough of a fuss that we'll hear what's going on.'

'You've got the right person for that, then,' AJ deadpans, as his mum gives him a regal wave.

Once they're sorted, they traipse up Alice's path. Some people nearby seem to have realised what's happening, and shouts of encouragement and promises to not let anything happen to their homes follow them towards Alice's door.

Alice gives Bill her arm to lean on. Everyone's gone quiet. Alice hears Levon's voice in her head, the words *unlimited fine* giving her a cold flush of fear.

Everyone's uncertain. And worried.

'Well, if nowt else, this has brought them and me out of the woodwork, hasn't it?' Bill mutters in a gloomy tone, nodding towards Danny, Kiki, Kyle and the others. 'S'pose I've got more options now than before.'

Alice squeezes his arm in an attempt to make him stop. 'Still,' Bill adds, with a dark sidelong smirk in her direction. 'Can't pretend this int a bit like going to the gallows, eh, lass?'

They get inside, the kitchen cool and shadowy after being outside so long.

'Come through, Bill, you sit down there,' Alice tells him, distracting herself from her fury towards Paul. 'You've been on your feet ages, you must be knackered.'

'Always fussing,' he grumbles, but winks at Alice once he's creaked into a chair.

The others assemble around the table.

Paul's fidgeting, his distracted state similar to how he was that night in hospital. AJ gets the sudden impulse to ask after Benji. *Better not*, he thinks, swallowing the weird bubble of hysterical laughter that lodges in his throat. *Not really the time or place for that, is it?*

For a moment, Paul hesitates, looking anywhere but at them. Alice doesn't offer him anything. And it's not only because she's got no tea, milk or biscuits left.

'Come on then, man,' Bill huffs. 'Out with it.'

Paul gives an irritable sigh at being bossed about, then plasters on an oily smile.

'I'm here with an offer for you. The offer I originally made to Alice,' he says, with a nod in her direction. 'I've been authorised to extend that to you all. Council rates for state-of-the-art luxury apartments. Here. You can stay on the street you love so much, and it gets the regeneration it so desperately needs.' He fans his hands open as though revealing a magic trick.

Alice's first instinct is to snort with laughter at his nerve, but then terror thrills through her. *What if the others are up for it?*

But AJ's already leaning forward. 'Mate, not a chance,' he tells Paul, flatly. 'I don't want a fancy-pants flat and millionaire neighbours.' He glances round at the others. 'I like the neighbours I've got, ta.'

The others mumble their assent.

Levon speaks next. 'The way I see it, Mr Buchanan, we're

the ones with the leverage here. And an offer like that – which by the way would still leave us homeless for a significant period of time while the new flats were built – ultimately comes across as hollow. With respect, it doesn't seem like you've really understood what we're fighting for.'

A vein in Paul's forehead throbs. He clenches his jaw. 'Am I to understand you all feel that way?'

They glance at each other and nod, one by one.

'Fine!' He sneers. 'We've lined up an alternative site, we'll move ahead with that instead.'

A shock wave follows his sentence. Everyone stares at each other, no one daring to believe what they've just heard.

'What does that mean?' Alice demands. 'What does that mean for us?'

Paul gives her a filthy look. 'That we're not moving ahead with the demolition.'

'Is this a joke?' Jessie demands, her voice coming out crackly and high. 'It had better not be a joke.'

'It's not,' he gripes. 'We've had too much negative publicity, and the investors are concerned about how that would impact the viability of the new properties we were planning to build.'

Jessie whoops, devil-hands double-fisted to the ceiling, tipping her chair back onto two legs. 'In your face, suck-aaaa. We *won*.'

'Wait, so you're not going ahead at all?'

'We will,' he tells them, and there's a collective inhale and bracing. 'But not here. There are other areas of Leeds that are less risky, so your eviction notices have been revoked. Your original contracts with the council remain in place.'

'So we can stay?'

'That's between you and them, but looks like it. You've got a lot of attention on you, and right now we're the bad guys.

The council won't want to risk that getting turned on them. Not with all that going on out there.'

AJ swears under his breath, still disbelieving. And then they all start laughing, talking over each other at top volume.

'Well,' Paul says, bracing his hands on the table to stand up. 'If that's everything, I'll leave you to it. Lots to do, you know how it is.'

'Okay, man,' AJ tells him, rising like someone should see Paul out. 'Thanks for coming,' he adds, unable to keep a straight face.

'Yeah.' Paul makes a faltering hand gesture, first holding out his hand as if to shake AJ's then changing his mind, turning it into an awkward wave then shoving his hand in his pocket, and finally meeting AJ's eyes. Neither of them mentions the night in hospital, but it crackles unsaid between them. Paul gives AJ a nod of acknowledgment, and AJ wants to read all sorts of things into it. Like, *thank you for what you did for my kid. Thanks for what you said. You were part of this. What you said got to me. It made a difference.*

But all he gets is that close-to-nothing nod as Paul slips out the door.

AJ returns to the kitchen. Everyone's still chattering in a non-stop animated rush. Alice is on her phone, sending a message to Sam, wanting him to bring Mollie down so they can celebrate. Jessie's on her phone too, scanning through all the pictures and videos from the protest that have been shared online. Levon and Bill are talking about how they're going to communicate their victory to everyone outside.

'Speaking of them lot,' Bill says. 'They're going to be wondering about us, aren't they?'

'See if that reporter's still there,' Jessie suggests. 'Bet she'd love a follow-up interview with Bill.'

'Come on then, let's get out there,' Bill says, heaving himself up from the table. 'The street's overdue a proper knees-up.'

'Shame there's no jam sponge for you, Bill,' Alice teases.

'Cheeky sod.'

'Bet someone's got some,' AJ puts in.

'I'm going home,' Bill threatens, but links his arm with Alice as they step back out into the sun.

As they emerge onto the step, a hush falls over the crowd. All those faces waiting, staring. Alice's vertigo returns. Then Jessie starts to laugh, a bright, loud cackle as she swings between AJ's and Levon's shoulders. Alice slides her hand from the crook of Bill's arm to his wrist, laces their fingers together and raises their fists into the air.

'We *won*!' Jessie yells, the words coming out like a howl, and the responding roar from the crowd is enough to start the rest of them laughing too.

# ONE YEAR LATER

'What happened to the banners?' Liam, back in his EAT THE RICH T-shirt for the anniversary of the protest, scoops Dolly the dachshund off the floor and onto his knee. He leans back on his camping stool to gaze round at the terraces on either side of the street. Beer barrels donated by the local pub have been transformed into fat planters that now house a riot of pansies and other flowers on each corner. After all the press, the council put more money into the street. All the street lamps work now, the potholes have been fixed; the road is a patchwork of black tar and asphalt, but the surface is smooth enough for Mollie to skate on. Alice took her to see the roller derby after talking to some of the players who came to the protest, and the toddler became *obsessed*. There have been other improvements, too, like the revamp for the nearby park, with its brand-new benches and playground. The rest they've done themselves. The end wall of the terrace has been turned into a giant spray-paint mural, swirly cosmic letters saying WELCOME TO LEODIS STREET. Bunting, another of Jessie's creations, wraps around each lamp post, back and forth across the street, her wobbling on AJ's shoulders earlier that day to get it into place. Holographic flags and rainbows flap on silvery ribbon, casting disco reflections onto all their walls.

On Liam's lap, Dolly takes immediate advantage of the extra space, trampling in a circle then resting her head on the table, black eyes paying close attention to the nearby plates of food. A long line of tables has been dragged out into the street for the occasion, draped with tablecloths and groaning under the weight of the pot-luck banquet assembled by the neighbours and everyone else who's come by.

'The banners? Jessie's got 'em,' AJ answers, leaning forward so the younger man can hear him over the music. Eli's already treated them to a live saxophone set and now they've defaulted back to various speakers playing music from phones: clashing pockets of reggae, punk and pop rise from the various clusters of people sitting and talking, eating or dancing, the entire thing blending into one upbeat bopping background. 'They stayed up until we got our new contracts from the council. There was some debate after that. Levon wanted them for the library, but Jessie claimed them. Said she wanted them for an art project. That was before she got into university, but she must've had some idea about what she was going to do. She's using them for something she's doing this term, anyway.'

'That's it,' Liam says, scruffing his blue mohawk back and forth, his face lighting up as he connects the dots. ' "The connections between protest and subculture", right?' He gestures towards his boyfriend, sitting in the sun on Alice's front lawn with some others, eating from paper plates on their knees. 'Jessie took some amazing pictures of our band, for the same project. I'm trying to persuade her to come on tour with us. Be our official photographer.'

'And like I said,' Jessie puts in, coming over and overhearing the last part of this conversation. Her hair is a mix of candyfloss-pink and tangerine, and she's had more piercings in the past year. 'When you've got dates, I'll decide. But if it clashes with uni stuff, it's not happening. I've worked too hard to let my grades slip now.'

'But you're glad you stayed here and didn't move into halls?' AJ asks, slinging his arm around her and pulling her into his side. It's a sibling-like scuffle, him messing up her hair before she gives up struggling and lets him hug her for a moment.

'Deffo the right decision,' she says, disentangling herself and stealing an oreo from AJ's plate. 'Some of the people on my course have told me some right horror stories about being in halls. Anyway, what would you lot have done without me?'

Levon comes over and joins them. He's in his usual denim jacket, over a protest T-shirt. LESBIANS & GAYS SUPPORT THE MINERS, it says. Liam reaches forward in appreciation, clinking a beer bottle with Levon's mug.

'I don't know how I ever did without you at the library,' Levon tells Jessie, when they recap their conversation for him. 'I wouldn't have thought one day a week would make such a difference, but it does.'

Levon got approached by Bill's foster son, Kyle, after everything that happened, offering him a job with his non-profit in Manchester. Levon turned it down, but still wanted to help. Together, he and Jessie run a monthly surgery at the library, using Kyle's housing know-how and Levon's community experience to help people facing their own housing issues. He also helped Jessie navigate the process of getting her new rental contract from the council put in her own name rather than her mum's.

Alice has barely sat down all day. Her teapot collection has been put to use again and she's been flitting in and out of her house to keep them filled. But she comes and joins them now, supervising Mollie carrying out a tray containing a plate with a jammy Victoria sponge cake. As they make their way down the path, Alice glances back over her shoulder at Bill's house, with its closed door and drawn curtains.

'What are we talking about?' Alice asks, as Mollie presents the plate, swipes her finger through the jam and cream oozing between the layers of sponge and darts off before Alice can grab her.

'How we can't believe it's been a year.'

'I know.' Alice gives an emotional sigh, then rallies. 'But *that's* certainly not what was happening this time last year, is it?' She cuts her eyes towards AJ's house, where his mum sits on his front step, in an animated conversation with a man about AJ's age.

'Don't,' AJ says, pillowing his head on his hands as he gives a despairing laugh-groan. 'I'm pretending that's not happening.'

For the minute they were all micro-famous, AJ was in high demand. The clip where his mum mentioned his being single went viral, and for a few days the internet seemed full of people thirsting for him, sending sexy selfies and begging for dates. His mum tried to make #FindAJAHusband happen, her friends taking up the challenge with glee. AJ found the entire thing ridiculous and mostly ignored it, but when Damian came up to him in the hospital canteen and asked where he recognised AJ from, he'd been too flustered to deny it. Damian was cute, with ashy-blonde hair and a short-sleeved shirt in an abstract print of multi-coloured stars and triangles. He was over from Huddersfield to visit his uncle who'd just had a hip replacement. Once they started talking, it turned out they had a couple of mutual friends.

'Does that make this more weird or less?' AJ had asked.

'Here,' Damian said, taking AJ's phone from his hand and thumbing in his number. 'You can let me know what you decide.'

AJ decided to message him, and they'd been seeing each other ever since. Nothing too serious, yet, and AJ hopes his mum isn't embarrassing him too much by mentioning wedding bells.

AJ's developing romance makes Alice reflect on her own love life just as Sam's car purrs to a stop at the end of the street. Things between them are better than ever – closer and more collaborative. She and Sam are finally getting the hang of being partners in parenting, and Alice still trusts her decision that they're not supposed to be anything more.

Mollie bolts over to greet him and his passenger, Sam coming round to open the door for Bill and help him out. Alice shades her eyes from the sun with her hand, examining Bill closely as he makes his way over.

'What time do you call this?' she teases.

'Train were delayed,' he grunts, leaning on Alice's shoulder as he eases himself into a seat.

'You've caught the sun,' she tells him, craning her neck to examine the pink patches – his bald patch and the tips of his ears.

'Aye, well,' he says, reaching for a slice of cake. 'Alisha wanted to go to the beach before I came home.'

Bill had been highly unsure of leaving Leeds for an entire weekend, but after making numerous day trips over to see him, Kiki had finally persuaded him to visit her and Alisha at their home in Whitby.

287

'So go on, then,' Alice prompts. 'What else did you do?'

'Arcades. Bairn kept telling everyone how her grandad had magic powers every time we got some coppers off the penny falls.' He gives an incredulous chuckle at the memory of being given this title.

'Anyway, Kiki says you've got to teach me how to internet so that Alisha can do that video-call thing instead of just phone.'

The others exchange grins. 'We'll teach you how to internet,' Alice promises in a grave tone.

'Good,' he says. 'It were good this weekend, but I'm too old to be doing that long train journey more than once in a blue moon. So she can come here next time, I told her to coordinate it with Danny and Kyle and the others. And if Alisha can video-call, she can talk to Mollie 'n' all. Make a wee friend for when she comes up for visits.'

As if she knows she's been being talked about, Mollie wanders back to the table, carrying a preposterously huge ice-cream cone from the van parked up at the end of the road.

She hands the ice-cream to Bill.

'No thank you, treasure,' he tells her, and gestures to his plate. 'I've got me cake.'

But Mollie pushes it into his hand, then climbs onto his knee and takes it back. Alice laughs at her kid.

'Can't blame a girl for knowing what she wants,' she quips, as Bill shuffles Mollie into a more comfortable position snuggled against his chest.

'Wonder where she learnt that from,' Bill grumps through his smile.

'I've got everything I want right here,' Alice says, making her voice schmaltzy to undercut the sentiment, but meaning it all the same.

'You're not sad about your mum not being able to make it, Jessie?' Levon asks.

'I'm good,' Jessie says, leaning her head back on AJ's shoulder.

'Besides,' Alice says, watching Bill take a giant bite of Victoria sponge, the jam and cream smearing everywhere, 'family's more than just blood, isn't it?'

'Aye,' Bill says, through his mouthful of cake, mugging for the camera as Jessie takes his picture. 'It is.'

# ACKNOWLEDGEMENTS

All the gratitude to my incredible editor, Cal Kenny, for their endless wisdom, kindness and support, and for having so much trust in me. This book would not exist without their vision, dedication and tenacity. Likewise to Ruth Jones, Kirsteen Astor and all the team at Sphere, along with my brilliant agent, Silvia Molteni.

I am immensely grateful for the many incredible writer friends I've learned from and leaned on before, during and since writing this book, but especially Claire Askew, Rosie Garland, Debz Butler, Paul Forster and Holly Ringland, who have sorted out my head and heart too many times to count. My beautiful mates Laura Kidd, Damian Gray, Amy Bainbridge, Emma Grayson, Avadrian Night, Fiona Ledgard, Anne Louise Kershaw, Kerry Ryan, Greg Thorpe and Gaynor Jones have also been amazing, much-appreciated sources of joy, mutual care, insight and support. Massive thanks too to the For Books' Sake dream team, Jo Flynn and Bridget Hart, and to Tuesday night highlights Sophie Hanson, Sarah Mosedale, Gemma Fairclough, Abby Ledger-Lomas and Janelle Hardacre.

My local community played important roles in getting this book written, so to the gangs at Lounge 66 and Coffee Fix, thank you for the kind words and good coffee that brightened many writing days, and to Amanda at the train station for being such a reliable source of energy, compassion and cheer.

I'm someone whose life has been saved several times over by access to council housing, the NHS, libraries and education, so I'm forever grateful to everyone who works so tirelessly in those areas and others to give people the care, shelter, access and support they need. I'm sorry you have and continue to be so badly let down by those in power.

To Mum, Selina, Matt, Tash, Mike, Kath, Freda, Dave and Paul: I love you more than a novel's worth of words could properly express. Thank you for everything.

And to Zigs: Thank you for coming to visit me in my dilapidated Victorian terrace on a street in Leeds during that weird, dark time decades back. I couldn't have imagined anything that was to come but I'm grateful beyond everything that it's been with you.